BRIDGET

Recent Titles by Linda Sole from Severn House

THE TIES THAT BIND
THE BONDS THAT BREAK
THE HEARTS THAT HOLD

FLAME CHILD

THE ROSE ARCH
A CORNISH ROSE
A ROSE IN WINTER

BRIDGET

Linda Sole

This first world edition published in Great Britain 2002 by
SEVERN HOUSE PUBLISHERS LTD of
9–15 High Street, Sutton, Surrey SM1 1DF.
This first world edition published in the USA 2003 by
SEVERN HOUSE PUBLISHERS INC of
595 Madison Avenue, New York, N.Y. 10022

British Library Cataloguing in Publication Data

Sole, Linda
  Bridget
  1. Problem families - Fiction
  2. Docks - England - London - Fiction
  3. London (England) - Social conditions - 19th century - Fiction
  4. Love stories
  I. Title
  823.9'14 [F]

  ISBN 0-7278-5868-8

Except where actual historical events and characters are being
described for the storyline of this novel, all situations in this
publication are fictitious and any resemblance to living persons
is purely coincidental.

Typeset by Palimpsest Book Production Ltd.,
Polmont, Stirlingshire, Scotland.
Printed and bound in Great Britain by
MPG Books Ltd., Bodmin, Cornwall.

One

The sound of a foghorn somewhere out on the river was almost lost in the noise of chucking-out time at the Cock & Feathers, known locally simply as the Feathers. Lying in my bed in the little room at the back of the house, I heard the usual screams, yells and scuffles from the pub at the end of the lane. I was used to it and it was not the petty squabbles of my neighbours that had woken me. No, this was something much closer to home.

'Can I get into bed with you, Bridget?'

I smiled at the sight of my six-year-old brother dressed in a worn flannel shirt that was three sizes too big for him and reached down to his ankles. Beneath that ridiculous shirt was a painfully thin body; he was hardly more than skin and bone and worried me more than I'd ever let on to him or anyone else.

'O' course you can, Tommy. Was it them villains from the pub that woke you?'

'It's our mam,' Tommy whispered, and coughed as he tugged the thin blanket up to his chest and burrowed further down into the lumpy feather bed my sister and I usually shared. 'She's having a right old go at Lainie again.'

No sooner had he spoken than there was an almighty crash downstairs in the kitchen. Tommy shivered and I folded my arms about him protectively as our mother suddenly screamed out a torrent of abuse.

'You're a slut and a whore – and 'tis after throwing you out of the house, I am.'

The spiteful words could be clearly heard by us as we lay in

1

bed, Tommy shivering against my side as he always did when Mam was in one of her rages.

'Whatever I am, it's what you made me, and if I go you'll be the one to lose by it, Martha O'Rourke. It's four shillings a week you'll be missin' if I leave,' Lainie shrieked, full of anger. 'You're a cold-hearted bitch and I'll be glad to see the back of this place, but you'll not take too kindly to going without your drop of the good stuff.'

'And we all know where the money comes from! You've been down the Seamen's Mission again, selling yourself to them foreigners.'

'Hans loves me and one day he'll be wedding me. You know he's the only one, Mam. I don't know why you take on so. Our da was working the ships when you met him – and our Jamie was on the way before the wedd—'

There was a scream of rage from downstairs and then more crashing sounds as furniture was sent flying. Our mother and sister were having one of their frequent fights, which always upset Tommy. They weren't the only ones to indulge – similar fights went on in houses up and down the street, especially on a Friday night – but Martha O'Rourke could be vicious and I was anxious for my sister.

'If your father was here, he'd take his belt to you!'

'Give over, Mam . . .' Lainie gave a little scream.

I jumped out of bed and hastily pulled on my dress. I was worried about my sister leaving. Lainie wasn't going to put up with much more. She would walk out, and then where would the rest of us be?

'Where are you going?' Tommy said, alarmed.

'You stop here. I'm going to creep down and see what Mam's doing to our Lainie. She'll kill her one of these days if no one stops her.'

Tommy clutched at my hand, his wide, frightened eyes silently begging me not to leave him. He was terrified of Mam when she was in one of her rages, and with good cause. We had all felt the back of Martha O'Rourke's hand often enough. She was a terrible tyrant when she was in a temper.

Even as I hesitated, I heard Lainie slam the kitchen door and I knew I had to hurry, but Tommy was hanging on for dear life.

'You'll be all right here. I shan't let Mam see me, and I'll be back before you know it. There's no need to worry, me darlin'.'

Leaving Tommy, I crept along the painted boards of the landing on bare feet and began a careful descent of the stairs. They were uncovered stained wood and creaked if you stepped on the wrong spot, but I had become an expert at avoiding the creaks. This was hardly surprising since I was the one who scrubbed them three times a week from top to bottom.

'Lainie . . .' I whispered as I saw her at the door. 'Don't go . . .'

Either she didn't hear me or she was too angry to listen as she left the house and banged the door after her with a vengeance. I ran down the rest of the stairs as quickly as I could, forgetting to avoid the creaks in my hurry which brought Mam to the door of the kitchen.

'And where do you think you're going at this time of night? Off down the docks to be a whore like your slut of a sister, I suppose?'

'I'm going after Lainie. You can't throw her out, Mam. It isn't fair!'

'I'll give you the back of me hand, girl!' She started forward purposefully but I took a deep breath and dodged past her, knowing that I was risking retribution later. Lainie had to come back, it would be unbearable at home without her. Besides, where would she go at this time of night?

When I reached the street, I saw that she was almost at the end of the lane and I called to her desperately, running to catch up with her. She looked back reluctantly, then slowed her footsteps and finally waited for me at the top of the lane.

'What do you want?'

'You're not really going to leave us, are you? I can't bear it if you go, Lainie – I can't!'

The note of desperation in my voice must have got through

3

to her, because her sulky expression suddenly disappeared as she said, 'Sure, it's not the end of the world, Bridget darlin'. I'll only be living a few streets away, leastwise until Hans' ship gets back. After that, I don't know where I'll be – but I'll be seeing you before then. You can come to me if you want me. If I stay here Mam will kill me – or I'll do for her. I'm best out of the way. You know it's true, in your heart.'

'But we'll miss you – Tommy and me. You know Jamie can't stand to be around her . . .'

Jamie, our elder brother, was going on twenty and seldom in the house. Mam yelled at him if she got the chance, but he was a big-boned lad and she didn't dare hit him the way she did us. He took after Da, who had a reputation for being handy with his fists, and would have hit her back.

'I'll miss both of you, me darlin',' Lainie said and her eyes were bright with tears she would not shed. 'I can't stay another day, Bridget. Sure, I know 'tis hard for you, darlin', but you've Mr Phillips to help you – and our Jamie if you need him. Until he gets sent down the line, leastwise.'

'Oh, Lainie!' I cried fearfully. 'He's not in trouble again?'

'When have you ever known our Jamie not to be in trouble? He's like Da. He hits out first and thinks after. One of these days he'll do for someone – and then they'll hang him.'

'Please don't,' I begged. I stared at Lainie's pretty face, hoping that she was joking, but there was no sign of a smile in her soft green eyes. 'I can't bear it when you talk like that. Ever since Da drowned—'

'Huh!' Lainie flicked back her fair hair. She was as fair as I was dark and far prettier than I thought I could ever be. She also smelled of a sweet rose perfume that Hans had given her. 'Mam has been lying to us, our Bridget. There was no body – no proof he drowned. From the way the old bill haunted us for months, I reckon they know the truth. Jamie says he was away on a ship to America.'

'Do you think that's what happened?' I looked at her anxiously. I'd cried myself to sleep after Mam told us our father had drowned in the docks. I'd had nightmares about him being down there in the river somewhere, his body eaten by fish.

'I shouldn't be surprised,' Lainie said. 'They're always looking for someone to take on down the docks. When crew have jumped ship or drunk themselves silly and not signed back on. Hans says it's likely Da was taken on and no questions asked.'

'Then he might still be alive?'

'For all the good it will do any of us,' Lainie said and pulled a face. 'If he got away, he'll not be after coming back. He'd be arrested as soon as they saw him. It was months before the law stopped hunting him. They haunted our Jamie at work, and watched the house. Da knows he'd hang for sure.'

'Yes, I'm sure you're right. It was better in the house before he left, that's all.'

'Only because he put his fist in her mouth if she opened it too wide. Don't you remember all their rows?'

I remembered well enough, even though Sam O'Rourke had been gone for five years – years that his absence had made much harder for us all – but I also recalled Da giving me a halfpenny for sweets a few times. He had liked to ruffle my hair and call me his 'darlin' girl'.

'Yes, I remember.' I looked pleadingly at her. 'You won't change your mind and stay? Not even until the morning?'

'I can't,' Lainie said and her mouth set into a stubborn, sullen line, which told me there would be no changing her. 'Hans has begged me to leave home a thousand times. I only stayed as long as this for you and Tommy.'

'What about your things? What are you going to do, Lainie? You can't walk about all night—'

'There isn't much I want back at the house. I'm going to Bridie Macpherson. She's asked me to work for her and she'll provide uniforms. Hans will be back soon; he'll give me money for what I need and then I shall go away with him. You can have my stuff and if I think of anything I want, I'll let you know and you can smuggle it out to me.'

'Will Hans marry you, Lainie?'

5

'Yes.' She smiled confidently. 'He knows he's the only one. I've never had another feller, Bridget. Mam carries on the way she does because he's Swedish and not a Catholic, but Hans doesn't care about that. He says he'll convert if it's the only way he can wed me.'

'I'm glad for you.' I loved my sister and I was going to miss her like hell, but I couldn't hold her against her will. 'Yes, yes, you must go, Lainie. It's your chance of a better life.'

'You'll be all right,' Lainie replied. 'You're clever, Bridget. I think you must take after great grandfather O'Rourke. He came over to England in 1827 when they were clearing the land for St Katherine's Docks. They say he had a bit o' money behind him, but he died of the cholera – there used to be a lot of it in the lanes in them days.

'Grandfather O'Rourke was a lad of six years then, and his mother a widow with five small children. She had to struggle to bring them all up. When our grandfather was old enough to work, he started out as a labourer but ended as a foreman, running a gang under him. He would have done well for himself if he hadn't taken a virulent fever and died. Leastwise, that's what Granny always told us. Do you remember her at all?'

I had a vague memory of a white-haired woman in a black dress. 'Yes, I think so. She used to sit on her doorstep and smoke a long-stemmed clay pipe, didn't she?'

'Yes.' Lainie chuckled. 'She died when you were about three. She was forever talking about the Old Country – and her brogue was so thick that I couldn't always understand her.'

I stopped walking and looked back. We had already come a couple of streets and I knew Tommy would be waiting anxiously for my return.

'I'd better get back then,' I said and leaned towards her, kissing her cheek once more. 'Take care of yourself, Lainie.'

'You take care of yourself too, Bridget – and don't let Mam bully you too much.'

I nodded, but it was easy for Lainie to say. She was nearly eighteen and she had someone who cared for her. I was almost a year younger and I couldn't just walk out the way she had – someone had to watch out for Tommy.

Mam would be in a temper when I got back, but I was used to that. I hated to see Lainie go, but there was no point in making a fuss over spilled milk. I supposed Lainie ought to have left home long ago. She would be much happier working for Bridie – even though the hotel owner was a bit mean from all accounts.

I liked Mrs Macpherson, but then I didn't have to work for her. She was a widow who had come to live near St Katherine's Docks three years earlier and seemed to be a plump friendly person. When she had taken over the Sailor's Rest, it had been a run-down hovel, but she had built it into a thriving business.

My thoughts were still with my sister as I walked slowly home, deliberately loitering despite the bitter cold, which was chilling me through to the bone. I knew what was waiting for me when I got back and I wasn't looking forward to the row with Mam, who would take out her frustrations on me now that Lainie had gone.

It was only after a few minutes of walking on my own that I realized how late and dark it was in the lane. Most of the houses were shuttered, their lamps extinguished. I had never been out this late alone before. Nervously, I glanced over my shoulder as I sensed someone was watching me . . . following me even. Chills ran through me, giving me goose pimples all over; I was suddenly frightened.

The East End of London was a harsh dirty place in 1899, its air polluted by the smoke of the industrial revolution that had taken place throughout most of the past century. Crime was rife in the narrow lanes and alleyways that bordered the river and it was far from safe for a young woman to walk alone on a dark night. I began to walk faster, my heart jumping with fright.

The wind was blowing off the river bringing the stench of the oily water and refuse, dumped into the docks by the ships anchored out in the river, into the lanes, which already carried their own smell of decay. The houses here were better than the tenements a few streets away, but nearer to the river several deserted buildings harboured vagrants and rats.

I looked round again, but it was too dark to see anything. The suspicion that someone was following me sent prickles of fear down my spine. Lainie had often warned me about walking alone late at night. She'd told me that Hans always insisted that he walk her back to Farthing Lane after a night out.

When she was with him, Lainie was safe. Hans was a gentle man, but he was a blond giant with feet the size of meat plates and hands to match. One blow from him would knock most men's heads off their shoulders. I'd met him once and he'd made me laugh with his stories about the days when the Vikings used to raid the English coast.

I wished Hans were here with me now or that my brother Jamie would come whistling down the lane to meet me. There was a man following me, I was certain of it now.

'Where are you goin'? Bit late for you, ain't it? Or 'ave you taken to walkin' the streets for yer livin'?'

The voice was close behind me and made me jump. As I turned, I knew instantly who the voice belonged to and my fear abated slightly.

I lifted my head proudly, meeting that hateful, leering look on his face. Harry Wright had been after me since I was at school. Then he had been a snotty-nosed bully with no shoes and his arse hanging out of his trousers like all the rest of the kids in the lanes. Now he was dressed in a toff's suit and leather shoes. He had made good and there was only one way to do that round here.

'Who made it your business? Haven't they locked you up yet, Harry Wright?'

'Nah – and they ain't goin' ter neither,' Harry said, eyeing me speculatively. 'Leavin' home then? Martha chucked yer out?' he asked in his broad cockney accent. Harry was a Londoner through and through, but his manner was coarse and unlike most of the friendly people who lived in our lanes.

'Take yourself off where you're wanted,' I retorted angrily.

'Hoity toighty tonight, ain't we? Got somewhere to go,

'ave yer? Only I could offer yer a bed fer the night – mine!'

Something in the way he looked at me was beginning to make me uneasy. 'I'm going home – and I wouldn't come with you if I wasn't! I'd rather sleep under the bridge. So just you clear off, Harry Wright! I don't want anythin' to do with the likes of you . . .'

'You're too cocky for yer own good, Bridget O'Rourke!' His eyes narrowed as he looked at me. 'I bet yer a tart just like that bleedin' sister of yours. Bin with a bloke down the docks 'ave yer? Yeah, yer a slut just like that Lainie.'

'My sister isn't a whore. You're drunk, that's what's the matter with you. Just you leave me alone, Harry Wright! If you try anything I'll tell Jamie and he'll give you a thrashing.'

'Stuck up bitch!' he snarled and lurched at me, suddenly slamming me into the wall of the nearest house.

I could smell the stink of strong drink on his breath and knew I had guessed right: he was very drunk.

'You've been givin' it away to anyone who asks. Well, I'm takin', not askin'. I'll just 'ave a little taste of what yer've bin givin' away . . .'

He was so strong and the pressure of his body was holding me pinned to the wall. I screamed once before his hand covered my mouth. Fear whipped through me but I was determined not to give in.

His hand was smothering me, making it difficult to breathe. I bit it as hard as I could and he swore, jerking back in pain and then striking me so hard across the face that I tasted blood in my mouth.

I screamed again, clawing at his face with my nails. My head was reeling and I hardly knew what I did as I struggled desperately to save myself. He was dragging my skirts up, clawing at me down there, where no man had touched me. I gave another cry of fear and pushed hard against him. For a moment I was able to wrench free of him, but he grabbed me and swung me round. I kicked out at him and then he hit me so hard my head went spinning. I gave a moan of pain and

he punched me again, sending me crashing to the pavement.
I hit my head hard as I fell, and then I knew no more.

'What's happening . . . don't touch me!' I screamed as the man
bent over me and I stared wildly into the face of a stranger.
'What are you doing to me? Leave me alone . . . leave me
alone . . .' I was almost sobbing now, hysterical. 'Please leave
me alone . . .'

'Are you all right, lass?' The man's gentle voice was
concerned as he knelt over me, helping me to sit up. 'Someone
attacked you. I think he was trying to – well, I believe I got here
in time. You hit your head as you fell – does it hurt badly?'
He was touching my head as he spoke, feeling for the wound.
'You're bleeding. You must have fallen hard. It's a wonder the
bastard didn't kill you! You should get your mother to bathe it
for you. Where do you live – near here?'

'Just down the road . . .' I took a sobbing breath. I was
beginning to remember. It wasn't this man who had attacked
me, in fact he had probably saved me from Harry Wright's
attempt to rape me. Shame swept over me and I hardly dared
to look at him. 'I'm all right . . . thank you for helping me.
Are you sure he didn't . . . you know?'

'He was certainly attempting it,' the man said. 'I had been
visiting a friend of mine, Fred Pearce, and I came out just
as you fell.' He smiled at me, a flicker of amusement in his
greenish-brown eyes. 'I think you can be sure that he didn't
manage it. He ran off when I yelled at him or I'd have thrashed
the bugger for you!'

'Thank you,' I said again and blushed. I was overcome with
shame as I realized that Harry Wright would have succeeded
if it had not been for this stranger. I also wondered what I
must look like with my clothes all over the place. 'He . . . he
frightened me. I was walking home and he followed me . . .'

'Do you know him?'

I hesitated, then shook my head. If I told anyone that it was
Harry Wright who had attacked me, Jamie would go wild. He
would go after him and when he caught him, he would kill him.

I didn't care what happened to Harry Wright, but I couldn't risk my brother getting into trouble over this.

'No, I'd never seen him before in my life . . .' I gave a cry of distress as I looked down at myself and saw that my dress had been torn and was stained with dirt from the road. 'Mam will half kill me!' I said and scrambled to my feet. 'I've got to go . . .'

'I'll come with you,' he said, steadying me as I nearly lost my balance. 'Just in case that bastard is still hanging around. Besides, you look as if you need a hand.'

He was being kind but all I wanted to do was get away. My head hurt and I felt sick and dizzy and worst of all I thought that he must be thinking the worst of me – a common tart who'd fallen out with one of her clients.

'No, thanks all the same. I'll be all right in a moment. Mam will kill me for sure if she sees me with a feller. You can watch me until I get to me door, if you like?'

'All right,' he said and grinned as I dared to look at him again. He had a friendly smile, though he wasn't a real looker; his hair was short and wiry and a sandy colour in the light of the gas lamp from Farthing Lane, but he had a nice manner and I knew I was lucky that he'd happened along when he did. 'Cut along home then, lass. You'd best not keep your Mam waiting too long.'

'Thank you for helping me. I'm Bridget O'Rourke. I don't know your name . . . ?'

'I'm Joe Robinson,' he said. 'Take care of yourself. I'll wait here and see as no one tries anything until you get home.'

I sent him an awkward smile and started to run, my heart pounding as my feelings rose up to overcome me. Inside, I was shaking, my mouth dry and my stomach riled. My head was sore where I'd banged it, but it was the feeling of shame that was so unbearable.

I had been attacked and almost raped! Things like that didn't happen to decent girls, and I was certain Mam would go for me when I got in. She was already in a bad mood and when she saw the state I was in, she would lose her temper.

When I got to my house I turned and waved at Joe Robinson. He was still standing beneath the gaslight and nodded to me as I pointed to the door of my house, but he didn't make a move. He was going to make sure I got inside safely.

Most of the houses in the area were just two-up two-down with a lean-to scullery at the back and a privy of sorts in the back yard. Ours was an end of terrace and luckily we had an extra small room built on over the back washhouse. It was this extra room that had made it easier for Mam to take in a paying lodger after Sam O'Rourke disappeared. Had it not been for the lodger and the little bit of money the rest of us brought in, she would have had to go out scrubbing floors at one of the factories, like most of the women in the lane, which, knowing Mam, would have made her temper even worse.

As I reached the bottom of the stairs, the front door opened and our lodger looked at me. He was a small, thin man with a pale face and sad eyes, and was just coming back home after visiting a friend. He often stayed out late in the evenings, but Mam never objected. She needed his rent too much to risk losing him. I put a finger to my lips, warning him not to give me away.

'Don't let on I'm here, Mr Phillips. I want to get upstairs before Mam sees me.'

'What happened?' he asked, looking at me in concern. 'You've got mud on your dress – there's blood in your hair . . .'

'I'll wash it out when I—'

The door from the kitchen opened and I heard my mother shout, 'If that's you, Bridget, you'd better get in here before I lay me hand round your ears. I hope you're not after bringing that slut of a sister back with you . . .'

Mam came out into the hallway. She was a big-boned woman with a mottled complexion and dark hair streaked with grey dragged back into a bun at the nape of her neck. Her mouth was set in a grim line, her eyes cold with anger as she stared at me.

'Bridget has had an accident,' John Phillips said, standing in front of me as though prepared to defend me from her temper. He gave me a warning look and I took my cue from him.

'I slipped and fell in the mud in the lane, Mam – must have banged my head. Leastwise, it's bleeding.'

'Perhaps I should take a look at it,' Mr Phillips offered. 'Come into the kitchen, Bridget.'

I followed as he went through the parlour to the back kitchen. The parlour itself was furnished better than most in the lane, with a half-decent sofa and two chairs, a table with ends that folded down, four chairs to match it, an oak dresser with a mirror and shelves for a few bits and pieces of china and glass fairings.

Mam lunged at me as we passed, giving me a slap on the ear that nearly sent me flying. I gave a yelp of pain and the lodger turned to look at her reprovingly.

'Mrs O'Rourke! Surely such violence isn't necessary? The girl has already had a nasty accident.'

'You keep your nose out of it,' Mam retorted, forgetting to be polite to him in her temper. 'She's a slut and needs to be taught a lesson or she'll bring shame on us for sure. You ought to watch out, my girl. If your father were here he'd take his belt to you.'

'I've done nothing wrong, Mam. I had to go after Lainie, you know I did. I tried to get her to come home, but she wouldn't.'

Mam hit me again, making my head rock.

'That's enough, Mrs O'Rourke. I've told you before the girls *will* leave home if you continue to hit them like that. If you are trying to drive her on to the streets you are making an excellent job of it.'

'He's right, Mam. Lainie's gone and she says she won't come back – and if it weren't for our Tommy I'd go with her.'

'And where will you be going? No decent woman will take you into her home at this hour of the night. It's after pickin' up a man you'll be. You'll bide here and do as I tell you or you'll feel the back of my hand and harder than you've felt it before, my girl.'

'Bridie Macpherson will have me,' I said, my voice rising with anger now. 'She's always looking for girls to help out in that hotel of hers. That's where Lainie's gone and if you hit me again I'll go with her!'

My threat was not an idle one. Bridie Macpherson's small but scrupulously clean hotel was only three streets away from Farthing Lane. It was patronized by the captains and first officers who preferred somewhere better to stay than the Seamen's Mission, or the special hostel for foreign sailors. Jamie had told us the mission had been set up some forty years earlier, to protect the Lascars from being preyed on by river thieves. Before the hostels were built, they had often ended up penniless after being cheated or robbed of their pay by the rogues who lived in the dirty alleyways close to the docks.

Until now, both Lainie and I had worked in the brewery, which was just across the river from St Katherine's.

St Katherine's Dock was originally built on twenty-three acres between the Tower of London and the London Docks, making it conveniently near the city. The site had been home to more than a thousand families, a brewery and at one time St Katherine's hospital, which had always been owned by royalty. Its land had been cleared though, despite the hardship it caused, and the docks given a grand opening in 1828. Commodities such as tallow, rubber, sugar and tea had all been stored in the sturdy yellow-brick warehouses some six storeys high, but for some reason the docks were not a financial success and had become part of the London Docks in 1864. However, to the people of the lanes, especially those that worked there, they would always be known as St Katherine's.

There had been breweries near the river since the time of Queen Elizabeth when they supplied beer to the soldiers in the Low Countries, but Dawson's, where Lainie and I worked, had only been built in the last five years, and produced ginger beer as well as three kinds of ale.

Lainie worked in the brewing side, but I had recently been taken on in the office. Before that, I'd had occasional work down the market, helping Maisie Collins with her flower stall, and giving Mam a hand with work in the house. Being in the office at the brewery was much better. At the moment I made the tea, tidied up and ran errands for three shillings a week, but I was learning to help keep the ledgers because I could copy letters in a neat hand and I was quick at figures. Mr Dawson had promised me another two shillings a week soon.

I brought my thoughts back to the present as Mam started on at me again. 'Walk out of this house and you don't come back! I'll not have a slut livin' under my roof. You'll mend your ways or I'll see the back of you.'

'Now that's foolish talk,' Mr Phillips said. 'Bridget has always been a good girl, Mrs O'Rourke. You would find it hard to manage the house without her.'

Mam's face screwed up and I thought she was about to explode, but although she opened her mouth to tell him to mind his own business, she shut it again.

'Get to bed before I change me mind,' she said and scowled at me. 'You can think yourself lucky that Mr Phillips spoke up for you. If I had my way I'd give you a good thrashing!'

I turned and fled towards the stairs, not stopping until I was in my own room.

Tommy sat up and looked at me. 'Where's our Lainie?' he asked sleepily, clenched fists rubbing at his eyes.

'She's gone out to see a friend,' I said and hushed him with a kiss on the top of his head. He smelled so good after I'd had him in the bath and scrubbed his hair with strong soap – the same as I used to scrub the house. Tommy hated it, but he hated the nits worse and I made sure he went to bed clean – even if he came back filthy every night. 'Go back to sleep, darlin'.'

I held my brother closer, feeling protective towards him as I felt how thin and frail he was. There was no way I could ever walk out on him because he wouldn't stand a chance left alone with Mam.

'What happened to you, Bridget?' Tommy touched my cheek and found a smear of blood. 'Are you hurt?' He looked anxious, as if afraid that I might suddenly disappear too.

I glanced down at myself, repressing the shiver that ran through me as his words reminded me of what had almost happened. Rape was something all decent girls lived in fear of, which was why we took notice of our mothers and didn't go walking alone at night.

'It's nothing, darlin' – just a tumble on some mud in the lane. You know how dirty it gets at this time of year. It was probably a bit icy, it's freezin' out so it is. I fell and banged my head. It knocked me out for a moment, but I'm all right.'

'Let me look.' Tommy scrambled out of bed.

'Can you see anything?'

'It's cut open. Shall I bathe it for you, our Bridget?'

'Will you, darlin'?' I caught his hand as I saw the troubled look in his eyes. 'Don't look so worried, it's nothing much. I might have a bit of a headache, but I'm all right.'

I poured some water into the earthenware bowl from the washstand and sat on the bed for Tommy to bathe the cut on my head. He was as careful as he could be, but it stung and I winced a couple of times.

'I'm sorry, Bridget.'

'It's all right, Tommy. Let's get to bed, darlin', or you'll be too tired for school in the morning.'

We got into bed together, me holding him as he settled to sleep. I wished I could sleep as easily and I fought desperately to stop myself thinking about Harry Wright and what he had almost done to me. I knew Jamie would have gone after him if I'd told him, and he had such a temper there was no telling what he might do.

It was quiet down in the kitchen now. Mam would be having a drop of the good stuff with her lodger before they came up – to separate rooms. Mam had made it plain to her lodger there was to be no funny stuff. She slept with Tommy as a rule and Mr Phillips had the room that had been Jamie's and Tommy's before Da disappeared. If Jamie came home at all, he would sleep on the couch, but most nights he stayed with a friend, leastwise that's what he told Mam. I had heard stories that would make Martha O'Rourke's hair curl, but I kept them to myself. There was enough trouble in the house as it was without stirring up more. Still, now that Lainie had gone perhaps things would settle down for a while . . .

As I lay sleepless beside my brother, I wondered what had happened to turn Martha O'Rourke into the hard cold woman she was. Had it happened when her husband had killed a man in a violent fight on the docks?

I knew Mam's life had been hard these past years, but that didn't account for her violent rages. Some of our neighbours had it even harder than us – though we were going to miss Lainie's money. But there was real hatred in Martha O'Rourke.

Lainie was right when she said that Mam had always hated her. She'd never been as bad with me as she was with Lainie but that might change now I was the only daughter at home.

I shivered and snuggled into the warmth of my sleeping brother's body. There wasn't much point in worrying over something I couldn't change. I'd had a lucky escape thanks to Joe Robinson and I would take good care not to give Harry Wright another chance to attack me.

Sighing, I closed my eyes and willed myself to sleep. It would soon be morning and I had to be up early.

Two

M am looked heavy-eyed when she came down the next morning. She had slept late and I'd already scrubbed the front step and given Tommy his slice of bread and dripping. He hadn't wanted it, complaining that it made him feel sick, but I'd coaxed him into eating it.

'Have you done them stairs yet, you lazy little cat? You can tell that boss o' yours this mornin' that I want you setting on in the works. You'll earn more there than in that fancy office.'

'You know he won't give me Lainie's job. She was on the ales and I'm too young. He gave me my job because I can't start in the brewery proper until I'm eighteen. It's his policy and he won't change it for me.'

'His policy is it?' She sneered at me, an ugly expression on her face. 'What fancy talk is that? Don't you put on your posh airs with me, miss! You tell him what I said. If he won't pay you at least four shillings a week you can go scrubbin' floors.'

I didn't want to work on the ales or scrub floors, but knew better than to answer my mother back when she was in this mood.

'Get your brother ready first,' she said. 'I'm off down the market before the best stuff is gone.' The front door slammed as she went out.

'What do you want to take for your dinner at school, darlin'?'

'Nothing. I ain't hungry.' Tommy coughed, a harsh sound that made me look at him anxiously

'You must eat something,' I urged. He was so thin, a puff

18

of wind might blow him away! 'Bread and jam do, love?' He nodded unhappily. 'Take it with you and promise me you'll eat it and I'll get you an egg for your tea.'

'A whole egg just for me?' Tommy brightened a little. 'With bread and butter and not dripping?'

'I get my wages today. Mr Dawson promised me a rise. I'll keep a few pence back for us. Mam won't know any different. Just eat your dinner in the playground like a good boy. Then I promise I'll get that egg for your tea.'

'Mam will hit you if she finds out you didn't give her all your wages.'

'If she can catch me.' I was relieved to see a smile poke through at last. I loved this brother of mine more than anything or anyone in the whole world, and sometimes I was desperately afraid I was going to lose him. 'You and me won't tell her, will we? I'll let on Fred Pearce gave me the eggs.'

'Mam says he's a dirty old man.'

Fred lived at the end of the lane in a house that looked as if the windows hadn't been washed since he'd been there, and people often avoided him when he was trundling his little cart up the street, but I liked him and we often stopped for a chat when we met.

'He doesn't wash much, but I don't suppose he can afford the soap,' I said, deliberately ignoring what I knew was implied by Mam's harsh words.

'I don't think that's what Mam meant. She pulled a funny face the way she does, and said he'd have your knickers off you, if you don't watch it.'

'Mam says a lot of daft things – but don't tell her I said so. Fred Pearce isn't like that. He's kind and he just likes to talk to me, that's all. He's never tried to touch me – not like some of the blokes round here.'

Tommy stared at me. 'Does Mr Phillips try to touch you, our Bridget?'

'No, o' course not! I never heard the like. He's a decent bloke. I like him. I just hope he doesn't leave us. Mam would lose her rag. What made you ask me that, Tommy?'

'Nothing. I just wondered if he was one of them what tried it on with you.'

'No, he isn't. Mr Ryan from next door tries it on when he's drunk – pinchin' my bum that's all. He'd better not let Maggie see or she'll go for him with the rolling pin. Do you remember in the summer when she chased him all the way down the lane?'

Tommy nodded. He had lost interest in the conversation and said he was going out the back to the lavvy. I reminded him to wash his hands before he went to school. He nodded and promptly forgot my instructions as he shot through the kitchen without so much as a good morning to the lodger.

Mr Phillips was just preparing to leave for the day. I thought how smart he looked in his dark overcoat and bowler hat. He worked as an accountant in a big import firm on the docks and earned more in a week than I could in months. I knew how important it was that he continued to live with us and pay his rent of ten shillings a week.

'Was your breakfast satisfactory, Mr Phillips?

'The bacon you cooked was very nice.'

'Have a good day at work, sir.'

'I shall have a busy day,' he replied. 'I'm afraid no days are particularly good ones for me. Good morning, Bridget.'

I stared after him as he went out. I hadn't thought of him as being a miserable sort of man, though he was a bit odd sometimes.

However, I certainly hadn't got time to puzzle over it now. I'd better scrub the stairs and get off to the brewery or I would be late for work.

As I crossed the cobbled yard to the brewery office. I heard a shrill wolf whistle. Men were loading heavy barrels on to the wagons ready to deliver the beer to pubs all over the East End, and the smell of the horses mixed with the sharp odour from the brewery sheds. I didn't bother to turn my head at the whistle because I knew who was responsible. It was that Ernie Cole. The cheeky devil! He drove a wagon and two lovely great shire horses for Mr Dawson – and thought he owned the world.

Well, he might be a tall strong lad with a fine pair of shoulders, but I wasn't about to encourage his cheek. I wouldn't give him the satisfaction of showing I'd heard, so I stuck my head in the air and walked on by.

I supposed I liked him in a way, but I never gave him the chance to get too close. I rather enjoyed putting him down and seeing his face fall. He was too sure of himself for his own good!

He was after walking out with me, I knew, but I wasn't interested in anything like that. Not yet anyway. I was seventeen and a few months – too young for courting. Besides, I wanted to get on a bit in my job if I could and Mr Dawson thought a lot of me.

Mrs Dawson had told me that only the previous day: 'My husband thinks you might take my place as his secretary one day, Bridget. He would like me to take things a little easier, stay at home and meet my friends.'

'Take your place?' I had stared at her in surprise. 'But I could never do all the things you do, Mrs Dawson.' I had never dreamed of such a thing until she put the idea into my head, but I had liked it at once.

'Why not? You're bright, careful and industrious. I think it entirely possible that you could learn to do everything I do.'

'But how?'

'Well, I can teach you a lot of it,' Edith Dawson replied. 'But my husband feels it might be worth paying for you to have special tuition. There are places where you can learn in the evenings after work. You might even learn to use one of those machines – typewriters I think they are called.'

I hadn't known how to keep my joy to myself as I'd hurried home the previous evening. I had hoped to tell Lainie my good news when she came to bed, but the row had put it out of my head.

Stephen Dawson was waiting for me as I entered the office. He grinned at me. 'Pop the kettle on, Miss O'Rourke,' he said. He called me that sometimes just to tease me. 'We'll have a cuppa before we start, shall we?'

'Oh, yes, please,' I said. 'I didn't get one this morning and I'm proper parched, so I am.' I glanced round the small office. 'Mrs Dawson not in the mornin'?'

'No – she had some shopping up town,' he said. 'Wants to buy herself some fripperies I dare say. Our daughter is getting wed after Christmas. We heard the news last night.'

'That's grand news,' I said. 'Give Miss Jane my love and tell her I hope she will be very happy. Lainie might be getting wed soon. She told me last night that her feller had asked her.'

'That's good,' he said. 'Though I'll be sorry to lose your sister when she leaves. She's been a good worker.'

'She might have to leave before the wedding,' I said as I remembered she'd told me she was going to Mrs Macpherson's. 'You haven't heard from her the mornin'?'

'No – not yet, though she may have spoken to the foreman.' He glanced through the window, which had rivulets of water trickling down the glass because of the cold outside. 'Ah, I just need to speak to Ernie before he leaves.'

'You'll catch him if you hurry.'

I went through to the little kitchen at the back of the office. I filled a kettle from the tap over a deep stone sink, then lit the gas stove and put the water on to boil. I set the cups out on a tray – blue and white china they were and not one of them chipped – then poured milk from the can into a matching jug so that I wouldn't spill it as I served the tea. Mrs Dawson was most particular. She liked things nice and hated the smell of stale milk on her pretty tray cloths.

I picked up a thickly padded holder as the kettle began to whistle. The copper handle got hot and I didn't want to burn my fingers. I had a lot of copying to do that morning.

'Bridget . . .' I turned as Mr Dawson called to me from the doorway. 'Leave that for a moment. I want to talk to you.'

My heart caught with fright. 'Have I done something wrong, sir?'

He shook his head but looked displeased. 'You've done nothing, Bridget . . . but your brother, Jamie, is in trouble yet again.'

'What has he done?'

'Apparently he was in a fight last night. The police want someone to go down to the station and sign for him. He's in a bit of a state and they won't let him go unless a member of his family takes him home.'

'What do you mean in a state – is he hurt?'

'I think he may have been hurt during the arrest. The police couldn't find Mrs O'Rourke so they sent a young constable here. I really can't have this sort of thing, Bridget. This is a respectable business.'

'I'm sorry,' I said as I reached for my shawl. 'I'll come back as soon as I can, sir – and I'll make up the time later.'

Mr Dawson nodded, but he was still frowning. This was the second time in as many months that the police had sent for someone to fetch Jamie, and he wasn't pleased that his brewery should be associated with a known troublemaker.

I was anxious as I left the brewery office and hurried across the yard, ignoring Ernie Cole as he called out to me. He'd asked if I wanted a lift, which meant he knew where I was going. Everyone would know! I felt humiliated as I left the yard and set off in the direction of the police station, some ten minutes' walk away.

Jamie was such a fool to himself when the drink was in him. Most of the time he was a good-natured, cheerful and generous man. There was violence in Jamie; it simmered beneath the surface, erupting every now and then in uncontrollable anger. Instead of thinking, he went in with his fists just the way Da had.

Hearing the rattle of a wagon on cobbles behind me, I glanced back and saw that Ernie had almost caught me up. He slowed the horses as he drew level.

'Jump up, Bridget. You'll get there all the quicker and it's on my way, lass.'

'Thank you, but I would rather walk.'

'You're a stubborn girl, Bridget O'Rourke. You'll be quicker if you ride.'

'No, I shan't. I'm going to take the short cut by the river.'

'It's a rough area down there. Let me take you.' He gave a sigh of exasperation. 'Ah, Bridget, don't be daft, lass . . .'

Ignoring him, I ran down a side alley towards the river. It was one of the worst areas in this part of the docks and I would normally have avoided it, but I had to get away from Ernie's pestering. After the incident of the previous night, when Harry Wright had attacked me, I was less trusting than ever of men who wouldn't take no for an answer.

The river looked dirty and oily where the waste from the ships lay floating in the shallows, and it was cold enough to freeze over. There were vagrants by the dilapidated warehouses on the banks, some of them hunched by a fire burning in an old metal pot, others drinking and lying on sacks.

I felt their eyes on me as I hurried by and a couple of them called out to me, but they were harmless enough, too beaten down by life to bother. It was the cocky ones like Harry Wright you had to be careful of – and Ernie Cole.

As I turned the corner towards the police station, I saw a young woman loitering on the pavement and recognized her at once. Her name was Rosie Brown and she was what Mam would call a whore. I'd heard that she had been seen hanging around the pubs with Jamie a few times.

As soon as she saw me she came to meet me and said, 'Have you come for Jamie?' She was a pretty girl, though her fair hair looked as if it needed a good wash and her clothes weren't as clean as they might be. 'They won't let me in to see him, the rotten buggers.'

'How is he, Rosie? What happened last night?'

'Jamie got paid three shillin's,' she said and grinned wryly. 'It was the first work he'd had in days and he spent all the money on drink. There was an argument with some bloke he knows . . . turned into a bleedin' riot! They were smashin' the furniture when the bleedin' coppers arrived.'

'Was Jamie hurt?'

'Someone hit 'im from behind. I think it were a copper or it might 'ave bin one of the sailors he were fightin'. Your Jamie's a proper bruiser, Bridget. 'E ought ter do it fer a livin'. Layin' 'em out left and right he were, then someone cracked a bottle over his head, and the next thing the bleedin' coppers were all over the place and one of 'em knocked Jamie down, even though he were already dazed. They carted 'im orf and I ain't seen 'im since.'

'They ought to be ashamed of themselves.'

'I was worried about 'im,' Rosie said looking at me oddly. 'But I shan't hang around now that you're 'ere. Jamie will be all right wiv you, Bridget.'

'I'm not too sure about that,' I said ruefully. 'Mam will go wild if there's no money for her and if she finds out he spent his money on drink and spent the night in the cells, she'll likely throw him out.'

'She's a hard woman, your ma.' Rosie pulled a face. 'Jamie knows he can come to me if he's looking for a place to stay. You tell him that, Bridget.'

'That's kind of you,' I said, 'but you can't keep him, Rosie. He needs to work – he ought to work. There's nothing wrong with him, he's strong as a bull.'

'It ain't easy to find work round 'ere. 'You don't know what it's like for 'im, Bridget, the men standin' in line, waitin' to be set on. If you've been in trouble you get the worse jobs. Jamie was unloading bones for the soap factory – dirty, stinking and crawling with maggots, 'e said they was. Had to wash the taste out of 'is mouth. You can't blame 'im, Bridget.'

'No, I don't suppose so, but he's his own worst enemy, Rosie.'

'Jamie's Jamie,' she said and smiled, her eyes warm with affection. 'Don't nag 'im, luv. He's down enough as it is.'

I watched her walk away. I was well aware that it was hard for my brother having to wait in line to be given a job. Until a year previously he'd been in regular work, but some trouble on the docks had led to his being dismissed and since then he'd had to take whatever he could get.

As I entered the station the sergeant behind the desk gave me a sour look. 'Come for that brother of yours, I suppose?'

'Yes, please, Sergeant Jones. I am sorry he caused you some bother.'

'Not your fault,' Bill Jones replied, his frown lifting at the tone of my voice. 'He's a fool to himself. He's got a good brain, he should make some use of it.'

'It's only when the drink is in him, Sergeant Jones.'

'I know that. If I didn't I would have had him on a charge before this. As it is, the landlord didn't want to push charges. He's used to his customers causing trouble, and it wasn't him that called us in. Take Jamie home and see if you can make him see sense, will you, Miss O'Rourke? He's getting a bad name for himself. Tell him that it's only a matter of time before he'll be in serious trouble if he goes on this way. He might listen to you.'

'Yes, perhaps,' I said and smiled at him. 'And thank you for not sending him up before the magistrate.'

'One of these days he'll go too far . . . He's got a sore head and feels a bit sorry for himself. You'd best take him home and give him a cup of tea, miss.'

One of the younger policemen had been sent to fetch Jamie from the cells. He came in through a side door, his jacket slung carelessly over his shoulder and an air of defiance about him, but his expression changed as he saw me.

'So they sent for you,' he said, and just for a moment a flicker of shame showed in his eyes. 'There was no need. I'm sober now.'

'You were injured last night,' Sergeant Jones said and glared at him. 'Go home with your sister and think about your life, lad. You're wasting your time with all this drinking and brawling.'

Jamie scowled but made no answer, merely jerking his head at me as he left the station.

'Goodbye, Sergeant Jones,' I said. 'Thank you.'

'Why did you thank the bastard?' Jamie growled as we walked along the street. 'It was probably him that hit me.'

'You know it wasn't, Jamie. Rosie Brown said you were hit by one of them varmints you were fighting with, then

26

one of the coppers knocked you down, but you were half out anyway.' I looked at him anxiously. 'Does your head still hurt bad?' My own was feeling sore after the incident the previous night, but I wasn't going to tell him that. He was in enough trouble already.

'It aches a bit. The police surgeon patched me up earlier, said I should go to bed for a couple of days when I got home. But I'm off down the docks to see if I can get a few hours' work.'

'Surely it doesn't matter for one day? Have a rest, Jamie.'

'I can't afford to, Bridget. I've no money for Mam . . .'

'You'll likely earn some another day.'

'And when's that likely to be? I can't stand it, Bridget. Sometimes I think I'll run away – go to America like Da did.'

'Do you think that's where he is? Mam said he was drowned, but Lainie said she was lyin'.'

'Well, it was what we told the coppers,' Jamie said. 'Maybe Mam believes it now, but I reckon he got away. He'd spoken of going back to the old country and from there to America. Ah, it's a grand life there so they say – the streets are paved with gold, so they are.'

'You don't really believe that?'

Jamie grinned, his arrogant manner back in place. 'No, but there's more opportunity for a man to get on. I'm sick of bowing and scraping just to get a day's work . . .'

'Why don't you try something else, Jamie? Something better than casual work on the docks. Why let them humiliate you? Show them you're better than that!'

'There's nothing else on offer round here, Bridget. I've been everywhere and none of them would give me a chance, even if they wanted a man—'

'Then go further afield . . . don't just give up, Jamie. Try to make some sort of a life for yourself.'

'It might mean me being away for weeks – even months. There would be no money until I got a chance to come back for a visit.'

'We could manage. And if you went to America we might never see you again. At least this way you could come home now and again.'

'Would you miss me, darlin'?'

'You know I would, Jamie, but you're wasting your time around here. I'd like to see you settled . . .'

'I'll think about it,' he said and then frowned. 'Why don't you get back to work, Bridget? Mr Dawson won't be too pleased as it is, I'll wager?'

'No, he wasn't,' I admitted and studied his face. 'Are you sure you're all right? Sergeant Jones said I should make sure you got home safely.'

'I'll see Mam, then I'll be off. Make inquiries about work elsewhere. No doubt they'll be fallin' over themselves for me services . . .' He grinned at me, his old confidence coming through. 'If you don't see me for a while you'll know I've taken your advice.'

'You won't go to America?'

Jamie hesitated, then shook his head. 'No – not yet, anyway. I promise I'll tell you if I decide to go and I'll see you've got a bit o' money in your pocket. Get off then before Mr Dawson gives you up for lost.'

I ran all the way back to the brewery, terrified that I would lose my job. It was going to be hard enough without Lainie's money, and if Jamie didn't bring anything in either Mam would create, but I was glad I'd told him he ought to move on. Being out of work so often was making him bitter and I wanted the old, carefree Jamie back – even if it meant that I had to bear the brunt of Ma's temper.

Mr Dawson didn't dismiss me that day. Instead, he gave me a rise of two shillings and sixpence. It was more than he'd promised and I thought he wanted to make up for being sharp with me earlier.

I decided not to give this first rise to Mam and I bought some eggs at the shop on the way home and a tiny corner of butter for Tommy. I hesitated over some raspberry drops, then bought a small twist for him as a treat.

'Put these in your pocket and don't let Mam find them,' I told him as I gave him the sweets. 'It's our secret.'

'If she finds them I'll tell her I won them off a lad at school.'

Mam was in a bad temper when she came in from gossiping with Maggie Ryan. She looked at the eggs I'd cooked for our tea and then glared at me.

'I suppose I know where they came from!' she muttered and banged the pots on the stove. 'You just watch yourself with that Fred Pearce, my girl. He's up to no good – giving you things . . .'

'It's only a few eggs, Mam. I gave Tommy two because he's growing, but I saved one for you. Shall I boil it or fry it for you?'

'Neither. I'll put it in the pudding for Mr Phillips' dinner.' Her gaze narrowed menacingly as she looked me over. 'If I find out you've been up to something . . .'

'I wouldn't, Mam. You know I wouldn't do anything to shame you.'

'You'll rue the day you were born if I catch you hanging about with men.' She cuffed my ear in passing as I rose to gather the tea things. 'Did you speak to Mr Dawson about putting you on the ales?'

'No, Mam . . .' I ducked as she came at me again. 'Don't hit me! Mr Dawson is going to give me a rise next week – and Mrs Dawson is going to teach me to be a secretary.'

'You watch your language, my girl!' She stared at me suspiciously. 'What's that supposed to mean then? I know his sort, all hands. If you're lettin' him do things to you . . .'

'No, Mam! It means I'm going to keep the accounts and learn to use one of those typing machines. Mrs Dawson says I'll earn a lot more once I've learned than I will on the ales.'

'How much more?'

'Perhaps as much as fifteen shillings a week when I'm trained.'

Her mouth twisted in disbelief. 'She's having you on, Bridget. They'll never pay you that! Unless he's interfering with you? Bloody men, they never know when to keep their hands to themselves.'

'Of course he isn't doing anything – Mr Dawson isn't like that, you know he isn't. And I wouldn't let him if he tried. I shan't get that sort of money for a long time, but the more I learn the more they will pay me. Please don't make me leave, Mam. I like it there and Mr Dawson said he wouldn't put me on the ales yet anyway. I should have to go scrubbin' and then there would be no chance of anything better.'

'We'll be needing more money with that whore of a sister of yours leaving us in the lurch, and Jamie bringing home next to nothing.'

'Jamie hasn't been able to find regular work. It isn't his fault . . . the bosses won't give him a proper job.'

'And whose fault is that? He's a troublemaker like Sam. Always fighting! It was the worst day of my life when I met Sam O'Rourke. I had a good place in service until he . . .' She broke off and scowled. 'If you're lying to me about the money I'll make you sorry.'

'You'll see, Mam. I'll bring you extra money next week.'

'See you do,' she muttered, clipping my ear again. 'That's nothing to what you'll get if I catch you out, miss. Now you can go up the Feathers and get me a jar of whisky.' She took half a crown from the shelf and slapped it down on the table in front of me. 'Come straight back and don't lose the change.'

I was resentful as I made my way towards the pub at the end of the lane. It was still early in the evening and there were plenty of people about. Mr Ryan from next door was on his way home from work.

Tilly Cullen waved as she scurried home to get her husband's tea. She was the laziest woman in the street, spending most of her time gossiping with her friend. Maggie Ryan had told me that Tilly's house was a tip most of the time.

'I don't know how she gets away with it,' Maggie had said.

'My Mick would take his belt to me if I let things go the way she does.'

When I came out of the Feathers, I glanced round uneasily, half fearing that Harry Wright might be hanging around waiting to grab me again, but there was no sign of him. I breathed a sigh of relief and did my best to put the incident out of my mind; it wasn't likely that I would see Harry for a while. He couldn't be sure that I hadn't told Jamie, and he would be aware of my brother's reputation.

Even so, I walked home quickly. Ernie Cole and a group of other young men and women were walking up the lane towards me, obviously heading for the pub and a night out. Ernie waved to me but I ignored him as always, hurrying inside the house.

Mam snatched the whisky jar from me as soon as I went into the kitchen. I gave her the change, which she counted before putting it on the mantelpiece.

'Haven't you got anything better to do with yourself, Bridget O'Rourke? It's time you fetched Tommy to bed, and then you can do the ironing. Out of my way, girl! I've got to see to Mr Phillips' dinner.'

I turned away, feeling the resentment bite deep. What did Mam do with herself all day? She washed the clothes and sheets twice a week because of the lodger, but I did most of the other work.

For a few minutes rebellion flared inside me. The future seemed bleak despite the promise of a better job, and I wished I could just walk out the way Lainie had.

Thinking about my sister cheered me up a little. Maybe I could find a way to take Tommy to visit her that weekend. I still had a few pennies left in my pocket. Maisie would sell me a nice bunch of flowers for that.

I called Tommy in from the yard, where he had been playing with Billy Ryan and some of the other lads. He was the reason I stayed here. As long as I had him to take care of, I would put up with Mam and her temper.

Three

'Harry Wright did *what* to you?' Lainie stared at me in horror. 'Did he hurt you, Bridget? He didn't manage to . . . well, you know . . . ?'

'Careful,' I warned, 'I don't want Tommy to hear. If he were to tell Jamie – you know what would happen. I don't want Jamie in more trouble.' I glanced at Tommy, who was playing with a cat in Bridie Macpherson's back yard and eating an apple.

'He would go after that bastard for sure,' Lainie said. 'He deserves a thrashing for what he did to you.'

'But then Jamie would go to prison.'

'Let that devil wait until I see him,' she said. 'I'll have a thing or two to say to him. You should have told Sergeant Jones. He would have sorted him out for you.'

'I couldn't. It's too embarrassing. Don't let's talk about it any more. I'm all right. My head was sore for a bit and it gave me a nasty feeling inside, but I'm over it now.'

'Nothing bothers you for long, does it? If I'd been more like you maybe I wouldn't have quarrelled with Mam so much.'

'It was Mam's fault not yours. Her temper is getting worse all the time.'

'That's the drink,' Lainie said. 'She guzzles too much of that rot gut stuff from the Feathers. It's not like good whisky, Bridget. I'm after thinkin' it's turned her mind.'

'You don't mean that?'

'It seems that way to me. She wasn't this bad a few years back, but it's been coming on for a while . . . since Da left.'

'That made things hard for her, Lainie.'

'She was better off than a good many. I've tried to work it out, but I've never understood why she's so hard . . . so bitter.'

Mrs Macpherson had come into the yard to tell us there was a pot of tea and cakes waiting. 'You can have your tea with your sister, Lainie,' she said. 'Then I need you in the kitchen. We've an extra guest this evening and he wants his dinner at six.'

'I should be going soon anyway,' I said. 'It was good of you to let Lainie have time off to talk to us, Mrs Macpherson.'

People might say she was hard on her girls, but I thought Lainie was lucky. Mam would have me at it night and day if she could, and some nights I was so tired I could hardly wait to get my things off and go to bed.

'Lainie's a good worker,' she said. 'I was pleased to get her, but don't expect to visit every week. Once a month will suit me, and Lainie gets a half-day every other week.'

We followed Mrs Macpherson into the hotel. She'd set a tray in the little back parlour and she'd been generous with slices of seed cake and treacle tart. Tommy fell on them with delight, wolfing down two slices of each.

'Don't make yourself sick,' I warned, but Lainie smiled and ruffled his hair.

'Let him enjoy himself, Bridget. Bridie won't expect any left over. She's always generous with food, even if she does drive us girls hard.'

'Is it all right here, Lainie?'

'It's better than being at home with Mam after me all the time. And I shall go with Hans as soon as he gets back.'

'When will that be, Lainie?'

'He said it would be a short voyage this time. He always stays here and he'll be surprised to find me waiting for him.'

'I hope he comes soon,' I said and felt an odd chill that I couldn't explain at the back of my neck. 'I want you to be happy.'

'Don't worry about me . . .' She paused, wrinkling her nose. 'I'm going to talk to Hans about you and Tommy. When we're settled – I might send for you both.'

'Do you mean it? Would Hans let us? You don't want to spoil things for yourself.'

'You don't know Hans if you think that,' she said confidently. 'He's so good to me, Bridget. I think he would give me the moon if he could . . .'

Mrs Macpherson was looking at us from the doorway. I jumped up and caught Tommy's hand. 'Thank you for the lovely tea,' I said. 'We'll be going now.'

She nodded her approval, ruffling Tommy's hair as we passed by. 'You've got good manners, Bridget,' she said. 'If you ever want to leave home I could find work for you here.'

'Thank you. It's generous you are, Mrs Macpherson. I shan't forget.'

It was cold outside and I shivered, pulling my shawl tighter around me as we passed a gentleman who was about to enter the hotel. He was carrying a large bunch of crimson chrysanthemums and something about his manner made me look at him and smile.

'Someone is going to be lucky,' I said. 'Aren't they lovely – really big heads and that sort always smells so good.'

He glanced at me, surprised at first and then he replied with an answering smile, 'They are rather special, aren't they? I bought them for a friend.'

'Did you get them from Maisie?' I asked, chattering on because he seemed such a pleasant man. His clothes told me he didn't belong in the area; they were too smart – too expensive. I thought he must be gentry, perhaps a country gentleman in town on business and calling on a friend. 'She had some on her stall yesterday.'

'What an observant young lady you are,' he said. 'Yes, I bought them from Maisie. I usually visit her whenever I'm this way.'

'On business I suppose?'

I wondered at myself even as I spoke. Normally, I wouldn't have asked a stranger questions, but I was curious about him. He didn't look as if he were one of Mrs Macpherson's regular guests, but he was clearly about to go inside.

'Business and pleasure,' he replied looking amused. 'Bridie is a friend of mine – the flowers are for her. I visit her now and then . . . When I'm here on business, as you said.'

'Oh . . .' I flushed as I realized that he was laughing at me. 'I shouldn't have asked . . .'

'I don't mind.' He offered me his hand. 'I am Philip Maitland – and who do I have the honour of addressing?'

'Bridget O'Rourke,' I said, suddenly shy as I felt the warm clasp of his hand about mine. 'My sister Lainie is working for Mrs Macpherson and Tommy and me have been visiting – and I talk too much!'

'Ah – Miss Bridget O'Rourke,' he said and nodded. 'So that's the source of that delightful accent . . . just a trace of Irish and very attractive if I may be permitted to say so. Perhaps we shall meet again one day?'

'Yes, perhaps.' I was beginning to feel embarrassed. 'I have to go now.'

'In that case I must not delay you.'

'Did you know him?' Tommy asked when we were out of earshot. 'Mam will belt you if she knows you were makin' up to a toff, Bridget.'

'He was a gentleman. And Mam won't know, because I shan't tell her – and you mustn't either.'

'You know I wouldn't tell on you,' Tommy said giving me a reproachful look. 'But Tilly Cullen went past while you were laughin' with him, and you know what she's like.'

'Well, we'll just have to hope she doesn't tell Mam. Besides, we weren't doing anything wrong – just talking.'

But I crossed my fingers and hoped Mam wouldn't hear anything.

She was in an unusually mellow mood when we got in. She grumbled at me and asked where I'd been, but accepted it when I said we'd been to visit Lainie.

'Mrs Macpherson gave us tea,' I told her. 'She says we can visit again next month if we want.'

'If that slut of a sister of yours is still there. But at least you've had your tea so you can get on with cleaning the bedrooms. Mr Phillips has gone on a visit of his own, but he's paid his rent in full for next week – so we shan't have to feed him. And he bought me a present.' She stroked almost lovingly the bottle of good Irish whisky standing on the table in front of her. 'Well, what are you waiting for?'

'Do I have to do his room tonight, Mam? If he's away the week . . . All right, but I only polished it through two days ago.'

'Well, you can do it again – and less of your cheek, miss. Or you'll feel the back of me hand.'

She took a swipe at me as I went past her, but her heart wasn't in it for once and I was able to avoid the blow. She was pouring herself a glass of whisky as I collected my polishing rags and went through to the parlour. Tommy came clattering up the stairs after me. His face had lost the bright look it had worn all afternoon and I could see that he was close to tears.

'What's the matter, me darlin'?'

'Mam told me to get out of her way. What's wrong with her, Bridget? Maggie Ryan gets cross with Billy sometimes, but she's not like Mam.'

I took hold of his hand, leading him into my bedroom and we sat on the bed. He had a little coughing fit, so I waited for him to finish.

'I don't know why she's the way she is, Tommy. I don't mind her getting at me, but I wish she would be kinder to you.'

'I wish we could run away together. When I'm grown up I'm going to America to make my fortune and then you can come and live with me. I'll take care of you, Bridget. Mam won't shout at you then.'

'I don't mind her grumbling,' I told him and kissed the top of his head. 'Why don't you slip next door with Billy and Maggie? I'll come and fetch you when it's time for bed.'

He nodded, clearly still troubled, and rubbed at his chest as if it hurt him. 'Do you ever wish she would die, Bridget?'

'No, of course not – and nor must you. It would be a

mortal sin and you know what Father Brannigan would have to say about that, don't you?' The priest was his teacher at the Catholic school he attended, and Tommy respected him. He nodded but looked miserable as I continued: 'I know Mam has a terrible temper, darlin', but I don't wish her harm. One day you and me will go away together.'

'You should marry Ernie Cole,' Tommy said and grinned as I pulled a face. 'He's sweet on you, our Bridget. You're a real looker with them green eyes o' yours. Ernie would come courting if you gave him half a chance.'

'Get off next door, you cheeky monkey. I've work to do!'

I smiled to myself as he laughed and ran out, thinking about what he had said for a moment, but I sneaked a look at myself in the mirror. I supposed I wasn't bad looking, my hair had reddish tints sometimes and my eyes were a bit green. I knew Ernie liked me, but I doubted he had any thoughts of marriage. I'd seen him off to the pub on Friday and Saturday nights, and the company he chose told me that he wasn't thinking of settling yet.

I wasn't sure whether I wanted to be taken out by Ernie – or anyone else come to that. I supposed that I might think of marriage one day, though I was a bit wary of getting trapped into the kind of marriages that some of my neighbours endured.

Anyway, there wasn't much chance of my getting married, I didn't have time to go courting.

Tommy's cough was getting worse again. I wrapped a scarf I'd knitted around his neck as I sent him off to school.

'Don't stand about in the cold wind,' I told him. 'And ask Father Brannigan if you can stay in at break. Tell him I told you to ask.'

'I'm all right,' Tommy said, but he looked pale and he'd been awake half the night with his cough. 'Can we visit Lainie tomorrow?'

'Yes, I should think so. I spoke to Mrs Macpherson as I was walking home last night from the brewery. She said she was expecting us and I was to be sure to bring you, as she would have a special treat for you.'

Tommy's face lit up and he gave me a quick hug, then ran off to call for Billy Ryan. Mam was still in her room; she'd grumbled about having a headache and told me to cook the lodger's breakfast when I'd gone to call her earlier. I was still at the sink washing the dishes when Maggie Ryan opened the door and asked if she could come in.

'O' course you can.' I dried my hands on a bit of towel. 'I've done now, but I've time for a cuppa before I go to work if you fancy one? I could take one up to Mam – she's feeling a bit under the weather the mornin'.'

'Don't you bother for me, Bridget love,' Maggie said. She hesitated uncertainly for a moment. 'It was your Tommy I came about, Bridget. He's been after coughin' again all night. Tell me to mind my own business if you like, but shouldn't you be thinkin' of takin' him to the doctor?'

'Do you think I ought, Maggie?' Her words had echoed thoughts I had been trying to keep at bay. 'Does he seem poorly to you? I asked Mam but she said it was just a chill, told me she'd no money to waste on visits to doctors.'

'I've been wondering if I should tell you,' Maggie said and again she was hesitant. 'Our Billy says he was coughin' up blood the other day in the playground.'

'Blood? Maggie, no! Do you think he's got . . .'

I couldn't bring myself to say the word. Consumption was such a terrible illness. Children in the slum areas caught all kinds of nasty diseases, such as rickets and worms and a hundred and one other things, but consumption was contagious and they usually sent people in the final stages to the isolation infirmary, which was a horrible place.

'Ah, don't take on so, Bridget. Mick said as I shouldn't say anything – you've troubles enough so you have – but it's been on my mind.'

'I'm glad you told me. I shall have to speak to Lainie – see what she thinks. We're visiting her tomorrow. Tommy is looking forward to it.'

I glanced up at the ceiling as I heard a thumping noise upstairs. 'It sounds as though Mam's getting up. She had a headache this mornin'. Are you sure you won't stay for a cup of tea, Maggie?'

'No, I'm off to the market.' She paused, then: 'If there's anythin' I can do at any time, Bridget. I know it must be hard for you . . . the way things are with your mam.'

'Thank you, Maggie. I shall have to run now or I'll be late for work.'

'I'll call upstairs to your mam,' Maggie said. 'You get off, love. You're in more of a hurry than me.'

'Bless you, Maggie.'

I grabbed my shawl from the hook behind the door. Mrs Dawson had been quite sharp with me recently. She wouldn't be happy if I was late again.

As I hurried through the lane to the brewery, my thoughts were with my brother. What would happen to Tommy if he had consumption? I knew that sometimes people went away to places where the air was better to get over it, but that was bound to cost money. We couldn't afford to send Tommy to the mountains for a cure in some fancy hospital in Switzerland. Even the cost of a visit to the doctor was going to stretch my slim resources, but somehow I would find the money.

I thought of Tommy's pale face as I'd sent him off to school that morning, and my heart caught with pain. What would I do if anything happened to him?

Lainie was looking pleased with herself when I saw her that Saturday afternoon. I asked if she'd heard from Hans, but she shook her head, a little smile on her mouth.

'Why are you smiling like the cat that got the cream then?'

'Am I?' She touched something at her throat and I saw that she was wearing a heavy gold cross and chain. 'I wonder why . . .'

'Where did you get that? I've never seen you wear it before.'

'A friend gave it to me . . .' She laughed huskily, a sly look in her eyes. 'Don't look at me like that, Bridget. It was a gift, that's all. I didn't do anything for it – nothing wrong anyway.'

'What will Hans say if he sees you wearing it?'

'I can't help it if men find me attractive,' she said, looking sulky. 'Hans said he would be back before now. If he'd come when he promised I wouldn't have met . . . someone else.'

'I thought you said you loved Hans?'

'I do . . . in a way,' she said and there was guilt in her eyes. 'But . . . this other person . . . well, he treats me as if I were special.'

'Hans wants to marry you,' I reminded her.

'I shall marry him when he comes back,' she said, sounding cross. 'I'm just having a little fun, Bridget. Besides, what has it got to do with you? You're not my keeper. You're nearly as bad as Mam.'

'If that's the way you feel I might as well go . . .' I got up to leave but she caught at my hand.

'Ah no,' she said, giving me a shamefaced look. 'Don't go, me darlin'. I don't want to quarrel with you.'

'No, we shan't quarrel over it,' I said and sat down again. 'But be careful, Lainie. You've always told me that Hans was a good man. Don't throw his love away for a necklace.'

She smiled and tucked the cross inside her dress and I knew she wasn't listening. 'Forget it,' she said. 'I shall probably never see the other one again . . .' She frowned as she heard Tommy coughing. 'He doesn't seem to get any better.'

'Maggie said her Billy saw him coughing up blood in the playground.'

'Oh, Bridget! You'd better take him to the doctor. Here –' she felt in her pocket and brought out three florins – 'this should cover a visit, but send word if you need more and I'll get some for you.'

'Are you sure? Will it leave you short?'

'I can manage. Tommy is the important one. You take him

to the doctor, but don't let Mam take that money off you. She'll only spend it on the drink.'

'I know . . .' I sighed. 'Every morning she says she's got the headache. She doesn't get out of bed until I go to work and she hardly lifts a finger in the house.'

'You mean she lets you do everything? She's a lazy slut, Bridget. It would serve her right if you upped and left her.'

'I sometimes wish I could walk out like you did,' I said. 'But there's no sense in wishing for the moon. Tommy and me couldn't manage on our own – not until I'm earning more.'

Lainie nodded, a brief flash of guilt passing across her face. 'I know what I promised, Bridget, and as soon as Hans comes I'll talk to him. I can't understand why he hasn't come before this. He's usually only gone for two to three weeks.'

'Perhaps the ship was delayed.'

'Yes, that's probably it. They've had to wait for a cargo.'

'What about this other feller – you aren't serious about him?'

'O' course not, darlin'. He was just passin' the time o' day, and he gave me a cross because I happened to say I'd always wanted a nice one. He's a nice man, Bridget, and always polite. It made me think about another kind of life, away from the docks and all this, but I'll settle for Hans. Don't you worry . . .'

Lainie had told me not to worry about her, but I'd seen the sparkle in her eyes when she'd shown me the gold cross and chain, and I knew she was more taken with this other man than she would admit. I hoped she wouldn't be foolish over him – whoever he was – and not just because Lainie was my only hope of getting away from Mam.

I fingered the three florins in my pocket, thinking about where best to hide them. If Mam found them she wouldn't hesitate to take them for herself and I needed them for Tommy.

'And how are you this afternoon, Bridget?'

I was startled by the question, and turned round to see Fred Pearce just behind me. For once he wasn't trundling his old cart, which was why I hadn't been aware of his approach. Fred was usually to be seen collecting what other people left as rubbish in the streets, old bottles that he took back to the brewery for a few pence a load and other things he discovered on rubbish tips. The kids laughed and threw horse dung at him when they saw him, and most people turned the other way when he spoke to them, thinking him a dirty old tramp, but I had always found Fred pleasant to talk to. Sometimes he looked sad when we met, but he usually brightened up once we'd had a chat.

'I'm all right, thank you,' I said. 'How are you, Mr Pearce?'

'Well enough,' he said and frowned as Tommy started coughing. 'That's a nasty cough, lad.' He felt in his pocket and came out with two pennies, which he handed to Tommy. 'Get yourself some sweets . . .'

'Thanks, Mr Pearce . . .'

Tommy ran off towards the shop at the corner of our lane and I looked at the old man. 'That was kind of you,' I said, knowing that he worked hard for the coppers he earned from the brewery and the rag and bone yard. 'He's been coughing for a while now. I'm going to take him to the doctor this week, but he doesn't know yet. He won't like it much.'

'You take him just the same,' Fred said. 'I don't like the sound of that cough. You look after him, Bridget . . . before it's too late.'

'Yes, I will,' I said and watched as he shuffled off down the lane.

Fred Pearce was a mystery. No one seemed to know much about him, except that he lived in a detached house right at the end of our lane. He seldom opened the door to anyone, but Maude Brown, who lived opposite, said it was like a junkyard inside. I had sometimes wondered how he managed alone, but he was fiercely independent and would never accept help from anyone, preferring to keep himself to himself.

I remembered that the man who had come to my rescue the night I was attacked by Harry Wright had said he was visiting Fred Pearce . . . and that was odd in itself. I hadn't thought Fred encouraged visitors and Joe Robinson hadn't been from around here. At least, I hadn't seen him before or since that night, so I supposed he had come from away somewhere.

My mind returned to my own worries. I didn't know what to do about Mam's deterioration, which I believed was to do with her drinking, and now I had Tommy to think about – and that was much worse.

'And where would you be getting money for doctor's visits?' Mam lunged at me, trying to grab me, but I dodged back, avoiding her and the blow I knew was coming. 'If you've been down the docks with a man I'll flay the skin off your back!'

'Don't be daft, Mam. I told Lainie Tommy was coughing up blood and she gave me some money.'

'And we all know where that little tramp gets her money. She's a slut and a whore,' Mam said and grunted as she flopped down in her chair by the stove, clearly out of breath. She rubbed at her chest as though it hurt. 'She'll come to a bad end, your sister.'

'Lainie earns her money working for Mrs Macpherson. Why do you say those things about her?'

'I thought she was getting married? What's happened to that feller she was after marryin'?'

'Hans is still away. It's a longer voyage this time. He'll marry her when he gets home.'

'That remains to be seen.' Mam rubbed at her chest. 'So what did the doctor say then?'

'I've got to take Tommy back next week.'

'And what's that going to cost? I've trouble enough making ends meet as it is without paying for doctors.'

'Lainie said she'll give me the money.' Mam rubbed at her chest again. 'What's wrong, Mam? Have you got a pain in your chest?'

'It's all the worry of you and your brother,' she muttered. 'I've warned you, Bridget O'Rourke, you'll be the death of me yet. What if your brother turns out to have the consumption? Have you thought about that? They'll likely want to send him away – where will Lainie get the money for that? You should've left things as they were. Tommy will get over it—'

'Or he'll just get worse and die. Is that what you're thinking, Mam?' I noticed the fine red lines about her nose and a certain puffiness in her face. She was changing fast and it had to be the drinking that was dragging her down. 'Well, I'm not going to let that happen without a fight. I care about him even if you don't.'

'You little bitch!' She clawed up out of her chair suddenly and launched herself at me in a fury. Taken by surprise, I didn't move fast enough and she punched me hard in the face, splitting my lip and sending me crashing back against the stove. I knocked my arm on the kettle and felt the sting of hot water as it spilled on to my hand. 'I'll teach you to criticize me . . .'

'Stop it, Mrs O'Rourke!' The shocked voice from the doorway halted her as she was about to launch herself at me again. 'That is enough! Can't you see Bridget is hurt?'

'It was her own fault,' Mam muttered and slumped down in her chair again. 'Ah, but she's a hard girl that daughter of mine, Mr Phillips. You don't know how she talks to her poor old mother.' Tears of self-pity were filling her eyes. 'She's no feelings for me at all.'

Mr Phillips shot her a look of disgust. 'Was that water boiling, Bridget?' he asked. 'Let me look at it for you.'

'It's all right,' I said. 'It was just the shock. I'll put some cold water on it.'

'You should rub a little grease on it afterwards,' he advised, 'and bind it up with a bit of clean linen. And look, your lip is bleeding.'

'Don't worry, it will be all right,' I said. 'Was there something you wanted, Mr Phillips?'

'No, no, it doesn't matter,' he said. 'I was meaning to talk to Mrs O'Rourke but it will keep.' He turned and went out of the kitchen with a glance of disgust for Mam.

She started on at me the minute she heard the front door shut behind him. 'If he leaves we shall end up in the workhouse,' she said and glared at me. 'And it will be all your fault, Bridget.'

I was at the sink, plunging my hand in a bowl of cold water. The sting was beginning to go and I realized that I had been lucky – the water in the kettle had been hot but not at boiling point. I turned to look at her as I dried my hand.

'I do my best to help you, Mam,' I said. 'But Tommy comes first with me. I don't care what you do or say to me, but the minute you lay a finger on him we'll be out of this house and you can manage for yourself.'

'Get yourself out of my sight. Find yourself some work to do.'

'I never stop working,' I said as rebellion flared. 'I'm going next door to talk to Maggie.'

'You come back here! You'll feel the back of me hand, girl!'

I ignored her and went out without speaking again. As I emerged into the street I saw Fred Pearce trundling by with his cart. He smiled and waved at me. I waved back, holding on to the tears that threatened to overcome me.

It was a freezing cold night and there was only just over a week to Christmas now, but it would be much the same as any other day in our house. I had been saving a few pence to buy something for Tommy, but I wanted to make it special for him. Especially if it . . . The emotion rose up in my throat to choke me. I leaned against the wall outside Maggie's house, weeping.

'What's wrong, lass?' I hadn't noticed Ernie Cole approaching, but as I glanced up I saw that he was offering me a red-spotted handkerchief. 'Go on, it's clean,' he said, giving me an uncertain look. 'Ma washed and ironed it this mornin'.'

'Thank you.' I accepted it gratefully and blew my nose, gulping hard to stop myself crying. I gave him a watery smile. 'It's not clean now. I'd better keep it and wash it before I give it back to you.'

'You do whatever yer want, Bridget,' he said. 'Ma will ring a peal over me 'ead for losin' it, but I'll keep me mouth shut. Is there somethin' I can do to 'elp yer?'

His kindness and his broad cockney accent were comforting, as was the look of concern on his face. 'There's nothing you can do,' I told him. 'Tommy might be very ill – he might have to go away for a long time.'

'I'd 'eard somethin',' Ernie said and looked sympathetic. 'You mustn't give up, Bridget. If 'e's lucky he might get better at one of them places what they send 'em to sometimes.'

'If he's lucky. With our luck they'll stick him in the infirmary and he'll be dead within a year.'

The expression in Ernie's eyes told me that that was his own true opinion. He took a step towards me. I moved back as he reached out for me, a thrill of fear shooting through me as I recalled the night Harry Wright had tried to rape me.

'Don't you dare touch me, Ernie Cole!'

The sharpness of my voice startled him. He looked surprised and then a little offended. 'I wouldn't hurt you,' he said. 'Surely you know that, Bridget? I'd cut off my right arm before I did wrong to you.'

'I know . . .' I hesitated, wanting to tell him I was sorry I had spoken so harshly, to explain what had been in my mind, but it was too shaming. 'I am sorry, Ernie. I didn't mean to offend you. Please leave me alone now. I have to see Maggie . . .'

I turned away in a fluster of embarrassment, wondering why it had disturbed me to see that hurt look in his eyes. I wasn't going soft on him; I didn't have time to think of courting anyone.

Four

Maggie welcomed me warmly into her kitchen. It was no bigger than ours, but it always smelt of good things. She looked at me and tutted as she saw the dried blood on my lip.

'I suppose I don't need to ask how that happened. Martha been up to her usual tricks, has she?'

'We had an argument over Tommy. I wasn't quick enough at getting out of the way.'

Maggie looked savage and I knew she would have liked to have a go at Mam but didn't want to make things worse for me. 'I'll make a brew. Sit yourself down and tell me what's on your mind, love.'

'Mam says we can't afford to send Tommy away if he's got the consumption. I don't know what to do, Maggie. If he needs treatment . . . ?'

'Sure and wouldn't that be the best thing for the darlin' boy? It might do him the world of good if they sent him to one of them seaside places. The air will clean his lungs, so it will.'

'We couldn't afford to send him somewhere like that,' I said. 'He will probably finish up in the infirmary – and you know what that's like.' My throat felt tight as I blinked back my tears once more. 'I can't bear to think of him in there but I don't want to lose him, Maggie . . .'

'Ah, don't take on so, love,' Maggie said. 'There's something I heard that might help your Tommy.'

'I could do with some help,' I said, and blew my nose on Ernie's handkerchief. 'It's daft to get myself in a state but I can't help it, Maggie. I keep thinking about it all the time.'

'I know what you mean. I should feel just the same if it were our Billy – or the other boys, though they're grown up now with families of their own.' Maggie hesitated. 'I haven't said anythin' before because it's charity and I know how you feel about that, but this is the church, Bridget. Father O'Brien sent one of the boys from Billy's class at school to this place a few weeks ago. You don't pay anythin' unless you've got the money. It's near the sea somewhere . . .'

I stared at her in silence for a few moments, my stomach churning. I wanted to say that I wouldn't take charity but I knew I couldn't. Charity was a dirty word in my book, but if the Catholic Church ran this one I might just be able to accept it.

'I shall have to talk to Dr Morris. If he says Tommy has to go away to get better, I'll speak to Father O'Brien.'

'Tell you what. I've been doin' a bit o' sewin' for Father O'Brien's housekeeper. I'm takin' it back tomorrow afternoon. I'll ask to see him and find out a bit more about it.'

'You're a good friend, Maggie. You make me feel so much better.'

'That's what friends are for, me darlin'.' She poured me a cup of tea. 'Now drink that up if you can manage it, and then I'll bathe that lip for you.'

'Could you wrap a bandage round my hand?' I said. 'I spilt some hot water on it and it feels a bit sore.'

'More of Martha's doing?' She frowned as she saw the red patch on the back of my hand. 'She's a wicked woman that mother of yours. I'm tempted to give her a piece of me mind, so I am.'

'She's not wicked, Maggie,' I said. 'Just selfish and bitter. I wish I knew why she was like it, then I might be able to feel some sympathy for her.'

'Don't waste your pity on her,' Maggie said. 'It's you and Tommy I bother about, not Martha.'

'I'm all right,' I said. 'I was just a bit upset over Tommy, that's all. I can put up with Mam and her temper as long as he's all right.'

'Don't you worry about him,' Maggie said, trying to cheer me up. 'It will be like a holiday for him, so it will.'

'He would like to visit the seaside,' I agreed. 'He's never been. Da took Jamie, Lainie and me once years ago – to Southend in a charabanc, but Tommy hasn't ever seen the sea.'

'Well, this might be a chance for him,' Maggie said. 'You'll see, love. It might all turn out for the best.'

I knew she was just trying to lift my spirits and I smiled to please her, but the growing certainty that my little brother was very ill was like a lump of stone in my breast.

I decided that I would try to see Lainie the next day, even if it meant taking half an hour off work. I wanted to tell my sister that Tommy might have to go away. Even if the charity paid the costs of his treatment he was going to need a few things.

Mrs Dawson frowned when she heard me asking for time off.

'You are being very thoughtless,' she said after her husband had told me it was all right as long as I was quick and didn't make a habit of it. 'You've been late a couple of times recently. You should be working extra time not less.'

'I'm sorry. I'll stay behind tomorrow to catch up, if you like.'

'And so I should think!'

'It's all right, Bridget,' Mr Dawson said. 'Just don't make it a regular thing.'

'No, sir. I'm sorry for the trouble I've caused.'

I left work the moment Mr Dawson said it was all right and ran all the way to the Sailor's Rest. By the time I got there I was out of breath and my chest hurt.

Mrs Macpherson was behind the counter in the lobby when I went in. A seaman was settling his account and I waited until she had finished serving him before approaching her.

'May I please see Lainie for a few minutes? I promise I won't stop her working. I have to get back myself—'

'I'm afraid you can't,' she interrupted, looking annoyed.

'I've got time off work specially. It's very important, Mrs Macpherson.'

'I dare say it is,' she said, a sharp note in her voice, 'but you can't see her because she isn't here. She took her things and left this morning.'

'Where did she go? Did Hans come for her?'

'Not to my knowledge. She didn't say where she was going. She told me she'd had a better offer and went, just like that. It didn't matter that I would be one short in my staff, but that's your sister all over. I'm disappointed in her, Bridget. It's my opinion she went off with a man.' Her mouth had gone thin and hard, her eyes cold.

'But who? She was going to marry Hans . . . She cared for Hans. I know she did . . . Why would she go off just like that with someone else?'

'Perhaps she had big ideas all of a sudden. Don't ask me what your sister had in mind – and don't ask any more questions. I've too much work to do to stand gossiping to you!'

She turned her back on me and went through to her office, leaving me to stare after her in bewilderment. Bridie was very angry and I sensed that there was more to it than simply being let down by a girl who worked for her.

Lainie's sudden disappearance left me concerned as to how I would pay for my next visit to the doctor, but when I went back there just three days before Christmas he told me I wasn't to worry.

'You can pay me when you have the money,' he said kindly and I could see that he was wondering how to tell me the news about Tommy. 'I am afraid Tommy is a very sick boy, Miss O'Rourke. I suspected it last week when I examined him and the tests I did seem to indicate that he has all the early symptoms of consumption.'

'Does that mean he's going to die?' I asked fearfully.

'Because he is still at an early stage, Tommy may be treatable,' Dr Morris said. 'We don't really know enough about the disease, but in some cases rest, fresh air and good food may help – none of which is available to him in his present circumstances. Your brother is seriously undernourished, Miss O'Rourke.'

'He doesn't always eat what I give him,' I said, feeling hot all over. He made it sound as if we starved Tommy, but I made sure he got the best I could manage. 'He likes fruit but we can't often afford that . . .' I took a deep breath. 'Someone told me about a place the church runs at the seaside . . .'

'That would certainly be a good idea. I am afraid I can only offer the infirmary – unless you can find the money to send him away yourself.'

'You won't send him there yet? Not before Christmas?' I asked, my stomach beginning to tie itself up in knots.

'No, but you are going to have to keep him away from school. He could be infectious to other children – and your own family. I can give you a little time, but eventually it will have to be isolation at the infirmary if this charity thing doesn't come through.'

'As long as we have Christmas. I need a little time to prepare him . . .'

'Yes, of course. I understand perfectly,' the doctor said. 'I don't like this any more than you do, Miss O'Rourke, but I don't have a choice. If neglected, Tommy is just going to get worse.'

'Yes, I know,' I said. 'I know what I have to do, doctor, but not until after Christmas.'

Mam was sitting in her chair by the stove when I went in. She hadn't done a thing all day and there was a pile of ironing waiting for me to start. 'So you're back then,' she said sourly. 'You can go up—'

There was a knock at the door before she could finish and I went to answer it. Ernie Cole was standing on the doorstep, cap in hand. He looked at me awkwardly, as if unsure of my reaction.

'Ma sent this,' he said and held out a parcel wrapped in

greaseproof paper. 'She made too much cake mixture and this was left over . . .'

I glared at him, tempted to thrust his gift back in his face, but then I remembered Tommy. A cake was a cake and I had little enough to spend on my brother as it was.

'Thank Mrs Cole for me,' I said stiffly. 'It was kind of her to think of us. Tommy will enjoy it.'

'It's nuthin' much,' he said, seeming relieved that I hadn't yelled at him. 'Is there anythin' I can do fer yer, Bridget? Chop wood or—'

'Thanks but I did that this morning.' He nodded and turned away. 'If I don't see you before – Happy Christmas, Ernie, to you and your ma.'

He looked back at me and grinned. 'You'll see me, lass. Don't forget Mr Dawson has promised us a bit of a do at the brewery Christmas Eve. He's closin' at two so we can all 'ave a mince tart and a glass of ale before we go home.'

'Bridget!' Mam's voice called from the kitchen. 'Stop gossiping and come here.'

'I have to go,' I said. 'Thank your ma for the cake.'

Mam glared at me as I returned to the kitchen. 'What have you got there?' she demanded. 'We don't want charity.'

'It's a piece of cake for Tommy. He's entitled and he's having it.'

She sniffed and drew the whisky jar to her, pouring what was left into the glass. Finding there was no more than a mouthful she pulled a face and took some coins from the shelf.

'Go and fetch me a jar.'

'It's dark out, Mam. I'll get it in the morning.'

'You'll get it now!' She sprang up and lunged at me, catching my head with the flat of her hand. 'You'll do as you're told or I'll make you sorry.' She lifted the hot iron from the fire and threatened me with it. 'You'll get a taste of this in a minute.'

I went out without looking at her.

It was cold and dark in the lane and I hugged my shawl tightly about me. I hated having to go to the pub after dark because I was always afraid that Harry Wright might be hanging around, although I hadn't seen him since the night he attacked me.

I ran all the way to the Feathers. As I came out, I shivered in the cold wind, catching the stink of the river, and then I began to walk very fast in the direction of my home. When I heard the echo of footsteps behind me my heart took a leap of fear, but I refused to look back. I couldn't go on fearing an attack from Harry Wright for the rest of my life.

Besides, it wasn't Harry. Why should it be? I hadn't seen him in the lane since that night. He probably believed I had told Jamie what he'd done and would stay well clear.

'Bridget!' I heard the voice call to me. 'Bridget, wait for me!'

It was Jamie's voice. I stopped walking and turned as he came striding up to me.

'Oh, Jamie . . . Is it really you?' If it were not for the whisky jar I would have flung myself into his arms and hugged him.

'Sure and it's the very same,' he said, his eyes bright with devilment. 'Who else would it be?'

'I thought . . .' I stopped, remembering why I'd never told him about the attempted rape. 'It's dark and I was nervous.'

'You shouldn't be out on your own at this hour.' Jamie frowned as he saw what I was carrying. 'So, she's still up to her old tricks then? I might have known. She must be losing her mind, sending you out on a night like this for that.'

'I don't mind. It's so good to see you, Jamie. Where have you been? Did you find regular work?'

'That I did and more of it to come. What do you think these are, me darlin'?'

He was carrying several parcels and I smiled as I sensed his pleasure. 'Presents for Tommy I hope.'

'And for you, Bridget,' he said. 'I've money in my pocket for Mam and some to spare.'

'You sound as if you've done well, Jamie?'

'I have that, Bridget. It was good advice you were after givin' me. I've been workin' up Canning Town way.'

'Canning Town?' I looked at him in surprise. 'What were you doing there, Jamie?'

'A bit of building,' he said and grinned. 'Takin' the inside of a shop to pieces and puttin' in new counters.'

'That must have been a good job. You were lucky to find it.'

'That I was, me darlin'.' Jamie was cock-a-hoop at his success and it made me feel good. 'Joe Robinson leased the shop and he's going to open it after Christmas – or his sister is. It's to be a flower shop.'

'A flower shop like Maisie's stall on the market? I didn't know people sold flowers in a shop.'

'Nor did I until I met Mary Robinson,' he said. 'They're nice people, Bridget – Mrs Robinson, too. She's a widow but pleasant and cheerful . . . Mary's like her mother, but she's not very strong. She had rheumatic fever a few years ago and it left her with a weak chest. Not that she complains. She's always wanted a flower shop and Joe rented it for next to nothing, so he hired me to do it up for her.'

Jamie was full of himself and his new friends. I wondered if the Joe Robinson who had hired my brother was the same one who had been there the night I was attacked in the lane. It seemed unlikely and I hoped the name was just a coincidence.

The sparkle faded from Jamie's eyes as we went into the house and he heard Mam yell from the kitchen. 'Where's that jar? You've taken your time, you little . . .' She broke off as she saw Jamie, her face screwing up in temper. 'Come home at last, have you? And I suppose you expect me to feed you over Christmas?'

'No, Mam. I'm not stopping. I've friends to visit and then I'm back off where I came from for Christmas.' He took four gold sovereigns from his pocket and laid them on the table in front of her. 'That's for you and these parcels are for Bridget and Tommy.'

'Trust you to waste good money . . .' She stopped as she saw the look on Jamie's face. 'It's about time you gave me something . . . Weeks with nothing it's been.'

'The money is for food and coke,' Jamie said. 'Not whisky, Mam. By the looks of it you've had far too much of it recently. You'll kill yourself if you're not careful.'

'And who asked your opinion?'

'No one, but that's never stopped me giving it yet. I'm telling you, that stuff will do you in if you don't give it a rest.'

'You keep your mouth shut. Go back where you came from and leave me alone.' She gave him a surly look and grabbed the jar from me, holding it to her protectively as though she thought he might snatch it from her. 'Go on, clear off.'

'I'm going. I only came for Bridget's sake. If it wasn't for her and Tommy you wouldn't get another penny from me.'

'It's little enough I get now! That slut of a sister of yours can go scrubbin' floors after Christmas. It's about time she earned her keep, sittin' around in that office all day while I slave me fingers to the bone.'

'Well, don't expect any more from me for a while,' Jamie warned her. 'Make it last, Mam. I'll be back when I'm ready and not before.'

Jamie turned and left the kitchen, striding to the front door where I caught up with him, holding his arm to prevent him leaving.

'Won't you even go up and see Tommy? He's always asking after you.'

'It would only upset him if I said I was leavin' again. Besides, I'm expected.'

'Tommy isn't well . . .' I faltered as Jamie frowned and then I went on, telling him everything. 'I want to make this the best Christmas he's ever had . . .'

'In case it's his last? Poor little bugger. I could kill Mam for what she's done to him!'

'It isn't all her fault, Jamie. Tommy isn't the only one around here . . . and I'm going to see Father O'Brien soon. He says there may be a place for Tommy . . . at the seaside.'

Jamie nodded grimly. 'I can't tell you not to take charity when it's for Tommy,' he said. 'If I gave you everything I earned I couldn't give him all he needs, but take this for his Christmas.' He reached in his pocket and gave me thirty shillings.

'That's your money, Jamie. You've already given us so much. I can't take that.'

'I've another sovereign in my pocket,' he said and took it out to show me. 'I'll manage and I want Tommy to have it. Just don't let Mam know you've got it.'

'She's not getting a penny of it,' I said fervently and tucked it down the front of my bodice. 'Thank you, Jamie. I'm glad you came to see us, and I wish you could stay.'

'I'd do for her before the night was out. If I had to stay here I'd not be responsible for my actions. No, it's best I go, Bridget darlin'. Besides, I've got to see Rosie. I've a present in my pocket for her. Many's the time she's helped me out . . .' He saw the look in my eyes and laughed. 'No, I've finished with all that, but I owe Rosie. I've bought her something nice. She wouldn't take money but she'll like this.' He showed me a little velvet box with a gold brooch inside.

'That must have been expensive?'

'Joe got it second-hand for me. That's his business, Bridget – buying and sellin'. It was far less than I'd have paid in a shop. He got me one for Mary too . . .'

Something in his voice then made me look at him sharply. 'You like Mary Robinson, don't you?'

'Sure – anyone would like Mary,' he said. 'Mrs Robinson told me to bring you for tea one afternoon on a Saturday. Would you like to come if I fetch you?'

'Yes, please . . . but it depends on Tommy.' I caught back a sob. 'He doesn't know he's going away yet. I'm not going to tell him until after Christmas.'

'Poor little bugger,' Jamie said again. 'If you need me, Bridget, you can find me here . . .' He gave me a scrap of paper with an address in Canning Town. 'This is Joe's house. He'll always know where to find me. I'm going to be working for him on one of his barrows after Christmas.'

'I thought you said he bought and sold second-hand goods?'

'Joe's got his finger in a dozen pies,' Jamie said and

grinned. 'He's a bit of a goer, Bridget. I like him and I think you will.'

'Thank you for all you've done,' I said and tucked the paper away safely. 'When shall I see you again, Jamie?'

'Not for a while,' he said. He hesitated, then kissed my cheek awkwardly. 'Keep your chin up, Bridget. Things will get better. I'll do what I can for you.'

'You've done enough already.'

'I've a bit put by if you need it,' he said. 'I was savin' it for something but it will keep. Have a good Christmas – you and Tommy.'

'I'll be getting him some new boots with what you gave me. His old ones let water.'

'Buy what you think right. I went to see Bridie Macpherson earlier. She says Lainie doesn't work there now. Do you know where she went? Was it with Hans?'

'I don't know,' I replied truthfully. 'She didn't tell me she was going and I haven't heard from her, but Hans may have come back suddenly. Perhaps she'll bring Tommy something for Christmas.'

'She's a fool if she didn't wait for Hans,' Jamie said. 'I'll ask Rosie if she knows anything. She hears all sorts of tales when she's out and about.'

'Let me know if there's any news?'

'O' course, me darlin'. Enjoy yourself and tell Tommy I'll be thinkin' of him at Christmas.'

'He'll be pleased with his presents.'

I watched my brother walk down the lane before going back into the house. It was good that he had come home with money and gifts, but I felt an aching loneliness after he had gone.

Five

'So you were wanting to talk to me about Tommy?' Father O'Brien indicated that I should help myself to the jam tarts his housekeeper had set on the table in front of us. He had already done justice to them himself, which was perhaps the reason he was rather too plump for his height. 'The doctor confirmed your fears then, Bridget?'

'Yes, Father. Dr Morris said he's in the first stages of consumption and needs to get away to the sea. If you can't find a place for him they'll likely put him in the infirmary after Christmas.'

'Maggie Ryan told me she thought you would be coming to see me,' the priest said and nodded as I took a bite of the jam tart. 'Now, what has she told you?'

'That it might be possible for Tommy to have a holiday at the sea.'

'That isn't quite the way of it,' he began, then as he saw my expression of disappointment, he continued: 'No, it's not a question of money, Bridget. It's not simply a holiday for the boy. For a start he will be in a sanatorium. Tuberculosis is something that needs to be kept under strict supervision, and for a while the doctors might not want you to visit. As Tommy begins to get better, you'll be able to see him, and that's when he'll be able to spend time enjoying the seaside. We usually pass the children on to families once they're over the initial stages. It's so they can continue enjoying the fresh air and benefits without being in hospital.'

'How long will it be before I can see Tommy?'

'The doctors at the sanatorium would make that decision,'

he replied gently. 'If Tommy is definitely diagnosed by them as having consumption, you may have to be prepared for a separation of several months – perhaps more than a year or longer before he could come home.'

'I thought Dr Morris said he had the symptoms?'

'He made preliminary tests; the doctors at the sanatorium will do far more than he could, and then they will make their decision about his treatment.'

'I'm not sure Tommy would go if he thought it would be that long before he could see us again.'

'What is your alternative?' Father O'Brien asked. 'If Tommy doesn't go away now he'll get gradually worse – and you might end up taking it from him. Dr Morris might have no alternative but to send him to the infirmary. What good is any of that going to do him – or you?'

I looked at him in silence, my throat too tight to answer at once.

'Could you find a place for him?' I managed at last.

'Yes, I think I can promise that. It isn't always as easy as that to get in, Bridget, but a new place has recently been opened on the East Coast near Skegness. I was asked only last week if I knew of any deserving cases. It is a fortunate thing, Bridget – there's a good many would be glad of the chance.'

'I shall have to ask Mam – and talk to Tommy after Christmas.'

'If you have any bother with that young man you bring him to me,' Father O'Brien said. 'And I can always speak to your mother. It's a while now since she came to church, Bridget.'

'She hasn't been well, Father.' I made the excuse but we both knew it wasn't exactly true. 'But I come as often as I can.'

Father O'Brien nodded, not arguing his case. He knew that I still attended church at least once every week and he had heard my confession himself only two weeks earlier.

'You get home now before it gets dark,' he said. 'And I wish you a Happy Christmas, Bridget.'

I thanked him and began my walk home. As I passed the Feathers, I saw Ernie Cole standing with his arm about a girl's waist. I knew her slightly but I wasn't sure of her name. I thought perhaps he was courting her and I turned away as he glanced at me, a flush in my cheeks.

So much for what he'd said to me the other evening! He was like all the other young men in the lanes – only after one thing. He'd made out he cared for me and now he was with another girl, and from the way he'd had his arm around her, he was doing more than passing the time of day!

Mr Dawson was in a jovial mood on Christmas Eve morning, laughing and chatting to his workers as he distributed food and drink from behind the long table he had set up in one of the sheds. His cheeks looked rather red and I knew he had been sipping whisky from a little flask in his pocket from mid-morning onwards.

'So there you are, Bridget,' he said to me as I approached the table for a slice of the rich Christmas cake and a glass of drink. 'Eat up, lass – there's plenty more where that came from.'

'Could I take a piece for Tommy?' I asked. 'He's never had a cake with almond icing on it before.'

'Yes, of course you can,' he said and cut me a chunk, which he placed on a napkin of white linen. 'Just bring the napkin back or Mrs Dawson will have my guts for garters. What are you drinking, Bridget? Wouldn't you like something better than ginger beer? What about a nice drop of sherry? I've got a sweet one in the office just for you to try.'

'This is lovely,' I said. 'I don't think I'll have anything stronger, thanks all the same.'

I took my cake to a bench and sat down, carefully tucking Tommy's chunk of cake into my pocket, and then began to eat my own. It was delicious and I licked my fingers when I'd finished, feeling startled when I heard someone laugh.

'Was it that good, Bridget?'

I turned to look at Ernie Cole and flushed. 'Yes,' I said defiantly and lifted my head. 'Not that it's any business of yours.'

'Now don't be like that. It's Christmas, Bridget, and I was

wantin' to give yer this.' He held out a parcel wrapped in brown paper and tied with a red ribbon.'

'What is it?' I stared at him suspiciously.

'It's a present,' he said. 'Don't look at me like that, Bridget. It ain't goin' ter blow up in yer face.'

'I can't take a present from you,' I said. 'We aren't courtin'.'

'I know you saw me with Grace Barker last night,' Ernie said and scowled. 'I go out with 'er now and then, but she ain't me girl, Bridget. We're just friends.'

'Friends, is it?' I pulled a face at him. 'It didn't look that way to me, Ernie Cole.'

'Don't be such a prude,' Ernie said, looking annoyed. 'It's just a box of chocolates. I'm not trying to bribe you into droppin' yer bloomers!'

'You just wash your mouth out with carbolic! I'm not goin' to listen to filthy talk from you.' I jumped up and walked away from him, going out into the yard and heading for the office. Ernie was following me but I was determined not to look back at him. Who did he think I was, talking to me that way? He caught up with me as I went inside the office, grabbing at my arm. 'Leave me alone. I'm not one of your loose women, Ernie Cole!'

'Don't be daft, Bridget. I'd have to be barmy to think I could get round you with a box of chocolates. Everyone knows you're not like that – I just thought you might like them for Tommy?'

'For Tommy?' I hesitated, knowing how my brother would love a proper box of chocolates. 'I couldn't take them for myself but . . .'

'Take them for your brother,' Ernie said and thrust the parcel at me in an embarrassed way. As I took it reluctantly, he bent his head and gave me a quick kiss on the cheek then shot out of the door before I had time to give him his present back.

I started to gather up my things. Mr Dawson had given me two pounds as a Christmas present 'for all your hard work' he'd said.

The money was safely tucked inside my purse. I had never

61

been given so many presents, or had as much money to spend before. I couldn't wait to take my things home and then get off down the market to see what I could buy.

'Ah, Bridget,' Mr Dawson's voice behind me made me jump. 'I was hoping to catch you before you left . . .'

As I turned I saw that he was holding a sprig of mistletoe and his cheeks looked redder than ever. He really was three sheets to the wind, I thought, and laughed inside.

'It's tradition to kiss under the mistletoe, you know,' he continued.

I hesitated, feeling embarrassed. I wasn't sure about Mr Dawson in this mood. He had obviously been drinking and I knew he was more than a bit tiddly, but he was my boss and he had been kind to me – and it was Christmas after all.

'Yes, I know,' I said and stood still as he came up to me, smiling and offering my cheek for the peck I expected. Instead of that, he seized me around the waist and crushed me to him in a stifling embrace, his mouth covering mine greedily in a wet kiss that I found unpleasant. I struggled, pushing both hands against his chest, but instead of letting me go, he started fondling my breast through my gown.

'You're a lovely girl, Bridget,' he muttered thickly as I struggled to push him away. 'A lovely girl . . . and I've fancied you for a long time . . .'

'And what do you think you're doing?' The cold voice from the doorway made him let me go in a hurry and for a moment I caught a glimpse of shame in his face before he turned to look at his wife. 'I knew you were after that slut. She's no better than her sister. I demand that you let her go immediately, Stephen.'

'I've let her go, dearest,' he replied, a stupid look on his face as he blinked at her. 'It was just a little Christmas kiss under the mistletoe.'

'I've seen the way you look at her,' Mrs Dawson went on angrily. 'I'm telling you to sack her – or I'll walk out on you myself. It's either her or me, Stephen.'

'But . . .' He stared at her in dismay, then at me and back

at his wife again. 'You can't mean that. What would Jane say? The business . . . ?'

'It's your choice,' she said and her eyes narrowed as she looked at me. 'It might interest you to know that my money started this brewery, Miss O'Rourke, and I still hold over half the business in my own name. I made sure of that before I put my money in. If I pulled out, he would lose the brewery. But perhaps you're willing to settle for what's left? He couldn't marry you, of course, but I dare say that wouldn't worry you. You and your sister both . . .'

I was feeling sick as I heard her tirade of bitter words. It was almost as bad as being at home with Mam. What had I done to make her hate me like this?

'I didn't do anything,' I said in a whisper. 'He just came and grabbed me . . . He's been drinking . . .'

'I am aware of my husband's nasty little habits,' she said. 'You can collect your wages after Christmas, Miss O'Rourke. We'll pay you a month's wages.' She looked at her husband. 'Go on, Stephen – tell her!'

He looked at me helplessly, a plea for understanding in his eyes, and then looked away as if he couldn't bear to see the accusation in mine.

'I'll be in to fetch my money,' I said. 'Thank you for the presents and I wish you both a Happy Christmas.'

My stomach was churning, but I was too shocked to feel much as I began to walk home. Everything had seemed so good and I was feeling better than I had for a while – and now I had lost my job.

I was stunned, unable to think what I was going to do. Mam would blame me if I told her what had happened. A lot of other people would too. They would think I had encouraged my boss by making eyes at him.

It was still light as I set out for the market, but wouldn't be for much longer. When I got there I saw that the lamps the traders hung round their stalls were already lit, which added to the air of festivity. I could hear people calling out seasonal greetings to each other and I felt the happy excited atmosphere taking me along with it despite the nagging worry at the back of my mind.

I was wondering what best to get for our Christmas dinner. A turkey was out of the question, of course, but I thought I might be able to make a good nourishing stew, and if I was lucky I might get a boiling fowl to cook for supper and the following day. I stopped to buy some oranges and nuts which I put in my basket, then went to have a word with Maisie Collins, who was standing by her flower stall.

'Happy Christmas,' I said. 'How are you, Maisie? You look as if you've been busy.' There were only a few bunches of holly left and one straggly bunch of chrysanthemums.

'I'm doin' all right,' Maisie said and gave me a toothless grin. 'I 'aven't seen much of you lately, lass. 'Ow's yer Ma?'

'She seems about the same. I've come to do my Christmas shopping – a few treats for Tommy.'

'That's right, luv.' Maisie nodded her approval, then noticed a youth lurking behind me. 'Watch it! He's after yer purse . . .'

I felt the hand in my coat pocket even as she spoke and whirled round, but it was too late. The youth had my purse and was running through the market, dodging in and out of the stalls and the crowds.

'Stop!' I yelled. 'Stop thief!'

I started to run after him, shouting for all I was worth. All my money was in that purse and without it I wouldn't be able to buy any of the things I had planned.

'Stop him! Please stop him. He stole my purse . . .'

I knew I was never going to catch up with the pickpocket and I was close to tears. I couldn't lose that money. I just couldn't! How could I have been so careless? I'd known there would be pickpockets hanging about the market – what had possessed me to put all my money in the purse? The youth must have seen it as I was buying something and followed me, waiting for his chance.

He was getting away from me. I gave another despairing cry, almost ready to give up. My chest was beginning to hurt and I knew it was hopeless, but then I saw a man dart out from the crowd and launch himself at the youth. There was a scuffle and some shouting as they both tumbled to the ground, then the youth got up and ran off again.

'Bugger it!' the man said as he got to his feet just as I reached him. 'He's gone – still I got your purse off him, miss.'

I looked at my saviour in delight, then blinked as I realized this was the second time in as many months that he had come to my aid. As I stared at him, I saw that his features were a little harsh, his mouth stern, but when he smiled his face changed altogether.

'You're a hero, Mr Robinson,' I said, sure that I knew him. 'It is Mr Robinson, isn't it?'

'Yes . . .' He looked at me for a moment before realization dawned. 'You're Bridget O'Rourke,' he said. 'I am right, aren't I?'

'Yes. This is the second time you've helped me. All my Christmas shopping money is in this purse. I don't know what I would have done if I'd lost it.'

'It's a pleasure to have helped you,' he said and grinned. 'It's lucky I was here. I live in Canning Town – just off Rathbone, but I don't suppose you know it?' I shook my head. 'I've got a couple of market stalls there and I'd heard there was one going here, but it's gone. It would have been a wasted journey, but now I'm glad I came.'

'You've done me a good turn,' I said, feeling a little shy as he gazed at me with warm approval.

'It was nothing,' he said. 'Could I buy you a cuppa some-where – to celebrate?'

'It's lovely of you to ask,' I said. 'I ought to be buying you a drink, Mr Robinson, but I've got too much shopping to do. This is the only chance I've had to get my Christmas things.'

'Yes, I understand,' Joe said. 'As a matter of fact, I know more than you might think. Your brother, Jamie, has been doing a bit of work for me . . . and before you ask, I haven't told him about your unhappy experience. I reckoned you would tell him yourself if you wanted him to know.'

'Jamie told me he was working for someone called Robinson, but I wasn't sure it was you. I'm grateful you didn't mention anything. He gets in a temper and I was afraid he might . . . well, you know.'

'You should have gone to the police, Miss O'Rourke.'

'It would cause gossip,' I said. 'Besides, I was all right – thanks to you.'

'I was doin' a bit of business with Fred Pearce that night.'

'You're not buying up beer bottles are you?'

Joe laughed and shook his head. 'No, it's a bit of property. He doesn't talk about it but he owns a shop in Barking Road.'

'Owns a shop?' I stared at him in amazement. 'You're pulling my leg. He's never had that much money in his life – has he?'

'You would be surprised,' Joe said. 'But that's his business, not mine. You won't tell anyone else I told you about the shop? I dare say he would rather his neighbours didn't know.'

'Is it really true then?' I laughed as he nodded. 'The crafty old devil. I think it's wonderful – and I shan't tell a soul.'

'I'll tell you what,' Joe said suddenly. 'I'm going to see him on Boxing Day – would it be all right if I came to see you?'

I hesitated and then shook my head. 'I'm sorry, Mr Robinson. I should like to ask you to tea, but my Mam . . . she isn't well.'

'Oh, I see.' He nodded as if he understood. 'Yes, of course, well, then, perhaps I'll see you around some time.'

I would have liked to ask him to the house, but Mam would throw a blue fit, and I would be embarrassed for someone like him to meet her if she was in one of her moods.

Joe was a Londoner through and through, but he spoke better than most of the lads in the lanes, and I could see from the way he dressed that he had got on in life. He wasn't quite a gentleman, but he was the next best thing to it.

I returned to Maisie, having tucked all but a few shillings away inside my clothes.

'Yer got yer purse back then, luv,' she said. 'That were a

bit o' luck. That young chap what 'elped yer is all right. Joe Robinson . . . 'E were askin' me about what flowers I sell earlier this afternoon. Seems 'is sister wants ter sell flowers in a shop.'

'What did you tell him, Maisie?'

'Nuffin' much I could tell 'im. I do all right 'ere, but I've 'ad this pitch fer years. I dunno about a shop.'

'Well, I shall have to go,' I said. 'I've got some baking to do tonight and I want to get things ready for Tommy – I've got things to wrap up for his stocking.'

'You get off then. I'm packin' up now.' She handed me the last bunch of holly. 'You take this, luv. I'm orf 'ome and I shan't sell it now. 'Ave a good Christmas, Bridget.'

'Thanks, Maisie . . .' I hesitated, then. 'If I were lookin' for work after Christmas . . .'

'Won't be much about then,' she said. 'Not fer a while, but I could always use a 'and. Not that I can pay yer more than a few pennies.'

'Have a lovely time yourself,' I said. 'I might come to see you in a couple of weeks . . .'

'You do that, luv. I'll see if I 'ear of anythin' fer yer . . .'

I nodded and turned homeward, my basket full of good things. Somehow I was feeling better now. I was young and strong and I would find a job . . . even if it was only scrubbing floors.

'Bridget . . .' I stopped as I heard a voice calling and looked round as Rosie Brown came up to me. 'I wanted a word wiv yer . . .' she said. 'Jamie was askin' if I'd 'eard anythin' about your Lainie. I don't know much, but I think she might 'ave gone off with a bloke what I've 'eard of. I ain't sure so I don't want to say no more but if I 'ear anything I'll let you know.'

Rosie was frowning and I thought she seemed anxious. 'Is something wrong?'

She hesitated, then: 'I don't want ter worry yer for nuthin', but if it is the bloke I think . . . he ain't very nice, Bridget.'

'Tell me his name, Rosie. Why don't you like him?'

67

She glanced uneasily over her shoulder. 'Not 'ere, Bridget – too many ears round this place. If I find out . . . I'll meet yer somewhere.'

'All right, thanks Rosie. But perhaps she didn't go with a man at all. She told Bridie Macpherson that she had a better job.'

'I 'ope that were the truth,' she said and smiled. ''Appy Christmas, Bridget. I've seen your Jamie. He's doin' all right.'

'Yes, he is,' I said and watched as she walked off, suddenly feeling a cold chill through my body.

'I'll be back in the New Year.' Mr Phillips was in the kitchen talking to Mam when I got back from the market. He turned when I entered and put my shopping down, indicating a couple of parcels on the table. 'They are for you and Tommy, Bridget. I was just telling your mother that I shall be away for several days, but I would like it if you will keep my room for me.'

'Yes, of course,' I said. 'We should be very sorry to lose you, sir.'

'Good.' He nodded to me. 'Have a lovely Christmas, Bridget. I'm leaving now.'

He walked out into the parlour and picked up the small suitcase and a few parcels he had left there.

'I wonder where he goes when he stays away for a few days,' I said to my mother as I began to unpack my basket. 'Do you think he has any family, Mam?'

'How should I know?' she muttered. 'He might have brought me some whisky rather than wasting it on presents for you and Tommy.'

'Perhaps he thought Tommy could do with it more.'

'Well, he was wrong. And where did you get money for all this, then?'

'It was a Christmas present from Mr Dawson,' I told her, turning away so that she couldn't see my face. 'And I've been saving a few pence myself. I wanted to give Tommy as much as I could this year.'

'You never think about me,' she said. 'If there was extra on your wages, you should have given it to me.'

'Why, so that you can spend it on whisky?' I asked and her head snapped up, eyes glittering with temper. 'Not this time, Mam. This time Tommy comes first.'

'You're lucky I don't take a strap to you,' she muttered and rubbed at her chest. 'It's sufferin' I am, Bridget O'Rourke, and you a cold hard daughter to me.'

I looked at her until she dropped her eyes, but neither of us said a word. And then I went upstairs to do Tommy's stocking. I was going to make sure this was the best Christmas he had ever known.

'Cor – thanks, our Bridget,' Tommy said as he ripped the wrapping paper off yet another parcel. 'This is just what I wanted.'

There were scraps of torn wrapping around the bed and a pile of sweets, oranges and nuts on the counterpane beside him. I had also bought him a pair of nearly new boots, a warm scarf and a pullover – and a toy tin car that I'd got cheap from the market. The box of chocolates from Ernie was already opened and we had both eaten two each, Tommy insisting that I have the same as him. From Jamie there was a tin of toffees that was also a pencil box and some colouring pencils and a shiny half a crown to spend as he pleased.

Mr Phillips' present lay unopened beside him as he munched happily at one of Jamie's toffees.

'Aren't you going to open that one?' I asked. 'Mr Phillips left it for you. I should be surprised if it isn't some more sweets and perhaps a book or something.'

'Don't want nothin' from him,' he said and hung his head as I looked at him. 'I don't like him, Bridget.'

'Why? What has he done to upset you?'

Tommy shook his head and I could see that he wasn't going to answer. Because it was Christmas, I didn't press the point, simply removing the parcel and putting it on the chest at the opposite side of the room.

It was unlike Tommy to refuse to open a gift and it worried

me a little. However, this was Christmas and I wasn't going to let anything spoil it.

'I think Billy must be up by now,' I said. 'Why don't you get dressed and go next door to show him your presents?'

Tommy grinned at me. 'I'll take him a couple of my chocolates, but I'm not taking the box – he'd scoff the lot.'

I laughed and ruffled his hair, thinking that Ernie's present seemed to have pleased him as much or more than anything else had. Perhaps because they were in a fancy box. A box that had been meant for me . . .

It made me feel a little odd that he should have bought me something like that, but I shrugged off my faint regrets as I dressed and went downstairs to start preparing the stew for dinner.

There was no sound of Mam stirring upstairs and I presumed she must have gone to bed in a drunken stupor again. She would get up soon enough and anyway I was relieved that she was out of the way for a while. It was much easier to get round without her sitting there glaring at me.

Once everything was ready I went upstairs to have a look at my mother. She seemed to be sleeping, a dribble of saliva on her chin. As I stood there, she opened her eyes and grunted.

'What are you staring at?'

'Happy Christmas, Mam.'

'Get out of here, you slut,' she said and turned over on her side.

I went downstairs and sat down at the kitchen table. Just for a moment despair seemed to sweep over me. The thought of being here alone with Mam after Tommy had gone away was making me feel low. I wasn't sure I could bear it, but what else could I do?

I had to keep a home going for Tommy to come back to one day. Besides, I would never be able to earn enough to keep both of us – especially now all my dreams of becoming Mr Dawson's secretary had vanished.

What was I going to tell Mam about that? I could just imagine what she would say, and suddenly I didn't feel I could face it. I leaned my elbows on the table, burying my face in my hands as the hopelessness swept over me.

'What's wrong, our Bridget?' Tommy's voice behind me made me jump. 'Has she been on at you again?'

I raised my head to look at him, glad that I hadn't given way to tears. Forcing a smile I said, 'No, of course she hasn't, Tommy darlin'. I'm fine . . . just a bit tired that's all.'

'That's 'cause you're always workin' and *she* don't do nothin',' Tommy said and his face creased with anger. 'I hate her, Bridget. I wish she was dead!'

'Don't say that . . .' I began but he turned and ran from the room. I heard the clatter of his feet as he went upstairs and I wondered if I ought to go after him, but I didn't. I couldn't think of anything to say to him. There were times now when I hated Mam myself; it was wrong and I knew I shouldn't feel like that, but what right had she to make all our lives a misery?

Hearing the thump from upstairs, I frowned. She was banging on the floor – her usual way of summoning me when she wanted something. I almost resisted, but then I got up and went to the bottom of the stairs.

'What do you want, Mam?'

'Bring me some whisky and make it quick.'

'I'm busy,' I said, resentment flaring. 'Get up and come down if you want it.'

'Do as I tell you, you little slut.'

I ignored her and went back into the kitchen, beginning to prepare the custard I was making to go with the pudding. I heard Mam yell a few times, then there was a loud noise as she half fell out of bed. I heard her walk heavily across the bedroom floor and then she halted at the top of the stairs. I could hear a commotion going on and stopped what I was doing to listen.

She was talking to Tommy. I couldn't quite hear the words, but it sounded as if she was shouting at him. Now, what was wrong with her? I stopped a moment to remove the custard from the heat then went out into the hall to investigate just as I heard a scuffling noise and a scream.

71

As I entered the parlour I heard thudding sounds and running towards the stairs I was in time to see Mam come tumbling all the way down to the bottom. I looked up to see Tommy standing at the top, his face pale with shock.

'I didn't mean to push her,' he said. 'She was trying to hit me and I just touched her – not hard. I didn't push her hard, Bridget. Honest I didn't.'

'Of course you didn't, darlin',' I said quickly. 'It was an accident. She fell . . . She probably turned dizzy and fell. It's all the drinking . . .'

I knelt down by Mam's side, trying to discover whether she was alive or dead, but I couldn't be sure.

'Go next door and tell Maggie that Mam fell down the stairs,' I said. 'That's all you have to say, Tommy. You didn't touch her – you weren't near her and nor was I. She just fell . . . Do you understand?'

Tommy nodded, but his face was as white as a sheet and he was shaking as he came downstairs, avoiding his mother as he stepped over her unconscious body.

The sickness churned inside me as I remembered the look of guilt on Tommy's face. Had he pushed her? I knew he hated her; he'd said it often enough, but he wouldn't actually try to harm her – would he?

No, no, of course he wouldn't. She had been shouting at him as usual, trying to hit him. Tommy had simply tried to fend her off. It was my fault anyway. If I had taken the whisky up to her it wouldn't have happened.

I was still kneeling by Mam's side, trying to bring her round when both Maggie and Mick came in. Mick knelt beside me and felt for a pulse, then he breathed a sigh of relief and looked at me.

'She's not dead, Bridget. Just out for the count. I'll go and fetch the doctor to her. He won't be pleased to leave his Christmas dinner, but he'll come for me.'

'Thank goodness she isn't dead,' I said. 'I don't know what happened to her – I think she must have turned dizzy . . .'

'And is it any wonder?' Maggie asked as her husband went

off. 'I don't think we'd better try and move her until the doctor comes back, Bridget. Just in case she's injured her back or somethin'.'

'No . . .' I looked at my mother, as she seemed to stir. 'I think she might be coming round.'

'Martha –' Maggie bent over her, patting her cheek – 'Martha . . . you had a little fall . . .'

Mam's eyes were open, but she seemed not to be hearing properly, and I saw the saliva dribbling on to her chin. Her eyes looked peculiar and she flopped as we tried to sit her up, falling over to one side.

'She's had a turn,' Maggie said. 'That's what must have caused her fall, Bridget. It's what they call a stroke – my old granny went just the same.'

'Is she going to die?' Tommy asked from behind me.

'I don't know, love,' I said as I turned to him. 'People sometimes get over strokes, but sometimes they don't. It was just unfortunate that she was at the top of the stairs when she had it. I should have taken the whisky up to her. It was my fault . . . It might have happened anyway, but it was my fault she fell . . .'

Tommy looked at me, then dodged past me and ran up the stairs.

'It's a shock for him to see his Mam like this,' Maggie said. 'Troubles never come singly, do they, Bridget? Do you want me to take him next door with me?'

'I don't think he'll come for the moment,' I said. 'You go back home, Maggie, and look after your family. I'll send Tommy round later if I can get him to come.'

'Well, your mam won't be going anywhere,' she said. 'Fetch a blanket to her, Bridget, and then leave her to the doctor.'

After Maggie had gone next door, I went up and found Tommy sitting on the bed. He wasn't crying, but I would almost have rather he had than sit there so pale and still.

'It wasn't your fault,' I told him again as he stared at me, his eyes dark with guilt. 'She has been unwell for a while – it's all the drinking. If I'd gone up to her she might not have fallen.'

'I pushed her,' he said. 'I was angry with her for shoutin' at you and I pushed her. If she dies it will be my fault.'

'No, that's not true,' I said. 'She was ill and I should've gone up to her. If she hadn't turned dizzy you couldn't have pushed her, Tommy. She was too strong for you. She was ill and that's why she fell. You must remember that. It's what everyone thinks and that's the way it's going to stay. Do you hear me?'

'Yes . . .' He nodded. 'Can I go next door with Billy until . . .'

'O' course you can, my darlin',' I said. 'I'll save the stew for this evening. You stay with Maggie for as long as you like.'

I watched him as he went slowly past me and down the stairs. I had tried so hard to make this Christmas special for him and now it would always remind him of what had happened to Mam . . .

Six

The doctor confirmed that Mam hadn't broken anything, but she'd had some kind of a seizure and he told me there was a possibility she might be partially paralyzed.

'She will certainly need nursing for a while,' he said after some of the neighbours had carried her up to bed. 'Can you manage that, Miss O'Rourke, or do you want me to arrange for her to be taken to the infirmary?'

'I'll look after her,' I said. 'She would hate being sent to somewhere like that.'

He looked at me doubtfully. 'It may be a longer job than you imagine. Perhaps you should think it over and let me know in a week or two how you feel?'

'Yes, thank you,' I said. 'It was good of you to come out on Christmas Day, doctor.'

I was feeling numb, my mind still in shock after Mam's fall. Coming hard on the heels of all the rest, it had left me in a kind of limbo, wondering what could possibly happen next.

Maggie came in to see me that evening after Tommy was in bed and I had finished clearing up for the day. She sat down at the table as I brewed a pot of tea, watching me anxiously.

'You know I'll help when I can,' she said. 'But . . . how are you going to manage your job, Bridget?'

'I shan't be going to the brewery any more, except to pick up my wages.' I told Maggie what had happened and she made a sound of disgust in her throat.

'Bloody men!' she exclaimed. 'I've a good mind to go down there and give him a piece of my tongue.'

'Would you fetch my wages for me?' I asked. 'Mrs Dawson

said I would be paid a month's money and I really need that, Maggie. If you wouldn't mind asking for me?'

'O' course I will, love,' she said. 'I'll sit with your mam when you want to go down the market and help you turn her in bed, things like that, but it's going to be hard for you. Perhaps you should have let the doctor send her to the infirmary?'

'You know what Mam's like,' I said and sighed. 'She would kick up such a fuss. And you know what they say happens to people who cause too much trouble in a place like that . . .'

'They'd soon keep her quiet,' Maggie said. 'I remember my old grandda – he kept wetting the bed and calling out. Granny looked after him for nearly a year, and then they took him in to give her a rest – dead within the week. She vowed she would never have let him go if she'd known.'

'I've heard it from others,' I said. 'I don't know what it is about that place – whether people just give up hope when they go there. I can't do that to Mam – even if I wish I could, Maggie. But I shall have to leave her for a day when I take Tommy to the sanatorium.'

'That's no problem,' Maggie said. 'You've got friends, Bridget, and you know we'll rally round to help you. When are you going to tell Tommy?'

'In a day or two,' I said. 'He's upset enough as it is over Mam . . . I wish there was some alternative, but I know there isn't.'

Maggie's look was sympathetic but there was nothing more she could say.

I looked in on Mam before I went to bed. She was snoring and dribbling in her sleep. The doctor had told me there was nothing anyone could do for the moment except leave her to rest.

'Oh, Mam,' I sighed as I stood gazing down at her. 'What am I going to do?'

The thought flashed into my mind that it would be so easy to finish what had begun with her tumble down the stairs. A pillow held over her face for a few minutes and . . . but that was a terrible sin.

'You should be ashamed of yourself, Bridget O'Rourke!' I spoke the words aloud. It was a wicked thing to wish for someone to die!

I couldn't do that to Mam no matter how much trouble she was. She was still my mother and I had to look after her.

As I went into my bedroom to undress, I saw that Tommy was sound asleep and I bent down to kiss the top of his head. He had been so scared when Mam fell, and I knew he blamed himself. It was possible that he had contributed to her fall, but he hadn't meant to kill her. Of course he hadn't! He might say he hated her when he was upset, but he didn't mean it – it was just like that brief moment when I'd felt it would be easy to hold the pillow over her face.

Mam slept for a couple of days, waking once or twice and accepting the drinks of water I gave her from a little cup I held to her lips, but saying nothing. I wondered if the seizure had affected her speech or her mind, but it was just exhaustion. On the morning of the third day I went into her room and saw that she was wide awake and staring at me.

'I feel as if I've been flattened by a bloody steamroller,' she said. 'What happened to me, Bridget?'

'Don't you remember, Mam?'

'I wouldn't bloody ask if I did!'

Her mood hadn't improved for her illness! I sighed as she struggled to sit up but flopped back, obviously too weak to manage it. I heard her fart and knew that she had messed the bed again as we tried to move her, but it wasn't her fault and I was getting used to it now.

'You've had a stroke, Mam,' I told her as I went to help prop her up against the pillows. 'The doctor says you've got to rest.'

'Who told you to fetch that quack?' she asked and glared at me. 'Why can't I move anything on the left side of my body?'

'I don't know. Can't you?'

'I've just said, haven't I? What are you – bloody stupid now?'

Mam had never sworn as often as she was doing now, and I realized that this was another change in her.

'I'll ask the doctor to come and have another look at you, Mam.'

'I don't want that bloody fool poking round me,' she said. 'You can help me get out of bed, that's what you can do.'

'Mam, I don't think you should . . .'

'Help me, you slut, or I'll thrash you when I get out of here.'

I sighed and went to the bed, throwing back the covers. She struggled to bring her legs over the side of the bed, but even with me trying to support her she couldn't manage it, and eventually she flopped back against the pillows with a grunt.

'I'm buggered,' she said. 'You'll have to see to me, Bridget. I've messed me bloody self and it stinks something awful.'

'It's all right, Mam,' I said. 'Next time tell me and I'll get you the pot . . .'

It took me nearly an hour to get her cleaned up and settled, by which time Tommy was downstairs waiting for his breakfast. He looked at me anxiously.

'Am I going to school today, Bridget?'

I took a deep breath, knowing that I would have to tell him.

'You won't be going to school for a while, Tommy darlin'.'

'Am I stayin' home to help you with Mam?'

'You can help me with little things,' I said. 'But do you remember when we went to the doctor, Tommy?' He nodded, looking at me warily, and I sensed that he had already guessed a part of what was coming next. That was hardly surprising the way people talked around here. Billy would have heard his mam and da discussing his illness. 'Well, he says you're not very well and you need treatment.'

'Billy says I've got consumption and I'm infectious,' he said. 'Am I, Bridget?'

'Well, the illness you have might be passed on to others,' I said carefully. 'But it doesn't always happen – we've slept in the same bed and I haven't got it, have I?'

'I don't know . . .' He looked at me anxiously. 'I don't want to make you ill, Bridget.'

'The doctors want you to go away for a while,' I said and hesitated as I saw his face turn pale. 'It's at the seaside, Tommy. You would like to see the sea, wouldn't you?'

He nodded but his eyes were dark with fear. 'Are you coming with me?'

'I shall take you there, darlin', but I can't stay with you. The doctors have to make tests and—'

'You're sendin' me away 'cause of what I did to Mam.'

'No, o' course I'm not, Tommy!' I cried. 'You mustn't think that – not for a moment. You didn't do anything wrong. Mam fell because she was ill.'

Tommy stared at me, his eyes wide with fright, accusing me. He imagined I was punishing him for what he had done. 'I don't want to go away from you. Please don't make me, Bridget.'

'Oh, Tommy . . .' This was so difficult and it was breaking my heart, but I couldn't weaken – for his sake. 'It isn't that I want you to go, but the only other place is the infirmary and you would hate that. It will be much better at the seaside. When you're feeling a little better you will be able to go on the beach and look at the seagulls.'

'Why can't I just stay here? I'll be good. I promise I won't be a trouble to you and I won't say nothin' about Mr Phillips. I promise . . .'

'What about Mr Phillips?'

Tommy hung his head. 'I don't like him that's all. Don't send me away, Bridget.'

'Please don't be upset, Tommy.' I was too worried to wonder why he was so insistent that he didn't like our lodger. 'Will you talk to Father O'Brien about this? He will explain about the sanatorium and why you need to go there for a while.'

Tommy hung his head, but I knew he liked the priest and he would do what I asked when he'd thought about it.

'But I can't go to school?'

'Not for the moment – not until you're better.'

'What can I do then?'

'You can help me,' I said and sighed as I heard Mam start shouting upstairs. 'Run up and ask what she wants, darlin'. I'll have your breakfast ready when you come down.'

Maggie came in later that morning. I was ironing one of Mam's nightdresses, and she watched me for a moment before laying a newspaper on the table in front of me. I glanced at the headlines. It was something about the changes the new century was going to bring and the hope that the relief of Ladysmith was only few days away.

'That's good,' I said, but wondered why Maggie thought I should be interested in the Boer War.

'Not the war,' she said. 'That small paragraph at the bottom – about a girl being found battered half to death.'

I put my iron on the range and picked up the paper, frowning as I understood why Maggie had brought it to me. 'That's Rosie . . . the girl Jamie used to visit sometimes. I spoke to her in the market just before Christmas.'

'I knew Jamie used to hang around with her,' Maggie said. 'That's why I showed it to you. I know she was a tart, but there was no need for someone to do that to her. She was lying in the street half-naked when they found her.'

'No . . .' I frowned as I put the paper down. 'That's terrible, Maggie. She might have been no better than she ought, but I liked her. She was going to see if she could find out where Lainie was.'

'They've taken Rosie to the infirmary,' Maggie said. 'I don't know whether she'll live.'

'Do you think I should go and see her – or write to Jamie?'

'You've got more than enough on your plate,' Maggie said. 'Write to Jamie. If she needs help, he might be able to do something. You can't, you haven't got time.'

'No . . .' I glanced ruefully at the pile of ironing. 'Our lodger will be back any day now. You're right, I'll let Jamie know and he'll probably pop in and see her. She would like that.'

Mr Phillips came back the next morning. He looked concerned when I told him that my mother was ill in bed, and seemed to consider for a moment before he spoke.

'Would you prefer it if I left, Bridget?' he asked. 'If it's going to be too much trouble for you . . .'

'Oh, no, please don't think that,' I said quickly. 'I can manage, really I can. Your meals will be cooked just as you like them – everything will be just the same. I'm going to stay home and look after Mam, and I couldn't manage without . . .' My voice tailed off in embarrassment.

'Then we'll say no more about it.' He smiled and nodded. 'And how is Tommy? Did he enjoy his Christmas?'

'Yes, thank you,' I said. 'Did you have a good time, sir?'

'It was a change,' he replied and frowned. 'Well, I'll go up and get settled in then, Bridget. If I could have a cup of tea later?'

'Yes, o' course you can. Shall I bring a tray up or would you rather come down to the kitchen?'

'I'll have it on a tray in my room, if that's all right? We don't want to start the neighbours talking, do we?'

'No . . .' I hadn't thought about that. People might start to gossip if they discovered I was sitting alone with him in the kitchen.

He went off upstairs and a moment later Tommy came clattering down the stairs. He was at the front door when I caught up with him.

'What's the matter, Tommy?'

'I'm off next door,' he said, giving me an odd look. 'Maggie don't mind me being infectious. She said I could go round when I like . . .'

He gave me a rebellious stare and banged the door after him when he went out. As I turned away, I looked up and saw Mr Phillips standing at the top of the stairs. There was a very strange expression on his face and it made me wonder what he was thinking.

I remembered his remark about the neighbours talking and I wondered if I'd done right in telling him he could

81

stay. Supposing he tried it on now that Mam was tied to her bed?

I discussed it with Maggie later that day.

'Will people talk? With Mam in bed the way she is? I mean Mr Phillips isn't a problem to me. He's never so much as looked at me in that way, but you never know now that Mam is ill and you know what the gossips are like . . .'

Maggie looked at me a bit oddly. 'Oh, I shouldn't worry about that, Bridget. I don't think anyone will suspect there's something going on between you and Mr Phillips.'

Something in her voice made me wonder. 'Why wouldn't they? He's a man after all – older than me, I know, but that doesn't stop people talking.'

'You've no idea, have you?' Maggie hesitated. 'He's . . . well, he's what some folk call queer. He doesn't like women, not in that way. He likes men . . . and boys. Your Tommy is in more danger than you are.'

'What do you mean?' I felt a cold thrill of horror trickle down my spine as I stared at her and I remembered the way my brother had bolted the minute Mr Phillips had gone upstairs on his return. 'You don't mean he interferes with . . . He wouldn't try to touch Tommy, would he?'

'I don't know, love.' Maggie hesitated. 'Perhaps I shouldn't have told you,' she said. 'Your mam knew all about him when he came for the room, but she said he wouldn't touch Tommy or she'd give him the fright of his life . . .'

'But Mam is ill now. You think he might, don't you?'

'I don't know,' she admitted with a sigh. 'Have you ever noticed anythin' . . . anythin' strange when Tommy's around?'

'Tommy doesn't like him,' I said. 'He avoids him as much as possible and he wouldn't open the Christmas present Mr Phillips gave him. I didn't ask why because I didn't want to upset him . . . If that's the way he is, he'll have to go, Maggie. I can't risk him upsetting Tommy. It makes me feel sick to think of him . . .'

'I would never have taken him in the first place,' Maggie said agreeing with me. 'I can stick most things, but not them what interfere with children. I'd hang the lot of 'em! But how will you manage without his rent, Bridget?'

'I don't know,' I said. The realization that I'd have to manage worried me sick, but it would have to be faced. 'I might manage for a few weeks, but then I would have to get a new lodger.'

'Let him stay for a while,' Maggie advised. 'Tommy is going away soon and then it won't matter. He won't be a bother to you and his habits are his own business.'

I thought it over for a few days and then I asked Tommy why he didn't like our lodger.

'Has he ever said anything strange to you, darlin'?' I asked carefully. 'I know you don't like him and I wondered if there was a reason. You're not afraid of him, are you?'

Tommy looked at me, two bright spots of red in his cheek. 'I ain't said nothin' to you, Bridget, 'cause I know you can't manage without his rent.'

'It doesn't matter about that,' I said. 'Just tell me – has he touched you? Has he said anything unpleasant to you?'

'No . . . but he showed me his thing once,' Tommy said looking ashamed. 'He wanted me to touch him but I ran off. He was strange then, Bridget, breathin' funny and his eyes went queer. He frightened me. And he stroked my face the day he came back – that's why I went next door to Maggie.'

'He hasn't touched you anywhere else?'

'He's always touchin' me,' Tommy said. 'He tried to put his arm round me when I was coughin' the other day.' He shivered. 'He gives me the creeps, Bridget. I don't like him.'

'No,' I said and frowned. 'I don't think I do either, darlin'. I think I might ask him to leave.'

'Don't do that for me,' Tommy said quickly. 'I shouldn't have told you.'

'I wish you'd told me before,' I said. 'If he tries to touch you again, you let me know straight away. In the meantime, I'll give him a month's notice.'

Mr Phillips looked at me oddly that evening when I told him I had changed my mind about having a lodger.

'I'm very sorry,' I said, not meeting his eyes. 'I thought I could manage, but I find I can't. Naturally, I shall give you time to find another room.'

A hot red flush was creeping up his neck, and it was obvious he had guessed the truth. 'I don't know what people having been saying to you, Miss O'Rourke, but I want you to believe I would never harm your brother.'

I gave him a straight look then. 'Perhaps not, sir – but my brother told me you . . . made suggestions to him. I am very sorry, but I have to ask you to leave as soon as possible – within a month anyway.'

'Very well,' he said and now there was a glint of anger in his eyes. 'I've tried to be good to your family, because I liked you and Tommy, but this place hasn't suited me for a while. Your mother is a drunken slut and your sister was a whore. I don't think you have cause to preach to me, Bridget . . .' He broke off as he saw my expression. 'I don't think I need to wait. I'll leave in the morning.' He took a purse from his pocket, extracted a guinea and laid it on the table. 'I think that more than covers what I owe you. Good evening. I shan't bother with breakfast in the morning.'

Mam had a blue fit when she found out that Mr Phillips had left us.

'What did you do to upset him!' she yelled at me, clawing at the bedcovers as though she wanted to get out and go for me. Her frustration at being tied to her bed didn't help her temper. 'I know it's your fault, Bridget. You said something to him or he would never have left. He won't find it easy to get another room round here.'

'I found out what he was, Mam,' I said. 'Why didn't you tell me? He has been trying to interfere with Tommy.'

'He didn't try when I was about,' she said and glared at me. 'It's your fault if you can't look after your own brother.'

'I have. I asked him to leave and he's gone.'

'And what are we to do now?' she demanded. 'I'm stuck

84

in this bloody bed and you haven't been to work for days –
they'll sack you if you're not careful, my girl.'

'I'm not going back to the brewery, Mam.'

'Not goin' back . . . ?' Her eyes narrowed in suspicion. 'I
knew that bugger Dawson was no good. I suppose he was
tryin' it on?'

'He was a bit tiddly and silly on Christmas Eve,' I said.
'But Mrs Dawson didn't like it and told me I wasn't to go
back. They gave me a month's wages, and Mr Phillips paid
me a guinea before he left. We can manage for a few weeks,
even if I have to dodge the rent man.'

'Then what are you goin' to do?' she demanded. 'Scrubbin'
floors for a couple of hours in the mornings won't pay the rent
and coal, let alone my whisky.'

'I shall advertise for another lodger – a woman this time,'
I said. 'We'll manage somehow, Mam. I'll write to Jamie and
ask him if he can help us.'

'Fat lot of good that brother of yours will be. You'll not
see him from one year's end to the next once he gets settled
away from here. You'll rue the day you asked Mr Phillips to
leave, Bridget. He was clean and always paid his rent on time
– you'll find out there's a lot worse.'

'Well, it's done now,' I said. 'He's gone and we shall just
have to make the best of it. I'll pop down the corner shop later
and ask them to put a card in the window.'

'You can get me a jar while you're out,' she said. 'And
bring it here where I can get at it. I can't rest without a drop
o' the good stuff. You don't know what pain I'm in, girl.'

Jamie came to see me a couple of days after Mr Phillips
left. He listened to what I had to say about the lodger, and
frowned.

'It's a good thing you told him to go, Bridget. I'd have killed
the bugger if he'd harmed our Tommy.'

'Well, he didn't, so forget it,' I said. 'What about Rosie?
Did you go and see her?'

Jamie's face clouded. 'For all the good it did. She just lay
there staring at me, her face blank. She didn't know me and

the nurses say she never will. Her mind's gone, Bridget. Whatever that bastard did to her has finished her. She's like a cabbage.'

'Oh, I'm so sorry. I liked her, Jamie. I really did.'

I didn't tell him what Rosie said about trying to find something out about where Lainie had gone. There was no point. One of her customers had beaten her almost to death and she wasn't going to be telling anyone anything any more.

'I've only got a few bob on me,' Jamie said, taking five shillings from his pocket. 'Take this for now, Bridget, and I'll come to see you when I can.'

'Are you sure you can manage this?' I asked. 'I don't like taking it, Jamie. You gave us a lot at Christmas.'

'I want you to have it,' he said. 'If you're in trouble let me know and I'll come over.'

'Thanks, I said and kissed his cheek. 'You get off now and don't worry about me too much. I'll manage.'

'Yes,' he said. 'I expect you will.'

The next few weeks were the hardest of my life. Mam was a difficult patient and had me up and down the stairs fifty times a day. At first I tried to resist her demands for whisky, but then I gave in and took her a small measure in a glass when she put herself out. It wasn't enough for her because she had become dependant on it, but if I gave her more, the jar would soon be empty and I couldn't afford to buy it very often.

I had put a card in the shop window advertising for someone, but no one had called to ask about the room and I knew it wouldn't be easy. Especially as I'd said I wanted a woman. There weren't many women looking for work in our area, other than those that worked in the brewery and lived at home with their families. In the end I might have to take a man, but for the moment I was managing, though I knew it couldn't go on much longer.

I tried not to take advantage of Maggie's good nature, but when Father O'Brien told me they were ready for Tommy, I asked her if she would stay with my mother.

'She wouldn't have anyone else,' I said. 'I know it's a lot to ask, Maggie. I shall be gone from early in the morning until late in the evening, but I want to take Tommy myself.'

'O' course you'll be takin' him,' she said. 'Don't you worry, love. Mick can buy a pie from the shop for his tea for once – it won't hurt him. Make him appreciate what he's got.' She grinned at me. 'I'll handle Martha all right. You take your brother and don't worry about hurryin' back.'

'I want to have an hour or two by the sea before I take him to the sanatorium,' I said. 'It's his first time by the sea.'

'That's it, make it special,' Maggie agreed and smiled at me. 'And stop blaming yourself, Bridget. There's nothin' more you can do for him and you know it in your heart.'

She was right, of course, but that didn't make it any easier.

I sat staring out of the train window on the journey home, the memory of Tommy's pale, scared face nagging at me. He hadn't cried when I'd handed him over to the matron, but I knew he'd been crying inside. It had taken all my strength to hold back the tears, but somehow I'd managed to smile and tell him I would see him as soon as the doctors said it was all right for me to come. He hadn't answered and I knew he thought I was abandoning him.

At least he'd had a good couple of hours walking by the sea and sucking a lollipop I'd bought for him at a shop near the seafront. I had done my best to make it seem like a treat, but all the time a shadow had been hanging over us and in the end I'd had to leave him with strangers.

It felt as if I'd committed a crime and I had wanted to rush back, scoop him up in my arms and take him home with me, but I knew that he would just get worse and eventually he would end up in the infirmary. At least he had a chance where he was now. I had to believe that. I had to!

Seven

T he house seemed horribly empty with Tommy gone and I felt restless as the days passed.

I went to the door and looked out one wet February evening. It was miserable, but not as cold as it had been in January. At the seaside, the weather had seemed almost mild and the sun had shone as we walked on the front. Perhaps Tommy was better off there.

I heard laughter and turned my head to look down the lane. Ernie Cole was with that girl again. As I watched, she put her arms about him and kissed him there in the middle of the lane – and he kissed her back. Neither of them seemed in the least bothered that someone might see them.

I went inside and shut the door. Ernie had a perfect right to go courting if he wished. I had blocked every attempt he had made towards getting to know me better, and it was my own fault if he had given up. Besides, I couldn't go courting – with Ernie or anyone else.

I returned to the kitchen and started on the pile of sheets that needed ironing, feeling startled as I heard the front door open. Who could that be?

I put the iron back on the range and went to the door as it opened. For a moment I stared in disbelief as I saw my sister standing on the threshold. She was drenched through to the skin and shivering with cold, wearing only a thin dress and no shawl or coat.

'Lainie!' I cried. 'You're wet through! What happened? Where's your coat?'

She stared at me in silence, her face pale. 'Bridget,' she

whispered. 'Can I stay here? Just for tonight? I'll go tomorrow before . . .' She choked and put a hand to her eyes as if she felt faint.

'What's wrong?' I said and went to her quickly, supporting her towards the chair next to the fire. 'Sit down, love. I'll get you a towel.'

She caught my arm as I turned away. 'What about Mam?'

'She's asleep in bed,' I said. 'She can't get out of bed, Lainie. She had a stroke and she's paralyzed down one side.'

She nodded, her eyes dropping from mine. 'I heard something or I wouldn't have dared to come. If I can just stay tonight . . .'

'We'll talk in a moment,' I said. 'Sit there and don't move until I come back.'

I raced upstairs to fetch a towel and one of the dresses Lainie had left behind when she walked out. I was half-afraid that she would have disappeared by the time I got back, but she was still sitting there when I returned, staring into space, seemingly dazed. I gave her the towel and hung her dress by the fire to warm.

'Change into this,' I said. 'I'll make a cup of tea and there's some soup I made for Mam earlier. I'll warm that up for you, if you're hungry?'

'I could drink the tea, but I don't want anythin' to eat, not yet,' she said, taking the towel and beginning to dry her hair. She turned her back as she pulled off her wet dress and I gasped as I saw the bruises on her shoulders and buttocks. 'Ah, don't, Bridget . . .' she cried as I tried to touch her. 'Don't touch me. I'm not fit . . .'

'Don't be daft,' I said. 'You're my sister, Lainie. Who did this to you – was it a man?'

'It's nothin',' she lied. 'I had an accident that's all . . .'

'That's not true, Lainie. Those bruises look as if you've been beaten. Did he do that to you – the man you went off with?'

'So you know . . .' She blushed for shame. 'I suppose everyone knows. I'll bring disgrace on you, Bridget. Do you want me to go?'

'As if I would,' I said. 'Surely you know me better than that?'

'You wouldn't turn me away, but Mam will when she knows I'm here.'

'Mam might not have any say in the matter,' I said. 'Do you want to talk about it, Lainie?'

Lainie was silent for a moment, then, 'I wouldn't have come if there were any other way. I went to Bridie's first but she wouldn't have me back.'

'She was very angry when you went off. She said you might have gone with a man. But it wasn't Hans, was it?'

'I wish it had been. I waited for Hans, but he didn't come and then this man . . . He tempted me, Bridget.' She caught back a sob. 'I should never have listened to him. I should have been patient . . . Bridie told me Hans came back to look for me just before Christmas.'

'He didn't come here as far as I know, but if he had Mam wouldn't have told me. She would have told him to clear off.'

'I can imagine how she would be,' Lainie said bitterly.

She stared at me and I could feel her misery, sense her defeat.

'If I'd only waited a little longer, but it seemed such a wonderful chance to make something of myself.'

'What did he promise you?'

'Oh, so many things,' Lainie said. 'A decent place to live, nice clothes, money. I should have known he was lying.'

'Did he beat you?'

She shook her head, a look of shame in her eyes. 'He hit me a couple of times but it was his bully boys who beat me like this. He told me I was beautiful, that I could be an actress. He was so sweet to me at first, Bridget. He was going to make me a hostess in his nightclub. But when he had me where he wanted me, he tried . . . I'm so ashamed. I thought he cared for me, but he wanted me to sleep with other men for money.'

'Oh, Lainie!' I cried, staring at her in horror. 'What did you do?'

'I refused,' she said, her head coming up, a flash of pride in her eyes. 'I had slept with him, but I wasn't going to do *that* for him or anyone. He kept me locked up for days, threatening and coaxing by turn. Sometimes I was given food, sometimes I was starved for a day. Then . . . he let his henchman teach me a lesson. He raped me and then he beat me, and then he said that was only a taste of what was coming if I didn't do as I was told.'

'Lainie . . . Lainie . . .' I moved towards her, my heart aching for her pain and fear, wanting to take her in my arms and somehow soothe away all that she had suffered.

She put out her hand, warding me off. 'Hear me out before you decide if you want me near you,' she said in a shaking voice. 'I couldn't fight any more, Bridget. I did what they told me – there were twenty or more. I gave up counting after a while . . .'

'It doesn't matter,' I said. 'That wasn't you, Lainie. You didn't do it because you wanted to – they forced you. We'll face this together. You and me. I'm going to look after you.'

'They just kept coming and then . . .'

'It doesn't matter any more, darlin'. You're here now.'

'In the end they got careless,' Lainie said. 'They thought I couldn't fight them any more. Someone – one of the clients – left the door unlocked. I escaped when he was asleep and I came here. I couldn't think where else to go . . .'

'You came home,' I said. 'I'm glad you came, Lainie. You're my sister and I love you. I could kill that man for hurting you, but I don't care what happened. It's over and I'm going to look after you.'

She was sobbing as I put my arms about her. I stroked her hair, whispering words of comfort, but nothing could ease her pain or take away the bad memories. She felt thin and I could feel her trembling, feel how vulnerable she was, her spirit crushed.

'I'm sorry . . .' She moved away after a moment, brushing the tears from her face with the back of her hand. 'I didn't mean to cry all over you. I know I can't stay here.'

'Anyone would cry if they had been through that. He

deserves to be hanged! Have you been to the police, Lainie?'

'No!' She looked terrified. 'I can't, Bridget. He would kill me. You don't know – he's ruthless. He would make me suffer – make you suffer too, all my family. He's evil!'

'He should be punished,' I said. 'Men like that don't deserve to live. Jamie would go after him if he knew.'

'You mustn't tell him,' Lainie said. 'Oh, please, Bridget, don't tell anyone else. I couldn't bear it . . . I couldn't face Jamie if he knew – or the neighbours. No one must know. And it wouldn't do any good. Jamie couldn't deal with him. He's too powerful – too well protected. Jamie would be murdered if he tried to get near him. I would rather kill myself than go to the police.'

She looked so desperate that she might be capable of doing anything. 'You mustn't say that, Lainie. You mustn't ever think that.'

'Then promise me you won't ever tell anyone – no one, not ever.'

'I promise,' I said reluctantly. 'Though I would like to see him punished.'

'He's powerful and rich,' Lainie said. 'Even if I went to the police they wouldn't do anythin'. They probably wouldn't believe me. He would deny ever havin' known me or accuse me of stealing from him. You don't know, Bridget. You don't know what he's like . . .'

'Then we'll just forget it,' I said. I wasn't ever going to forget, but there was no point in upsetting her more. 'Why don't you go up and get in my bed, Lainie? I'll have Mr Phillips' old room.'

'Has he gone?' she asked. 'Good – I never liked his kind. But you'll be findin' it hard to manage with Mam in bed. Have you got any money?'

'Take your tea up and get some rest,' I said. 'We'll talk about how we're going to manage in the morning. One of us will have to find a job, Lainie. Or we'll both do part-time. I've been trying to find a lodger, but now you're home we'll manage somehow.'

She nodded, picked up her mug of tea and went out. I gathered her clothes up. The dress she had arrived in looked as if it were of good quality, but just to touch it made me shiver with disgust because it was a reminder of what they had done to my sister. I shoved it on the fire in the range and then went to wash my hands with carbolic.

Lainie might be afraid of the man who had captured her, but if he was here right now I would take Mam's carving knife and stick it in his stomach – and I would smile to see him lying dead at my feet!

It wasn't easy to sleep in a strange bed, but my instincts told me Lainie would want to be alone for a while and I thought she would prefer the room we had shared. We might have to share a room again if we found another lodger, but that was for the future. At the moment, all I could think about was what Lainie had told me, and as I dwelt on what had been done to her, the anger mounted inside me.

It was after I had been lying there for some time that the thought suddenly came into my mind that Rosie had been beaten senseless by a man and left for dead. She had been trying to find out where Lainie had gone for us and now she was lying in the infirmary with her mind gone, unable to speak and not knowing anyone.

Were the two things connected? Had Rosie been beaten because she knew too much?

I decided not to mention Rosie to my sister. If Lainie made the connection she might be more frightened than ever, but I couldn't help thinking about it myself.

Sleep was impossible and I was up early scrubbing the front doorstep before the men from the lane were on their way to work. I had finished the ironing and started preparing breakfast when I heard the raised voices upstairs and I knew that Lainie must have gone to Mam's room.

I went up the stairs, standing on the landing for a moment to listen to their quarrel.

'So you've slunk back with your tail between your legs. I knew you would.'

'I'm not stopping,' Lainie said. 'I just came to collect some things and see how Bridget was.'

'I knew you hadn't come to see me,' Mam's voice was sharp with bitterness. 'Why should you? You've been nothing but trouble to me from the day you were forced into my belly.'

'You can't blame me because you were raped,' Lainie yelled back. 'Da told me you were raped, but not by him. You were having Jamie before he touched you.'

'You lying little bitch!' Mam yelled. 'I'm not talking about your brother – though God help me, he's as good for nothin' as his father – I'm talking about your father. Sam was drunk the night you were got, same as he was a good many other nights.'

'You probably drove him to the drink,' Lainie said. 'And anything else he did to you. You're a cold bitch, Martha O'Rourke.'

I couldn't bear any more of this and I rushed into the room, shouting at them.

'Stop this!' I yelled. 'Shut up the pair of you. I won't have it, do you hear? Lainie, Mam's been ill, you'll have to ignore her, and Mam, Lainie is going to live here with us for a while whether you like it or not. And I want a bit of peace in the house or I'll walk out on the pair of you.'

They both stared at me in shock. Neither of them had ever heard that tone from me before and for a moment it silenced them.

'Do you want everyone in the lane to know all your business?' I said as they looked at me. 'I can't manage everything alone, Mam. We need money coming in, and even if someone comes for the room it won't be enough without one of us bringing in a bit more. I'm tired and I'm worried about Tommy and unless you two can just ignore each other and get on with things I'm off to the sea to be near him.'

'She would too,' Mam said. 'She's a hard woman that sister of yours, Lainie. I'm tied to my bed and dependent on her and she knows it.'

'I'm sorry, Bridget,' Lainie apologized. 'I know you've had

94

a lot to put up with and I'm going to help now as much as I can, but she'll never let up on me,' she said, indicating Mam slumped on the bed.

'Just ignore her,' I said. 'And keep away from her as much as you can.'

'I need to use the pot,' Mam muttered glaring at me. She struggled up against the pillows by sheer effort of will. 'And don't think you can ignore me, miss. I shan't be stuck in this bed forever.'

'Your breakfast is nearly ready,' I said to Lainie. 'I'll see to Mam and then I'm off to see if I can find work somewhere.'

Lainie nodded and went out without glancing at Mam. I fetched the pot to her and helped her as she relieved herself, receiving a sly pinch on my arm for my trouble.

'I'll have me revenge on you, Bridget O'Rourke. Just see if I don't.'

'Don't push me too far, Mam,' I said and looked at her hard. 'If you drive Lainie away with your nagging, I'll go too and you'll end up in the infirmary.'

I left Lainie to wash the breakfast dishes and went off to the market. We needed various things for the larder and I wanted to take the chance to ask Maisie if she'd heard of any work that might suit me.

'I could do wiv some help on a Saturday,' she told me. 'If you want to come for a few hours, but I did hear as they wanted someone to scrub floors at the tannery.'

'It stinks something awful down there,' I said and grimaced. 'No one will do the job for long, but beggars can't be choosers. Thanks for telling me, Maisie, and I would like to come on Saturday if I can?'

'I'd love to have yer,' Maisie said and grinned at me. 'That lovely smile o' yourn always brings the punters in.'

I smiled at her, feeling more cheerful than I had in a while. Now that Lainie was back I wouldn't be so tied to the house as I had been since Mam's stroke. And I didn't mind what I did if it brought in a few shillings a week, though I would have preferred to work on the market with Maisie every day if it were possible.

Lainie looked at me when I told her that I'd found two part-time jobs, then pulled a face. 'I hope you don't expect me to scrub floors. I've never done that and I don't feel like starting now.'

'I haven't asked you to,' I said. 'My job is from five to seven in the mornings. I'll be back to look after Mam after that, but I'll want a few hours free on Saturdays. I've promised Maisie I'll help her on the market.'

'You won't get much out of that,' Lainie said, looking sulky.

'Perhaps not, but it's what I want to do,' I said. 'You'll have to look for something. I don't know if Mr Dawson will let you help out on the ales?'

'I could ask him I suppose,' Lainie said. 'Don't worry, Bridget. I'll find something. I'll contribute my share somehow.'

'If we could get another lodger it wouldn't be so bad,' I said. 'I asked for a woman when it was just Mam and me, but I suppose I could change the card.'

'We don't want a man here,' Lainie said and gave a shudder, reminding me of what she had suffered. 'Wait and see if a woman comes first, Bridget. I promise I'll look for work when I've had my dinner.'

'All right,' I agreed. 'I am sure you will find something, love. You never had a problem before.' But she had walked out on both her previous employers without notice and in a small community like ours word got round.

After Lainie had gone out, I looked after Mam and then started on the housework. It was past six in the evening when Lainie came back. One look at her face told me all I needed to know.

'Never mind,' I said. 'Give yourself a chance, Lainie. You'll find something before long.'

'Not round here,' she said and pulled a face. 'Talk about giving a dog a bad name. They all said work was short, but I know some of them were lying.'

'Just keep trying,' I said. 'I couldn't go down the brewery, but I might try somewhere else – if you were prepared to look after Mam?'

'I'd probably hold a pillow to her face before the week was out,' she said. 'No, Bridget. If it comes to the worst, I'll go scrubbin' same as you.' She looked a bit shamefaced. 'I was offered a job cleanin' at the soap factory, but that stinks even more than the tannery.'

'Well, there's no rush,' I said. 'You being here makes it easier for me to get out, and that's something. We'll manage and someone might come for the room.'

Lainie was being sick in the privy when I came home from work a few mornings later. I had taken a bucket of slops out to empty and she came out, wiping her mouth on the back of her hand.

'It stinks in there. I'd forgotten how bad it gets at times.'

'The night soil man only comes once a week. What's the matter – are you ill?'

'Can't you guess? I didn't tell you – I'm having a baby and I'm trying to get rid of it.' She looked ashamed. 'I shouldn't have come.'

'Of course you should.'

'Mam will sing a different tune – so will others.'

I could just imagine what they would say behind her back – and some of them to her face!

'It doesn't matter what other people say.'

'You won't tell anyone what happened?' She looked at me pleadingly. 'Let them think I went off with a man who let me down . . . I couldn't bear for anyone to know.'

'If that's what you want,' I said and looked at her sadly.

'It's the only way I can stay here.'

'Then I promise,' I said. 'Of course I do, Lainie. I want you to stay.'

'And I will find work. I can work almost to the last minute. I promise I won't be more of a trouble to you than I can help.'

'You aren't any trouble to me,' I said. 'But we ought to try and get a lodger if we can – just until the baby is born. Do you think you could bear to sleep with me if I get the chance to let the room?'

'Yes – if you can put up with me dreamin',' she said and smiled. 'I could always come down and sleep on the couch if you kick me out.'

Lainie spent the next two weeks looking for work without success. I saw the way her shoulders drooped when she came back at the end of the day and I sensed her humiliation. We still hadn't found a lodger and I'd had to dodge the rent man the last time he called, which was something that had hardly ever happened before. We had always paid our rent on time even if we went without other things. I couldn't leave it for long or we would be out on the street.

I decided that I would swallow my pride and go back to the brewery. If I could see Mr Dawson alone he might give me a job on the bottling.

I screwed up my courage, making sure he was alone in the office before I went in. He stared at me as I made my request, seeming to hesitate before he shook his head.

'I'm sorry, Bridget,' he said at last. 'I would really like to take you on, but at the moment we're laying girls off. Perhaps there might be something in the summer. We shall start to get busy again then.'

As I left the office a woman entered and I heard her speak to Mr Dawson about some letters she had taken to the post office. So, she was his new secretary. She had looked a plain, serious sort of woman in her early thirties and I suspected that Mrs Dawson was happier with her as my replacement.

As I crossed the yard, Ernie Cole came up to me. 'No luck?' he asked and looked grim. 'It's a bad time, Bridget. Dawson let five go last week.'

'He told me but I thought he was lying.'

'Why should he lie?' He stared at me as I remained silent.

'Excuse me,' I said hurriedly before Ernie guessed the truth, 'I have to get back.'

'I heard your Lainie's home.'

'Yes.' I hesitated, then, 'She went to visit a friend because she hadn't been well. The doctor said some country air would do her good.'

The expression in his eyes told me he didn't believe me, but he was willing to go along with my story if I wanted it that way.

'You'll be glad to have 'er back?'

'Yes, very glad, but she's finding it difficult to get a job.'

'I know of something. It's a pub I deliver beer to a couple of miles away. They want a girl to serve in the middle of the day – dinners and drinks and things. She might have to help out in the kitchen as well. I could put a word in for 'er and let you know?'

'Would you? It's quite a way to walk, but she might take it.'

'She could probably get a ride on the tram for part of the way,' Ernie said. 'I'm goin' there later today. I'll ask and call round this evening – shall I?'

'Yes, thanks. I may be busy, but Lainie will be there.'

'Fair enough,' he said. 'I dare say you've plenty to do with your Mam and all – if there's anythin' I can do . . . ?'

'We manage all right, thanks. We don't need help.'

'There's such a thing as bein' too proud, Bridget.'

He turned and walked off and I knew I had offended him. I hoped he wouldn't change his mind about trying to help Lainie. A part of me wanted to call out and tell him I was sorry, but pride held me back – that and a feeling that it was better not to get involved.

It was past seven that evening when Ernie came to the door. I sent Lainie to answer it, making the excuse that I had to go up and see to Mam, and I heard them talking on the doorstep.

When I came down, I saw by Lainie's face that it was good news.

'Ernie told me there's a job going,' she said. 'He's going to pick me up on Saturday morning and take me there on his wagon.'

'Saturday morning.' I pulled a face. 'I'll have to ask Maggie if she will pop in and look at Mam now and then. I've promised Maisie I'll help her out for a few hours.'

'I'll get back as soon as I can,' she promised. 'Besides, Maggie won't mind looking in on Mam when she can.'

'I'll pop round and ask her now,' I said. 'If she can't manage it I might be able to find someone else.'

Eight

'I'll be glad of a bit of 'elp, dearie.' Maisie's kind old eyes
had a new tiredness about them. 'This winter 'as played 'ell
wiv me rheumatics, Bridget luv. You come whenever you can.
I can't pay you much, but every little bit 'elps, don't it?'

'Thank you,' I said and smiled at her. I felt like hugging
her, but she would probably groan with pain if I did. Her
fingers were knotted, bent double like skinny claws, and her
movements were slow. 'I'll be here by seven to help you set
up, Maisie. I don't have to go to the tannery on Saturdays.'

Maisie nodded her approval. 'You always were a good girl,
Bridget. We'll set up the stall and then I can go home and have
a rest for an hour or two if I feel poorly. You can manage on
yer own fer a while, can't yer?'

'O' course I can, Maisie,' I said and looked at her anxiously.
I hadn't realized she'd been that ill. She seemed to have aged
rapidly since Christmas. 'You know you can trust me.'

Maisie's gnarled hands gripped mine. 'I'll see yer tomorrow
then, Bridget. Mind you wrap up warm. It's still winter fer all
it should be spring around the corner.'

As I turned into Farthing Lane, Fred Pearce was trundling
his barrow over the cobbles. He waved and called out a
friendly greeting. I paused for a moment, though it was
too cold for either of us to stand about in the street for
long.

'Cold isn't it?' I noticed he had a newspaper tucked under
his arm. 'Anything interesting in the news?'

'Not a lot. Seems them Boers are still stirring up trouble.
And that Ada Williams what they said were a baby farmer

101

has been hanged in Newgate for what she done to that little girl. Serves her right an' all!'

'Yes, it does,' I agreed. 'It's wicked the way some of those women mistreat the children left in their care. Anyway, how are you, Fred?'

'All the better for seeing you, Bridget. How's your mam and your sister?'

'They're all right,' I said. 'What about you?'

'I've got a chill settled on my chest,' he told me. 'I'll be all right when I get a tot of hot whisky inside me.'

'That's right,' I said. 'Hurry on home and get something warm inside you.'

Lainie had been washing her hair when I got home. She looked much better than she had since her return and I knew the prospect of a job in a pub had brightened her mood.

'If they pay what Ernie said, I'll be giving you ten bob a week,' she said, a gleam in her eyes. 'You'll be able to pay the rent then, Bridget.'

'That's a lot of money,' I said, feeling happy at her excitement. 'Far more than Maisie could pay me on the market, even if I worked all week.'

'I thought you were only going for a few hours on Saturday?'

'Yes, that's what I'd agreed,' I said. 'But she's not well, Lainie. She might not be able to keep the stall going without help and you know what the market controller is like. Any stallholder who doesn't turn up loses their pitch after a couple of days.'

'Well, both of us can't go out to work full-time,' Lainie said. 'Someone has to look after Mam. That girl Maggie recommended is all right for a couple of hours on Saturday, but she'll be at school in the week and you can't ask Maggie to come in every day.'

'No, I know that,' I said. 'I'll have to tell Maisie I can only manage Saturdays.'

'I don't know why you want to work there at all,' Lainie said. 'Surely you're doing enough as it is?'

I didn't answer her. It was hard to explain how I felt about working with Maisie – it just made things seem better.

'Well, we'll just have to see how things go.'

I went up to see Mam and then cooked the supper. Lainie had peeled the potatoes but she said she didn't know what else needed doing, and sat fiddling with her hair as I fried eggs and bubble and squeak for our supper.

It was as we were washing up that we heard a loud knocking noise at the door. When I went to open it, I was surprised to see Tilly Cullen standing there. She had a wild look about her and her chest was heaving as though she had been running.

'Whatever is the matter?' I asked. 'Come in and sit down, Tilly.'

'No!' she gasped. 'I've come to fetch you. It's Fred Pearce. He's been attacked . . . Someone broke into his house and knocked him out. Maude saw his door was open and went over there. She says he's poorly, Bridget, but askin' fer you.'

'Askin' for Bridget?' Lainie had come to the door behind me. 'Why would he be askin' for her?'

'Yer sister allus stops to pass the time of day wiv 'im,' Tilly said. 'She's got a kind heart, your Bridget.'

'I'd better go and see him,' I said. 'Will you keep an eye on Mam, Lainie?'

She nodded but didn't say anything as I grabbed my shawl and followed Tilly into the lane.

'Why does he want to see me, Tilly?'

'Blessed if I know, lass, less 'e wants ter leave yer all his worldy goods.' She went into a cackle of laughter as though it was a great joke. 'Pile of ginger beer bottles in 'is parlour so Maude says.'

'I wonder why someone attacked him,' I said as we hurried up the lane. 'Were they after stealing something?'

'Well, I did 'ear as he had a pile of gold sovereigns in a tin somewhere,' Tilly said. 'But I thought as that were a fool's tale. I mean 'e wouldn't go about the way 'e does if 'e 'ad, would 'e?'

'I shouldn't have thought so, but why would anyone want to harm Fred? He never hurt anyone in his life.'

'Me 'usband says there's been a rash of burglaries lately. The night watchman at St Katherine's was set on a week ago. Jud says it's more than the usual pilferin'. He reckons someone is organizing it.'

I didn't have time to think about what she'd said for we had reached Fred's house and Maude was at the door urging us on.

'He was askin' for you, Bridget,' she said. 'But I don't reckon 'e's in 'is right mind. Keeps wandering, 'e does, thinking he's back in the past, poor old sod.'

I followed her into the house. Fred was lying on the floor, but Maude had done her best to make him comfortable, covering him with a blanket and placing a cushion behind his head.

'I reckon whoever it was ransacked the place,' she said. 'They've ripped up the couch, though it never weren't much good, there ain't much left of it now. I don't know what the poor bugger 'ull do if 'e comes round proper.'

I glanced round the room. It looked as if whoever had been here was searching for something. They had thrown things all over the place, smashing ornaments and ripping up the old couch and chair that had formed the main part of Fred's furniture. There was so little of value that I wondered what they had been expecting to find – unless it was that tin of gold sovereigns?

'Who would do such a wicked thing?' I asked Maude, then as I heard Fred moan I went to bend over him, stroking his forehead. 'It's all right, Fred. We'll fetch the doctor to you. You'll be all right now.'

His face was a yellowish white and there was a bruise beginning to form over one eye. He moaned and then opened his eyes to look at me.

'You came then, Sally love,' he said and smiled at me. 'I knew you would. Have you forgiven me for what I done?'

'He must be talking about his wife,' Maude said in a hushed whisper. 'I 'eard as he was married once.'

I took the hand he held out to me, holding it gently. 'Yes, of course I came, Fred,' I said. 'It wasn't your fault . . . I'm sure it wasn't your fault.'

'I didn't mean you and the boy to die,' he muttered and my throat was tight with emotion as I saw a tear slip from the corner of his eye. 'I loved you, Sally. It was all for you. Everything I did was for your sake.'

'Hush then, Fred,' I said to try and soothe him. 'Don't upset yourself. The doctor will come soon.'

He closed his eyes and I knew he wasn't hearing me.

'I could look after 'im,' Maude said. 'They won't keep 'im five minutes in the infirmary. I looked after my Albert fer years.'

'That's kind of you,' I said to her. 'We'll see when the doctor comes.'

Fred had his eyes open again and now he seemed to be looking at me properly. 'Bridget,' he said. 'I wanted to see you, lass. Tell Joe . . . Joe Robinson. Tell him to look after you. It's for you, lass. It's all for you.'

'Fred, don't worry,' I said and bent over him. 'It's going to be all right.'

His eyes had closed again and his colour was terrible. I heard a horrid gurgling sound in his throat and then quite suddenly he stopped breathing.

'Fred . . .' I cried as his hand slipped from mine. 'Oh, Fred . . .' A sob broke from me and my eyes filled with tears. 'No . . . please . . .'

'Don't take on so, love.' Maude came up to me and put a hand on my shoulder. 'He's gone, Bridget,' she said. 'There's nothing anyone can do for 'im now, poor old bugger.'

'He thought I was his wife,' I said chokily. 'I'm sure that's what he thought.'

'Who was 'e talkin' about?' Tilly asked. 'Some bloke called Joe Robinson . . . Do you reckon 'e were the one what attacked Fred and done this?'

'Oh, no, it wouldn't have been him,' I said. 'Joe Robinson was his friend.' I didn't mention the shop Joe had leased, but

I realized that Fred had been trying to ask me to get in touch with Joe, though he had got muddled up in his mind and thought I was his wife.

'Well, you'd best get in touch with 'im if you know 'im,' Tilly said as Maude went to answer a knock at the door. We heard her speaking to someone. 'That 'ull be the doctor and the coppers will 'ave to be fetched now it's murder.'

'Oh, Tilly,' I said. 'That's such a horrible thing . . . murder . . .' I blinked hard as my throat tightened. 'Fred never harmed anyone.'

Maude had brought the doctor into the room and he was asking her questions about what she had seen and why she had come over to investigate.

After a brief examination, he confirmed that Fred was dead and said there was no point in taking the body to the infirmary.

'I can arrange for him to go to the mortuary in the morning,' he began but Maude stopped him with a shake of her head.

'We look after our own around here, doctor,' she said. 'I'll see to 'im and they can put the coffin in my parlour until the funeral. I've done it before and it ain't no bother to me.'

'Are you sure, Mrs Brown?' he asked. 'There will be expenses, you know. Why not leave it to the parish?'

'We'll see to 'im ourselves.'

The doctor nodded. 'I'll speak to the police about this and they may want to question you again.'

Maude looked at me as he went out. 'Will you get in touch with 'is friend, Bridget? This Joe Robinson – he'll likely want to see to things 'isself.'

'Yes, I'll do that, Maude,' I said. 'And don't worry about the money. I think Fred probably had enough put by.'

'That's if the bugger what done 'im in didn't pinch it,' Tilly said. 'Still, we'll all rally round if it comes to it – can't have the poor bugger stuck in a pauper's grave.'

'I'll send word first thing tomorrow,' I said and went over to Fred. Bending down, I kissed his cheek. 'I'm sorry for what happened to you – so sorry . . .'

I asked Mick Ryan if he knew someone who could get a message to Joe Robinson and he promised he would see to it. Fred might not have been the most popular resident in the lane while he lived, but people were angry about what happened to him. We had closed ranks and no one wanted to talk about anything else.

Maisie had tears in her eyes when she spoke of him. 'A sharp-tongued old bugger, that were Fred Pearce,' she said, 'but 'e 'ad a good 'eart.'

'I liked him,' I said. 'It makes me angry, Maisie, that anyone should do such a thing to an old man! I hope they catch whoever did it – he deserves to hang.'

'Aye, I reckon most feel that way,' Maisie said. 'Fred might 'ave been a funny old bugger, but 'e were one o' us.'

I told Lainie what Maisie had said when she came in that evening. She agreed, but she wasn't very interested. Her eyes were bright and I knew she was excited because she'd got the job and I could tell she'd been drinking.

'I shall have to work on Saturday evenings in future, but I don't have to start until five so you can keep your market job, Bridget. I don't mind stayin' here for a few hours, as long as it isn't too long.'

'Thanks,' I said, knowing she was reluctant to do things for Mam. 'We usually pack up about four so I'll be home in plenty of time.'

'I shall leave by three,' she said and frowned. 'But Maggie will probably come in for an hour or so. Anyway, Mam would be all right on her own for a while. It's my belief she could do more for herself if she wanted.'

I didn't argue, though I wasn't convinced. Mam was as stubborn as she was bad-tempered and I knew she was getting stronger, but she couldn't get out of bed by herself yet. Lainie knew that, but she just didn't want to be tied to the house or Mam. They argued every single time Lainie went near her, but not so fiercely that I'd considered carrying out my threat to leave.

There wasn't really much point in my going down to

Skegness to be near Tommy. I wouldn't be allowed to see him and though I'd written to him, I hadn't received a reply.

I worried about my brother all the time, but the matron had promised she would let me know how he was getting on and I had to be patient. The memory of his pale, scared face as I left him haunted me, mostly at night when I couldn't sleep.

Joe Robinson came to the house on Sunday morning. I was making a bacon pudding for dinner and Lainie answered the door. She brought him to the kitchen, then went straight upstairs.

'I didn't know your sister lived with you,' Joe said.

'She came back home a few weeks ago,' I told him, wiping my hands on the towel. 'I'm sorry, Mr Robinson. The kitchen smells of onions.'

'That bacon pudding smells good,' Joe said and smiled at me. 'Thank you for sending me word, Miss O'Rourke. I might have missed the announcement in the paper as it was only one line. I've spoken to the police and they have no objection to my arrangin' the funeral this week.'

It didn't seem right that the death of a man was only worth one line, but it was much the same as when Rosie was beaten. If she hadn't been found in the street, it might not have been mentioned at all.

'I should think they'd be glad of it,' I said. 'Fred wanted you to know. I'm not sure if he had any family.'

'No,' Joe said with a frown. 'There's no one. His wife and son died of diphtheria some years ago. Fred blamed himself. Said he'd neglected them. I think that's why he came here. He used to live over his shop – ran a pawnbroker's you know, but he couldn't bear to go near the place after they died. It was empty for years and had been broken into a score of times before I took it over. That's why it needed so much doin' to it. But Jamie soon sorted it for me.'

'What will happen to the shop now?'

'I shall have to sort things out with the lawyers,' Joe said. 'I'm not sure if he left a will, but he gave me a box to look after for him a couple of weeks ago. I visited about every couple of weeks, brought him a bottle of whisky. We got on all right, Fred and me. He said the box was important and he didn't want it left in the house – said he'd noticed some bloke hangin' around.'

'Did he say any more about the bloke?'

'He was worried about something. But he wouldn't say what. Just asked if I would look after his box. I put it in the bank but I'll get it out before the funeral, just in case he left any instructions about what he wanted.'

'Fred wasn't a Catholic, was he?'

'No. His funeral will be over the river, but I was thinking of givin' him a bit of a send-off in the lanes. Do you think he would've liked that, Miss O'Rourke?'

'Yes.' I smiled at him. 'Yes, I think Fred would have been pleased. People are upset about what happened. They would appreciate something like that.'

'Right, that's what we'll do then,' he said and took a small package from his pocket. 'This is from Jamie. He asked me to bring it over for him.'

I took the folded brown paper bag and opened it to reveal three pounds all in silver coins.

'Jamie shouldn't send so much,' I said. 'I'm working part-time now and Lainie has just found a job.'

'He wanted you to have it,' Joe said. 'Your brother is doing well for himself, Miss O'Rourke. I've given him a barrow to manage for me and we share the profits, so the harder he works the more he gets.'

'Oh . . .' I looked at Joe, wondering how he had come to understand my brother so well so quickly. Jamie responded to trust and independence in a way he never would for someone who treated him as if he were rubbish. 'I suppose it's all right then.' I put the money on the mantelpiece. 'How is your sister getting on with her flower shop?'

'Mary is doing just fine,' Joe said and his mouth curved in smile of affection. 'She is clever with her hands – makes lovely flower arrangements. A lot of hotels and restaurants ask her to do the flowers for them. I never expected her to make the shop pay with just flowers, but so far she's holding her head above water, as they say.'

'I wondered if people would buy flowers from a shop,' I said. 'I've only ever bought them from Maisie because she lets me have them cheap. I'm so pleased Mary is getting on well. Jamie told me she is nice.'

Perhaps there was a wistful note in my voice because he looked at me for a moment before replying. 'Yes, I think you would like each other,' he said at last. 'Perhaps you would like to come for tea one Sunday – if Jamie came to fetch you?'

'I suppose we could come on the tram,' I said, feeling pleased that he had invited me. 'I'd like that, Mr Robinson.'

'Why don't you call me Joe? I feel as if I know you well because of what Jamie tells us about you, Bridget.'

I blushed as he smiled at me, but he had been so kind that I could hardly refuse. 'I shall have to get someone to sit with Mam, but I should like to have tea with Mary and your mother, Joe.'

'We'll arrange it for next week then,' he said. 'I shan't keep you talkin' because I know you must be busy, but I'll see you at Fred's do, I hope?'

'Yes. I shall try to be there.'

'Good. I'll be on my way then.'

I went to the door with him, standing on the pavement to watch him walk down the lane. Just as I turned to go in, I saw Ernie Cole at the other side of the street. He was glaring at me as if he were angry over something. It was a while since I'd spoken to him, but I'd seen him walking to the pub at night. I waved to him but he didn't wave back, merely turned his back on me and walked away. Obviously he was annoyed about something, but I couldn't imagine what. Well, if that was how he wanted to be, it was all right with me!

Maggie offered to sit with Mam while I went to Fred's send-off.

'But don't you want to go?' I asked. 'It's bound to be a good do if Joe Robinson is arranging it.'

'Fred liked you, Bridget. You should be the one to go.'

'Thanks, Maggie. I don't know how I would have managed without you since Mam took sick.'

'Lainie could do more to help you with Martha.'

'She's starting work tomorrow,' I told her. 'She'll be working long hours then, Maggie. She can't do everything and I'm only working part-time.'

'What you're doin' is a lot harder than servin' in a pub,' Maggie said with a little sniff. I suspected that she didn't quite approve of Lainie coming back to the lanes. 'What about when the baby comes? Will she expect you to look after that while she goes swanning off somewhere?'

'What do you mean?' I felt hot and uncomfortable as she looked at me, but I knew I couldn't lie to her.

'Did you think I wouldn't guess, Bridget? It's in her eyes and I've heard her being sick out in the yard a couple of times. You can't keep a secret round here for long. You should know that.'

'You won't tell anyone else?'

'It won't be long before people start to talk,' Maggie said. 'But they won't hear it from me. Besides, she's not the only one. They say Ernie Cole has got to marry that girl he's been hangin' out with – more fool him!'

'Ernie Cole . . . ?' Maggie's remark had shocked me. I remembered the way he had scowled at me. Was that because he was resentful over the trouble he'd got himself into? 'Where did you hear that, Maggie?'

'His mother told me herself only this mornin',' Maggie said. 'Jean is furious with him over it. She doesn't like Grace Barker. She doubts the child is his because she says Grace has been with all sorts, but apparently he's going to do the right thing by the girl.'

'And so he should if it's his baby!'

'You don't mind then, Bridget? I thought you and Ernie might have got together one day?'

111

'I've never so much as looked at him that way,' I said.

I wasn't telling the whole truth. I had thought about going out with Ernie a few times. He was good-looking and I liked his smile, even though I'd never encouraged him, but I wasn't going to let anyone see that I minded.

Nine

It was raining on the afternoon of Fred's send-off. I put a shawl over my head and ran all the way to the church hall. The large, rather dingy room was full of people. Some of them I only knew slightly by sight. They didn't live in our lane or the brewery lane and I wondered if Fred had even known them.

'It's disgusting,' a voice said as I took off my wet shawl and hung it on a hook by the door to dry. 'Most of them have only come for the tea. I'll bet they never even knew Fred and they certainly didn't speak to him in the street.'

I turned to face Jean Cole. It was a while since I'd seen Ernie's mother who was a widow and lived at the far end of the brewery lane.

'I don't suppose Fred would mind,' I said. 'He would probably laugh and think it was funny. Besides, it looks as if there's plenty of food.'

'You can say that again,' Jean agreed. 'This Joe Robinson must 'ave a bit of money by him to afford all this.' Jean gave me a strange look. 'I don't know 'im but Ernie says as you're a friend of his. Saw him coming from your house the other day.'

'He came because I told him about Fred. I wouldn't say we're friends exactly. I do know him, but only slightly. He helped me a couple of times and my brother works for him. I think Mr Robinson knew Fred better than most people.'

'I suppose you've 'eard about our Ernie and that girl? I warned him not to get messed up with 'er, Bridget. But 'e wouldn't never listen and now 'e's got to wed 'er and where that will end no one knows.'

'I expect they will be happy if they love each other.'

She gave a crack of bitter laughter. 'Ernie's a fool, that's what 'e is, and so I've told 'im. She's not the one 'e wants, never was. Only went after 'er because 'e couldn't get the girl 'e wanted.'

'But he has to marry her if it's his child?'

'Who's to say who the father is?' Jean said angrily. 'I doubt if she knows 'erself. Ernie wasn't the first nor the last wiv 'er. I've told 'im to give 'er money and deny all knowledge of the brat, but 'e won't listen. Feels sorry for 'er 'cause she's 'ad a 'ard time. I told 'im there's plenty of others 'ad it as 'ard, but I might as well talk to meself!'

'Perhaps he loves her?'

'It's someone else our Ernie loves,' Jean said, giving me another odd stare. She was trying to tell me Ernie had wanted me, half blaming me because her son had gone off the tracks with this girl. 'She wouldn't 'ave 'im so 'e went looking for a bit of a laugh and now 'e 'as to pay the price.'

'I never gave Ernie any reason to hope, Mrs Cole.'

'I know that, lass,' she said and the accusing look died. 'He should 'ave waited. I told him to be patient and give you time to sort yourself out, but men never listen. Ernie went 'is own way and now 'e'll 'ave to live with it.'

'I'm sorry if I hurt Ernie,' I said. 'I never meant to do that. Please tell him that, Mrs Cole.'

'Aye, I'll tell 'im – and a lot more besides.'

'Bridget . . .'

I turned as I heard my name called and saw Joe walking towards me. 'Excuse me, I should have a word with Mr Robinson now.'

'You got here then,' Joe said, smiling in pleasure as he saw me. 'Have you had anything to eat yet?'

'Not yet,' I said and laughed. 'I wasn't sure I could get near the table. There's such a crowd.'

'I didn't know Fred had so many friends,' Joe said, grinning at me as we shared the joke. 'But I think he would've enjoyed this, don't you, Bridget?'

'Oh yes,' I said. 'I know he would, Joe. People thought Fred was surly and unfriendly, but he often used to have a little joke with me. We never passed in the street without speaking. I saw him on his way home the day he died . . . It upset me a lot when I saw him afterwards . . .'

'Yes, he told me he was fond of you,' Joe said and looked thoughtful. 'I'm going to be clearin' his house out soon, Bridget. If there's anything you want, you're very welcome to it.'

'That's very kind of you,' I said. 'I don't suppose there's anything I really want, but if you find a keepsake I wouldn't mind having somethin' to remind me of him.'

'I'll see what I come across,' Joe said. 'I've spoken to the lawyer and it seems Fred left me in charge of everythin'. He left a will of sorts, but the lawyer isn't sure if it will stand up. It isn't witnessed, and he didn't make it very clear.'

'Oh, well, I'm sure you will sort everything out, Joe. Fred obviously trusted you to do what's right.'

'I shall do my best.'

'I'm sure you will. I think you would take care of most things, Joe. I'm glad Fred had you for a friend.'

I thought about what Jean Cole had told me when I got home that afternoon. I was sorry if Ernie was unhappy about marrying that girl, but I didn't see what else he could do. If it was his baby, the only decent thing he could do was to marry her; I would have thought the less of him if he hadn't stood by her.

It was silly of me to feel that I had lost something. Ernie and I had never been more than friends – perhaps not even that – but there *had* been something between us, unspoken but felt and understood.

I tried to examine my own heart. Had I expected him to wait while I sorted my life out? I'd had reasons enough to distrust men and there were times when I felt that I hated each and every one of them, but that didn't stop the foolish ache in my heart every time I thought about Ernie marrying that girl.

No, that was foolish! I wasn't in love with Ernie and I didn't want to marry anyone. I couldn't have left Mam and Lainie if I had, and it was certain that Ernie could never have supported us all, even if he had been willing to take us on.

Mam was mine and Lainie's responsibility, not anyone else's. We had to look after her for as long as she needed us, and I had to have a home for Tommy to come back to when he was better. I didn't know what would happen when Lainie's child was born. She might take it and leave us – or perhaps Hans would come back and marry her despite what had happened.

Everyone was talking about Ernie and Grace now. Fred's murder had been a nine days' wonder and the splendid send-off Joe Robinson had provided had made people feel better about him. They still spoke of stringing the bastard who had done it to a lamppost if they got hold of him, but Ernie's wedding had now become the new source of gossip.

Maisie didn't like Grace much and she told me that she thought Ernie was a fool to marry her.

'It's probably not 'is,' she said. 'That girl 'as been around a bit, Bridget. She were just waitin' ter catch someone like 'im.'

'Perhaps . . .' I began and broke off as a man approached the stall. 'Yes, sir. What can I do for you?'

'Good morning, miss,' he said and tipped the smart bowler hat he was wearing. 'It is a better morning, isn't it? A little brighter today, I think.'

'Yes, sir. Not as cold as it was. We shall soon have spring here.'

'Yes, that will be something to look forward to. I am looking for some flowers for a friend by way of an apology. What do you recommend?'

Surely I had seen him before somewhere?

'These irises are lovely,' I suggested, taking them out of a tub. 'And the daffodils and tulips are pretty – you could make up a bouquet of these three bunches. Wrapped together they would make anyone forgive you – for most things at least.'

'Then I'll take them all,' he said and nodded his approval. 'You are an excellent saleswoman, Miss O'Rourke. I wouldn't mind employing you in one of my shops.'

'You're . . . Mr Maitland,' I said and blushed as he looked amused. 'I remember now. I saw you going into Bridie Macpherson's hotel last year. You had bought some chrysanthemums.'

'Yes, I thought I was right. It was your smile, you see. Once seen, never forgotten, I imagine? I believe you had a young lad with you that day?'

'Yes.' My smile dimmed. 'Tommy isn't well.'

'I am sorry to hear that. Very sorry. Let us hope he soon recovers. Perhaps I shall see you another day? When I am here on business, you know. Good afternoon, Miss O'Rourke.' He paid for his purchases, nodded to Maisie and walked away.

'Did you know 'im?' Maisie asked with a slight frown. 'Used to come 'ere often 'e did on a Saturday, but I ain't seen 'im for a while now.'

'I think he must know Bridie Macpherson,' I said. 'I was coming away from there once and I almost bumped into him. We got chatting. I thought he seemed nice.'

'Yer can never tell with 'is sort,' Maisie said. 'Gentry, 'e is and they're allus polite, but I never trust 'em . . . any of 'em.'

Maisie was always the same. If she took to someone she liked them, and if she didn't . . . well, that was just the way she was. I thought Mr Maitland was a gentleman and I hoped Bridie would forgive him for neglecting her.

Lainie was out when I got back that evening. Mam was alone in the house and I felt annoyed with my sister for going off and leaving her. She had promised she would go next door when she was ready to leave and ask Maggie to pop in and keep an eye on Mam.

When I went upstairs, I discovered that Mam was sleeping soundly and the reason was not far away. The whisky jar that had been almost a third full was lying empty by the side of the bed. Lainie must have given it to her before she left.

I went downstairs to the kitchen and made myself a cup of tea and then I started the ironing. The kitchen was in a mess with unwashed crockery in the sink. Lainie hadn't done a thing since I'd been gone. She was always telling me she would, but she never did and sometimes I resented the way she took it for granted that I would do all the chores around the house. I wondered what she would do when the baby came. Would she expect me to do everything then?

I attacked the sheets with the iron, knowing Lainie's behaviour wasn't the only reason I was in a bad mood. I shouldn't let it get to me, but all the talk about Ernie and that girl had unsettled me and I was restless. It wasn't my fault he had to marry her and yet I felt that it might not have happened if I'd been a bit nicer to him.

I had done about half the ironing when someone knocked at the door. I wasn't expecting anyone and I frowned as I went to answer it. The knocking was continuous and I wrenched the door open with a vengeance, glaring at the man who stood on the step.

Somehow I wasn't surprised to see who it was.

'What do you want?' I asked harshly. 'Mam's asleep. If you've woken her you'll feel the rough edge of my tongue, Ernie Cole. I don't know what you thought you were doing.'

'I thought you weren't going to answer,' he muttered. 'Can I come in, Bridget – just for a minute? I have to talk to you.'

I stared at him uncertainly for a moment and then I opened the door wider and let him follow me inside, leading the way to the kitchen. Then I turned to face him. I wasn't going to invite him to sit down. He could say what he had to say and then leave.

'You'd best say whatever you've come to say.'

'You've heard,' he said and looked at me. I could see the misery in his eyes and my heart caught with sudden pain. I felt responsible, even though I knew it wasn't my fault. 'You know what a bloody fool I've been?'

'I heard you got a girl into trouble.'

'It's my baby,' Ernie said and there was shame in his face

as he looked at me. 'I know what I've done and I'm not about to run away from my responsibility.'

'Well that's something,' I said. 'I wouldn't think much of you if you did. It's your duty to stand by her.'

'I knew you would say that. If I thought . . .' He broke off and swore. 'No, I didn't come here for that. I know there's no chance for me with you now. If I ever had one I threw it away.'

'We might have had a chance if things had been different,' I said and wondered at myself for saying it. Maybe it was the desperate look in his eyes or the way I had been feeling since I'd learned that he was going to marry Grace. 'I shouldn't have said that, Ernie – not now. Besides, I don't know that I want to marry anyone.'

'I would have been good to you,' Ernie said and now there was something else in his eyes – a look that was making me tremble inside. 'I love you, Bridget. I've loved you for as long as I can remember.'

'You never said it . . .'

'You never gave me a chance!'

'No, I didn't,' I admitted. 'I wasn't ready for courting and then . . .' I broke off and stared at him, my mouth tasting dry. 'There's no sense in this. You shouldn't have come here tonight, Ernie, and I shouldn't have let you in. It was wrong and stupid.'

'But you did.' He took a step towards me. The look in his eyes warned me but for some reason I couldn't move as he reached out for me. 'Bridget . . . It was always you.'

'No, Ernie . . .' I protested weakly, but I still didn't move as he put his arms around me. I just stood there as he drew me close and then bent his head to kiss me. I suppose I expected him to be rough, that his kiss would take from me rather than give, but I was wrong. His mouth was soft and gentle on mine, seeming to caress rather than bruise as the kiss just went on and on. 'Ernie . . .'

I couldn't help myself. It seemed as though he was tugging the heart from me. I clung to him as he held me and I wanted him to hold me forever, to go on kissing me and never let me go. This wasn't what I'd thought it would be like, but then the only other man to touch me had been Harry Wright and he had been trying to rape me. I was suddenly aware of all I was missing – and all that I would miss. My chance to love and be loved had slipped away without my ever realizing it.

Tears were slipping down my cheeks when Ernie let me go at last. He stood staring at me for several moments in silence and I saw that his eyes were also wet with tears.

'I'm sorry,' he said. 'I didn't mean that to happen. I just wanted to tell you. I wanted you to understand and I wanted you to forgive me. I'm sorry I let you down, Bridget. Ma told me to be patient, but I couldn't. I wanted you so bad and I thought it was hopeless. I went wild in my head and I got drunk a couple of times . . . That's when it happened. I never wanted her. I hardly knew it was happening. I'm so sorry, Bridget.'

'It was as much my fault as yours,' I said and the pain in my chest was so bad that I felt as if my heart had cracked in two. 'And it wouldn't make any difference if you hadn't gone with Grace. I can't marry you, Ernie. I've got Mam and Tommy to look after . . . and there's Lainie. And don't say you would have taken us on, because you couldn't. You know you couldn't manage all of us. You've got your mother.'

'And now I've got Grace and the baby,' Ernie said. 'People say she's bad, Bridget, but she's had a 'ard time of it one way and another. Her father abused her when she were little and she's had to fend for 'erself since she ran away from home. If she's done bad things, she's had no choice. It was either that or starve. I can't turn my back on 'er.'

'I know that,' I said and smiled at him. 'That's why you're special, Ernie.' I felt the ache of loss inside me as I realized what I should have known long ago. He cared for me and I cared for him. I'd been too young and silly to realize it, and now it was too late. 'I was as much a fool as you. If I'd been nicer to you this might not have happened.'

'Oh, Bridget,' he groaned and I saw his face twist with pain. 'It wasn't your fault, lass. You've had enough to put up with.'

'You'd better go, Ernie. It's too late. We both made mistakes, but we mustn't make another one now.'

'No,' he said and there was a decisive note in his voice now. 'I shan't come again. I had to make my peace with you or I couldn't 'ave faced it.'

I smiled at him. 'I'm glad you did, Ernie. I hope you will be happy with Grace. Be good to her.'

'I'll do right by 'er,' he said, and his mouth set hard. 'Goodbye then, Bridget. I hope things work out for you and your family.'

'Can you see yourself out? I want to finish this ironing before Mam wakes up and starts shouting.'

He nodded and went out without another word. I looked at the iron but I didn't pick it up. Instead, I sat down at the table and buried my face in my hands. Tears trickled between my fingers and I didn't attempt to stop them. This ache inside me hurt so much and I didn't know what to do about it.

I was such a fool! Why hadn't I seen that I cared for Ernie? Why had I just spurned every attempt he'd made to be my friend? It was so stupid – so unlike me to refuse to be friendly. I should have known there was a reason for the way I felt when he was around.

Finally, I had cried myself out. I went to the sink and washed my face in cold water, scrubbing at it with the towel afterwards until my skin felt hot. There was no point in feeling sorry for myself. I would never consider asking Ernie to break his word to Grace. He believed the child was his and the only decent thing he could do was to marry her. Besides, I couldn't leave Mam . . .

Right on cue I heard something thump on the floor upstairs and the next minute Mam started yelling. I sighed as I got up and went to see to her. Nothing had changed and it wasn't likely to as far as I could see.

I was wearing my Sunday dress when Jamie came to fetch me the next day for tea. He smiled as he saw me and said I looked nice, but his smile faded as he saw Lainie.

121

'So you came back,' he said. 'I suppose whoever it was ditched you?'

'That's my business,' she said and scowled. 'I'm off to work, Bridget. I'll see you when I get back.'

'You shouldn't have said anything to her, Jamie,' I said when the door slammed behind her. 'She's had a hard time.'

'And whose fault is that?' He frowned. 'Is Maggie coming round to look after Mam?'

'Yes, I'll go and fetch her now,' I said. 'Pop upstairs and say hello to her, Jamie. I shan't be a moment.'

He pulled a face but I heard him start up the stairs as I went next door to tell Maggie we were off.

'You have a good time,' Maggie said. 'And don't worry about getting back too soon.'

'I'll make it up to you one day,' I promised her. 'That's twice I've been out this week, Maggie.'

'It's a terrible gadabout you are, Bridget O'Rourke,' she teased. 'Get off, lass, I've nothin' better to do with my time.'

I thanked her and ran back next door, leaving her to follow when she was ready. She had no need to sit with Mam all the time, just to keep an eye and see she was all right every now and then.

Jamie was waiting for me on the doorstep and I could see by his face that he hadn't enjoyed his brief visit with Mam.

'We'll take the omnibus in the High Street,' he said. 'It's slow but it's better than walking.'

'I don't mind how we go,' I said and slipped my arm through his. I was excited by the prospect of an afternoon out and I liked the idea of the horse-drawn omnibus. I had been on them occasionally when I went up to Bermondsey market which was much bigger than our local one and had a variety of stalls selling things we couldn't buy in the lanes. 'Will Mrs Robinson and Mary mind that I'm coming, Jamie?'

'Of course they won't,' Jamie said and grinned at me. 'As a matter of fact, I've got something to tell you . . .'

I saw the glow in his eyes and I had half guessed what

was coming but I didn't let on. 'What is it, Jamie? Is it good news?'

'I think so,' he said. 'I've asked Mary to walk out with me and she's said she will.'

'Oh, Jamie! I think that's the best news ever. When are you going to get married?'

'Hold your horses,' Jamie said and laughed. 'I couldn't afford to marry her – not for a long time yet, but we've got an understanding. Joe is going to let me have some money to buy a horse and cart of my own, and I'm going into business for myself.'

'What kind of business, Jamie?'

'It's clearing houses when folk move or die,' he said and as I pulled a face he continued: 'It isn't as bad as it sounds, Bridget. There's money to be made when folk leave rubbish behind they don't want, so there is. Sometimes I move their things to a new house for them and sometimes I just get paid for taking the stuff away. It's the way Joe started out, and he's done all right for himself. He said that if I stick at it for a year he'll consider letting us get married and he'll let us have the rooms over Mary's shop. At the moment he's using them to store stuff of his own, but I could soon do it up a treat.'

'Oh, Jamie.' I felt so pleased for my brother that some of the ache I was carrying inside eased away. 'It's wonderful news, the very best. Did you tell Mam?'

'And have her start on at me . . . ?' Jamie looked at me uncertainly. 'Mary isn't Catholic, Bridget. It will be a civil weddin'.'

'Oh, I see . . .' I swallowed hard as I realized what that meant. 'Father O'Brien won't be pleased about that.'

'He won't be consulted,' Jamie said. 'I can do without his lectures, but you'll come to our weddin'?'

'I wouldn't miss it for the world,' I told him and hugged his arm. 'Father O'Brien can say what he likes – I'm glad you've found someone you can love, Jamie.'

'All I want now is to see you happy, Bridget.'

'I'm afraid you'll be waitin' a long time,' I said. 'Don't let's talk about me, Jamie. Tell me more about your Mary.'

'It's lovely to see you, Bridget,' Mary said and kissed my cheek as she drew me into the comfortable parlour. 'I may call you Bridget, I hope?'

'Yes, of course,' I said and smiled at her. I had been a little surprised at my first sight of her as she wasn't that pretty, but she had lovely thick dark hair which was caught back in a knot at the nape and soft brown eyes. It was when she smiled that I knew why Jamie had fallen in love with her for there was a rare sweetness in Mary – and a fragility that worried me a little. 'I hope we shall be friends?'

'I know we shall,' she said. 'I've been asking Jamie to bring you to tea for weeks, but it was Joe who asked in the end.' She glanced at her brother. 'I might have known you were up to something, Joe.' She gave a little laugh. 'My brother is always planning something, Bridget.'

'Your brother makes too many plans altogether,' Mrs Robinson said and touched the gold cameo brooch she wore at the throat of her black gown. 'But this time I approve. It's very nice to meet you at last, Bridget. Jamie has talked about you often.'

I glanced round the room, noticing the heavy overstuffed furniture that was typical of most homes where they could afford something decent. In the corner was a piano with a skirt round its legs and a silver-framed picture of Queen Victoria standing on the top.

Mary saw me looking at it. 'My mother keeps the picture there to remind me I should be more conscientious about practising,' she said with a mischievous look at Mrs Robinson. 'Because Her Majesty is a model to us all.'

'Poor old Vicky, she does miss her Albert,' Joe said. 'She came out of retirement for her diamond jubilee but her heart wasn't in it.'

'You just watch your tongue, Joe Robinson,' Mrs Robinson said sharply. 'It's Prince Albert and Her Majesty to you. But you're right, she's never got over her husband's death. People were so pleased to see her when she visited London last month, but they say her health isn't good.'

'We shall have Bertie for king before long,' Joe said and grinned at his mother. 'God knows what we'll do then. She's been a good queen when all's said and done, our Vicky.'

Mrs Robinson slapped his arm. 'You'll show some respect for your betters, Joe Robinson, or I'll not be sitting in the parlour with you. You can have your tea in the kitchen, unless you show some manners. Whatever will Bridget think of you?'

'I'm only teasin' yer, Ma,' Joe said. 'I know when to show respect, but you've got to have a laugh sometimes.'

'You know what he is, Ma,' Mary said. 'Leave him alone and he'll behave.'

A warm feeling formed inside me as I looked at their smiling faces and realized that they weren't seriously quarrelling. It was such a warm, happy atmosphere and so different to anything I had ever known at home.

The tea Mrs Robinson had prepared was like no other I had ever seen; the table laden with good things. Ham that was cut thin and melted on your tongue, bread and butter, delicious jam and honey to be spread on warm scones and a trifle with sherry in it.

Mrs Robinson kept urging me to eat more, but in the end I had to shake my head as she pressed yet another slice of delicious fruitcake on me.

'I couldn't eat another morsel,' I told her, patting my stomach. 'I only wish Tommy were at home so that I could take a slice for him.'

'Your poor little brother,' Mrs Robinson said, giving me a sympathetic look. 'I expect he misses his family, Bridget. Does he manage to write to you at all?'

'No, I haven't heard from him,' I said and frowned. 'He can write, though it is still hard for him, but I did have a brief note from the matron the other day. She says he is receiving treatment and the doctors are hopeful.'

'Poor little boy,' Mary said. 'It isn't nice to be ill and to be so far from home. I shouldn't like that.'

I recalled that Jamie had told me she had been ill as a child. I thought she still looked delicate and it was clear she understood just how Tommy felt.

'Perhaps Jamie would bring you to have tea with me one Sunday,' I said. 'It won't be quite like this, but you would be very welcome.'

'I'm sure it would be lovely,' she said. 'I shall plague Jamie until he brings me.'

I was sorry when it was time to leave, and as we sat behind the horses listening to the steady clip-clop of their hooves on the cobbles as they pulled the tram, I told Jamie that he was lucky to have found her.

'I know that,' he told me and his expression was serious. 'I was a silly fool wastin' me life, Bridget, and I'd still be doin' it if you hadn't given me a talkin' to.'

'Oh, Jamie, I didn't – at least I only said you might do better if you went further afield to look for work.'

'And didn't that work the miracle?' he asked, putting on the thickest of Irish brogues. 'Sure it's after thankin' you I am, me darlin'. I've you to thank for me good fortune and I'll help you whenever I can.'

'You've already helped me,' I said. 'Meeting Mary and her mother was like seeing another world.'

'It's not fair that you should have all the responsibility of Mam, Bridget. I know that and I'll make it up to you one day.'

'It's not your fault, Jamie,' I told him. 'And maybe it isn't all Mam's either. She's had a hard life, perhaps more things have happened to her than we know. Besides, it isn't so bad now that Lainie is home. She's bringing in a bit of money.'

'But you'll want to marry one day.' He looked at me as I shook my head and I turned away. 'I thought you and Ernie Cole . . . ?'

'He'll be married in a couple of weeks,' I said. 'Don't worry about me, Jamie. I can manage.'

Ten

Lainie didn't come in that evening. In the morning I went to check on her bed and I saw it hadn't been slept in.

'Where's that slut of a sister of yours?' Mam asked when I went in to make her comfortable a bit later. 'Up to her old tricks, is she?'

'I expect she worked late,' I replied, not looking at her. 'She told me they asked her if she wanted to live in and I should think she decided to stay the night rather than come home.'

'She'll be off with a man,' Mam said darkly. 'You wait and see if I'm not right.'

'Don't be silly. You know that's not true, Mam. Lainie has been working hard, that's all.'

'Believe that and you'll believe anything. That slut has never worked hard in her life. She's not like you and don't you be taken in by her. She'll let you down, Bridget. You'll find out I'm right one day.'

Lainie hadn't arrived when I left for work, but Mam said she would be all right for a couple of hours so I didn't bother Maggie. Perhaps my sister would be there when I got back.

She wasn't there and I began to worry. Supposing something had happened to her? I thought about Rosie and the way she had been beaten senseless and wondered if the men who had abused Lainie had somehow found her. Perhaps they had dragged her off to be a prostitute again.

I was anxious all day as I did my chores in the house and cooked supper for Mam and me, my thoughts going round and round like a puppy after its tail, but at a quarter to eleven that

127

evening Lainie walked in. She was so casual as she just flopped down in a chair that my temper snapped.

'Where the hell have you been? I've been going out of my mind all day wondering what had happened to you,' I said and glared at her. 'Don't you care about anyone else, Lainie? Didn't you think that I might be worried?'

'For goodness sake,' she muttered sullenly. 'You're worse than Mam. I'm not a child, Bridget, and I don't have to tell you everything I do.'

'I don't want you to, but you might show some consideration. I thought you might have been hurt.'

'I had to work late last night,' she replied, but her eyes didn't quite meet mine. 'I've decided to stop at the pub at night, Bridget. It doesn't make sense me travelling back and forwards, but I'll come home on Saturdays for a few hours so you can go on the market.'

'Are you sure that's what you want?' I was doubtful about this new arrangement and still a little annoyed with her. 'What about when they find out about the baby?'

'I'm well in with my new boss,' Lainie said, a gleam in her eyes. 'He won't throw me out.'

I could smell drink on her breath and the gleam in her eyes told me that she was excited. What had she been doing the night before? Mam had said she would be with a man and now I wondered if she'd been right. But it couldn't be that after what had happened! Surely she wasn't about to trust another man after that?

'Be careful, Lainie,' I said. 'Of course you can always come back here but—'

'I'll give you the money just the same,' she replied, a sulky downturn to her mouth. 'Don't question me, Bridget. Just leave me alone. I know what I'm doin'.'

I heard the resentful note in her voice and decided not to press the argument further. There was no point in arguing. I didn't want to fight with my sister. It was up to her what she did, though I couldn't help feeling worried about her.

'I'm going to try and let your room then,' I said. 'I'll

go down and ask them to put another card in the shop window.'

Lainie shrugged her shoulders. 'Do what you want,' she said. 'I'll clear my things out in the mornin'.'

Mam's comment when she heard that Lainie was going to sleep at the pub was exactly what I had expected. She called her names, then demanded some whisky and forgot about it. I gave her the drink rather than face another argument. Perhaps it would be better with Lainie gone – we might have some peace in the house.

I went to the church and stood at the opposite side of the road to watch everyone arrive the day Ernie got married. He arrived early, looking handsome in his best suit, his ma wearing a new dress for the occasion.

Grace looked pale and miserable when she came out of church on his arm and I thought she was probably feeling unwell. There was a lot of laughing and cheering as their friends threw rice and rose petals at them and then everyone went off for a drink at the Feathers. I'd heard they were having a bit of a do there and Mrs Cole had invited me to the wedding, but I'd refused, although I hadn't been able to resist going to have a look.

There was a constant ache inside me when I thought about Ernie and what might have been, but I tried not to think about him often. I suppose I had hoped that a miracle might happen and he wouldn't have to marry her after all, but of course it hadn't. It wouldn't have made any difference to me if it had; I still couldn't have married him.

Lainie had gone when I got back from the market that Saturday afternoon despite her promise to stay with Mam. Maggie was there. She had popped in because she heard Mam yelling and she had just finished helping her to get back into bed.

'Lainie left her sitting on the commode,' she said. 'That sister of yours is thoughtless and bone idle, Bridget. I don't hold with Martha's temper – she would try the patience of a saint at times – but Lainie might have got her back to bed before she left. She could have sat there for an hour or more if I hadn't come in to see what she was yelling about.'

'I'll have a word with Lainie when she comes next week,' I said. 'Besides, I may not be going to the market on Saturday for much longer, Maggie. Maisie isn't well enough to keep the stall going and she's thinking of selling it.'

'That's a shame,' Maggie said. 'You enjoyed that, but I've got a bit of good news for you, Bridget . . .' She smiled as I raised my brows. 'There was someone after the room while you were out. I saw her standin' at the door and came out to her. She says her name is Miss Elton and she is comin' back to see you later this evenin'.'

'In that case I'd better hurry and get the room polished out,' I said. 'It is clean, but a bit of lavender polish makes it smell nice.'

'Yes, I like a bit o' polish,' she agreed. 'Is there anythin' I can do to help you, Bridget? I don't think Lainie did a thing while she was here.'

'She never does,' I said and laughed. 'Don't look like that, Maggie. I'm used to her. She doesn't like doing housework, she never has. It won't take me long to rush round and get things right. You've seen to Mam for me and I can do the rest.'

Maggie left me to it. I spent a hectic hour making sure everything was clean in the room that had once been Mr Phillips', and then sat down for a cup of tea and a slice of cake I'd made the previous day.

I was just finishing my meal when someone knocked at the door. I opened it, staring at the woman who stood on my doorstep. I had seen her before. She was Mr Dawson's secretary.

'Are you Miss O'Rourke?

'Yes, I'm Bridget O'Rourke. Have you come about the room?'

'I work at the brewery.' She offered me her hand. I took it and she gave mine a brisk shake. 'My present lodgings are not at all suitable. I wondered if I might see the room?'

'Yes, of course,' I said and stood back for her to enter. 'I'll show you the room first and then perhaps you would like to look at the kitchen. I'm afraid the lavvy is out in the back yard . . .'

'If I might see the room first? Then we'll talk.'

'My mother had a stroke,' I told Miss Elton as I opened the door of the spare room for her to look inside. 'Sometimes she calls out a bit, but she sleeps through the night.'

'Mr Dawson informed me of the situation,' she replied, looking down her prim nose at me. 'You were highly recommended, Miss O'Rourke. Mr Dawson thinks well of you.'

'Thank you.' I wondered what she would think if she knew why I'd had to leave the brewery, but of course I would never dream of telling her.

The room I was offering her was the best in the house; the furniture was quite good and everywhere smelled of polish and fresh linen. I could tell she was impressed when she went inside and spent several minutes looking round.

'Yes, this all seems very clean,' she said at last. 'My present landlady is not at all fussy about her bed linen.'

'I keep sheets just for this room. You won't get anything we use ourselves.'

'Well, that sounds satisfactory. I should like to see the kitchen now and the . . . private room.'

'That's out the back,' I said. 'We've got a tap in the kitchen. It works most of the time and there's a man comes to empty the night soil regular. I have it done once a week now, but I could ask him to come more often if you stay here.'

She nodded her approval. 'You are lucky to have your own water supply. Quite a few of the houses in this area still rely on a pump in the street that serves more than one. I must have clean hot water to wash every morning.'

'Yes, of course. I shall bring it up to you every morning at whatever time you like. They keep sayin' we'll have proper flush lavvies one day. It would be a grand thing, but I can't see it happening in Farthing Lane.'

'We are at the beginning of the twentieth century,' Miss

Elton replied. 'There are going to be a lot of changes soon, Miss O'Rourke. One day women will be allowed to vote and we shall sit in the Houses of Parliament. We shall shake up the men! They've had it all their own way for far too long.'

'I've heard about women like you,' I said. 'Are you a suffragette?'

'Yes.' Miss Elton looked pleased. 'I am glad you take an interest in such things, Miss O'Rourke.' She glanced round the kitchen and at the door to the yard, but didn't bother to go out there. I made up my mind to get the night soil taken away straightaway if she took the room. 'Yes, I think I could be comfortable here. You were asking ten shillings a week, I believe? That is too much. I will give you seven shillings and sixpence.'

I hesitated, then shook my head. 'I'm very sorry, Miss Elton, but it will cost me several shillings a week to provide meals. I couldn't let the room for what you're offering.'

'Meals? Breakfast and an evening meal?' Her eyes gleamed. 'I see. I did not properly understand. Ten shillings a week to cover everything – washing as well?'

'Sheets and towels,' I agreed. 'For another half a crown I'll do your personal washing as well.'

'I'm very particular about my things being clean.'

'So am I,' I said firmly. I might not have stood my ground if that gleam in her eyes hadn't betrayed her, but I wasn't going to let her bully me. 'Very particular about who I have in my house.'

Her eyes met mine and then her lips curved in a thin smile. Her pale, pinched face could never be called attractive, but I saw that she had a sense of humour even if she didn't let it show very often.

'Very well,' she said and opened her purse. 'I'll give you twelve and sixpence now and I'll bring my things round in the morning. Will that be convenient, Miss O'Rourke?'

'Perfectly, Miss Elton. I'll give the bed an airing – not that it needs it, but just to be certain. Will you be wanting dinner tomorrow? Or would you prefer supper?'

'I never eat more than a light meal in the middle of the day,' she said. 'As it happens I shall probably be out tomorrow at lunchtime. I have a meeting with friends of the movement.' She nodded her head. 'Good day, Miss O'Rourke. I shall see you at about nine tomorrow.'

'Everything will be ready for you.'

I was elated as I closed the door behind her. Twelve and sixpence a week – it was going to make things so much better for me. I wouldn't be able to go scrubbing floors, because I would have to get Miss Elton's meals and look after her room, but that would be so much easier than what I'd been doing.

Mam pulled a face when I told her she would have to be on her best behaviour now that we had a new lodger.

'Miss Elton is a very particular lady,' I said. 'No swearing and calling out, Mam – at least while she is in the house.'

'And who are you to tell me what I can do in me own house?' She pinched my arm as I bent over to tuck the sheets round her.

'Ouch,' I said. 'One of these days I'll pinch you back, Mam. I'm only telling you for your own good. We don't want to lose Miss Elton too soon. She's paying more than Mr Phillips ever did and it means I shan't have to go scrubbing floors, though I'll go in for an hour on Monday and let them know I won't be back. That's only fair and I can be back in time to get her breakfast and her hot water.'

'Oh yes, you'll do that for her right enough,' Mam said. 'It didn't matter about your poor old mother layin' here in pain while you were out, but a lodger is different.'

'Yes, she is,' I said, 'because it's her money that will keep a roof over our heads. I'm still a week behind with the rent because even with the money Lainie gives me I couldn't quite catch up, but I shall be able to now.'

Mam grunted but didn't say anything. I just hoped she would try to be sensible, at least when Miss Elton was in the house.

She brought her things round the next morning promptly at nine and I helped her carry several bags and boxes up the stairs. Some of it was very heavy.

'You never carried all this stuff yourself?'

'I paid a young lad to help me,' she said. 'He brought them on a little cart, but ran off the moment I gave him his money, of course. It's all my pamphlets. I prepare them for the movement, you see.'

'They are very heavy,' I said. 'They must keep you busy. Do you do them all yourself?'

'Oh no,' she said. 'I type them up first and then we have them printed – if we can find someone to do them for us. Some printers refuse because they say our material is inflammatory and incites women to disobey their husbands and the law. It is ridiculous, of course.'

'I should like to read one of them,' I said. 'It all sounds very interesting.'

'Well, I will let you have some of our literature,' she said and smiled thinly. 'And now if you will excuse me, I must get ready to go out.'

'Yes, of course.'

I left her to settle into her room. She wasn't particularly friendly, but as long as she paid her money I didn't mind.

I told Mary and Jamie about her when they came to tea that afternoon. Joe wasn't with them, although I had invited him. Mary told me he had taken his mother out for the afternoon.

'She likes to go to a Sunday afternoon concert,' Mary said. 'There is a bandstand in the park and it's nice today – warm for the time of year. Joe said he would take her for a special treat.'

'That was nice of him,' I said. 'I wanted to tell Joe something, but you can pass the message on, Mary. It's about a stall on the market.'

Mary nodded as I explained about Maisie finding it difficult to stand on the market all day now, and seemed sure that Joe would be interested enough to come over and have a word with the old lady.

'He's always looking for new opportunities,' Mary said. 'He has his fingers in so many pies, always running here and there, so much that I sometimes think he'll meet himself coming backwards. Ma says show Joe a guinea and he'll want two. I think he must forget what he's up to half the time.'

'Don't you believe it,' Jamie said. 'Joe knows what he's doing all right.'

Mary frowned. 'I hope you're right, Jamie, but I don't like some of the people he deals with. Ma would have a fit if she knew, but Joe says he doesn't have to like everyone he does business with.'

'What kind of men?' I asked and Mary shook her head.

'I don't really know much,' she said. 'But I heard one of them threatening Joe over something once – about a piece of property he had bought. This man said his boss wouldn't take kindly to Joe treading on his toes . . . but when I asked Joe about it he just laughed and said I'd got it all wrong.'

'You can't be intimidated by threats like that,' Jamie said. 'It's the same on the docks or down the market – blokes who want your job try to frighten you off. You have to stand up to them or you would never get anywhere.'

Mary nodded. She didn't say any more, but I could tell she worried about her brother.

She kissed me as she was leaving later that afternoon. 'It was a lovely tea and you are such a good cook,' she said. 'You must visit us again soon and I'll give Joe your message. He will probably pop over to see you. I think he would have liked to come with us today, but we couldn't all descend on you at once.'

'You would have been welcome,' I said, but I knew she was right. I couldn't really manage more than two guests. Especially when I had to get things ready for Miss Elton.

I had asked her what she would like for her supper that evening, and she'd asked for an omelet. That wouldn't take much getting ready, but I wanted to make a start with the ironing. Miss Elton had brought a pile of washing with her and it looked as if she was expecting value for her two and sixpence a week.

Maisie told me that Joe had offered her a fair price to take over her stall when I saw her the next Saturday.

'It's more than I expected, Bridget,' she said. 'It means I can give up now instead of waitin' till I drop in 'arness.' She grinned at me. 'I like that lad of yours, Bridget. Got a good 'eart, 'e 'as.'

'He isn't my lad,' I said and laughed as she pulled a face. 'But I thought he would be fair with you, Maisie. He's honest and generous with his family, so I knew he wouldn't cheat you.'

'Joe says you can work on the stall any time, Bridget, but 'e won't be forcin' yer ter make up yer mind. Says yer can work Saturdays or not as yer like.'

'I shall have to see if I can manage a few hours,' I said. 'I shall miss seeing all the customers, but I've got a new lodger and I must look after her.'

Miss Elton was taking a lot of looking after. She was fussy about her food and her washing and I had to take extra care over her clothes when I ironed them. She was very reserved most of the time, keeping to her room except when she took her meals in the parlour. She went out somewhere most nights and I tried to get Mam off to sleep early in the evening if I could. Sometimes, when she was busy with her pamphlets, she asked me to take a tray up to her room. It was all extra work, but I didn't mind as long as she paid her money on time.

Joe came to see me on the Sunday morning a week or two after he'd taken the stall over from Maisie. He had brought a bag of fruit for Mam and a small box of chocolates.

'I thought you might like these,' he said, looking slightly awkward as he took something from his coat pocket. 'And I found something of Fred's I thought you might like.'

I took the worn velvet box he offered and opened it, exclaiming over the pretty gold and peridot necklace I found inside. The chain was short enough to wear in the opening of a blouse and the pendant was very delicate with a central stone and two smaller ones set in the gold. I had never seen anything as pretty.

'Oh, this is beautiful,' I said. 'Where did you find it, Joe?'

'It was in Fred's box,' he replied. 'There were some papers

and a few pounds – ten pounds in all. He wanted you to have it, Bridget. He had left a letter asking me to see you were all right, and I think he meant you to have whatever he'd got.'

'You're joking,' I said. 'Didn't you tell me he owned a shop?'

'Yes, the one Mary rents for her flowers. But I'm not sure you will get it, Bridget, even though I'm sure from Fred's letter that it was what he wanted. I think I told you he had scribbled out a will of sorts?' I nodded and he went on, 'I've made some more inquiries, but the lawyers say it won't stand up. However, I took the money and the necklace for you and didn't tell them about that. I didn't see why you shouldn't have something. He obviously meant you to have what he'd got – and that means the shop and his house.'

'It must have belonged to his wife,' I said. 'I shall treasure it, Joe, and the money will be useful. I've never had ten pounds in my life.'

'The shop might be worth a couple of hundred,' Joe said. 'I would pay you that for it, Bridget, but as I said I don't think you will get it. Fred didn't make things clear enough. I know what he wanted, but the lawyer says it isn't enough for the law.'

'I wouldn't know what to do with two hundred pounds, Joe.'

'No,' he said. 'I didn't think you would, but I could have looked after it for you, seen you didn't go without . . . I'm sure that's what Fred meant me to do.'

'Well, it doesn't matter,' I said. 'You don't miss what you've never had, though I think you may be right. Fred said something about it all being for me before he died, but I thought he imagined he was talking to his wife.'

'He told me once you reminded him of her,' Joe said. 'I am sure he would have wanted you to have what he'd got, but the lawyers say it's got to go to some kind of arbitration and I doubt you will get it in the end. It will probably go to the Crown or something stupid like that.'

'Will they take the shop away from Mary?'

Joe shook his head. 'I made sure my agreement with Fred

was right and tight,' he said. 'But I would have given you the money if it had come to you.'

'Yes, I know,' I said and smiled at him. 'As long as Mary doesn't lose her shop that's all that matters.'

Joe nodded, but I could see it had annoyed him that Fred's wishes were to be ignored. 'Well, I shall have to be off,' he said. 'Let me know if you need anything, Bridget. You know where I am.'

'Yes, of course. I don't think I can manage to work on the stall for the moment, Joe, but I should like to if I ever get the chance.'

'The offer is always there,' he said and smiled as he went out.

I showed Lainie the necklace when she came the next Saturday. She took it to try it on and said it was nicer that anything she'd seen. I sensed she was a little envious and I wasn't surprised when she told me she hadn't any money to give me that week.

'I had a couple of days off sick,' she said. 'I'll make it up another time, Bridget.'

'It's all right,' I told her. 'You keep your money for the baby when it comes, Lainie.'

She was beginning to show more now and I wondered how long it would be before she was forced to tell her employers.

Eleven

'I've written to Tommy every week since he's been away, but he hasn't sent me even a line on a postcard. I'm worried about him, Maggie.'

'It's natural you would be,' she said. 'But didn't Father O'Brien say it only upsets the children if their families visit? If you wait a little longer they may write and tell you that you can go.'

'If I did go, would you look after Mam for me?'

'You don't need to ask. I'm just thinkin' to save you a wasted journey, Bridget.'

'Father O'Brien says the doctors there are wonderful.'

'There you are then,' Maggie said. 'Tommy is probably enjoyin' the seaside and too busy to think of you. Sure, it's a terrible worrier you are, Bridget.'

The memory of my brother's haunted eyes as I'd left him with strangers was coming back to me more and more of late, but it might upset him if I went down. Especially if they wouldn't let him come back with me.

'I suppose I should wait.'

'Just a few more weeks,' she said. 'Have you seen Maisie recently, Bridget? I used to meet her about the market when she first gave up her stall, but I haven't seen her for a week or more now.'

'I shall take her a few buns when I go on Saturday,' I told her. 'I didn't get there last week because Mam was playing up and I had too much to do, but I shall go tomorrow same as usual.'

'Give her my love,' Maggie said. 'I might have a bit of meat pie going in the mornin'.'

'I'm sure she would be glad of it. Her hands make it difficult for her to cook much these days.'

'It's standin' out in all weathers brings out the rheumatics. You're better off takin' a lodger, Bridget.'

'I sometimes wonder.' I pulled a wry face. 'Miss Elton is a difficult person. She's so fussy and I have to be extra careful when I do her ironing. If there's the smallest crease she creates something awful.'

Miss Elton's money had made things easier for me, but she wasn't very friendly, though she did talk about the people she met at her suffragette meetings sometimes.

'You should come to one of our meetings,' she'd said to me that morning before she went out. 'I'll give you some pamphlets written by Lucretia Coffin Mott and Elizabeth Cady Stanton.'

'Thank you,' I said. 'I should like to learn more about the National Union of Women's Suffrage Societies.'

'The Movement has been gathering strength for a long time. We've been helped by the Chartists, who fought for the promotion of human rights, but there have been too many influential people against us. Her Majesty Queen Victoria, Gladstone and Disraeli have all held us back.

'In America some of the states have already given women the vote. They have worked so hard: Lucretia, Elizabeth Cady Stanton, Henry Ward Beecher and Wendell Phillips. Their work encourages us. One day we shall win through – even if we have to use more violent methods of protest to gain attention. Some of us are becoming tired of peaceful protests. We want more action! Even if we have to break the law.'

'You wouldn't – would you?' I stared at her in amazement. To hear her speak of breaking the law was both surprising and shocking, but her zeal in promoting the cause seemed to burn in her like a bright light.

'Do you think women will ever get the vote?' I asked and frowned. 'Will it really make a difference? Will it mean an end to women having to hide when the rent man calls because their husband drank all their wages away on Friday night? Will it stop them having to take their husband's suit to the pawnbroker on Monday morning so that they can feed their children? Will it mean that none of us need ever go hungry again?'

'Goodness gracious me!' Miss Elton said, looking annoyed. 'You want miracles, Miss O'Rourke. Give women the vote and we may start to make things better, but we cannot be expected to do everything at once.'

She had gone off in a bit of a huff and I knew I had ruffled her feathers by asking questions she couldn't answer. I didn't see why women shouldn't be allowed to vote the same as the men, but it was going to take an awful lot more than that to get rid of the poverty that seemed to hang like a blight over certain areas of London.

Nothing was going to change for me. I would still have to look after Mam and it would still be a struggle to find money for the rent and coal every week.

I hadn't seen Ernie since his wedding day, but his wife sometimes walked up the lane on her way to the Feathers. She was big with child now and I thought her time must be closer than I'd imagined. I'd tried speaking to her a couple of times, but she wasn't very friendly.

Lainie didn't look anywhere near the size of Grace Cole. I wasn't sure how she was managing to hide it, but I thought she must be lacing her bodice tight which surely couldn't be good for the child. I hadn't said anything to her because she was moody these days and apt to fly off the handle if I questioned her.

Lainie looked ill when she came in the next Saturday morning. Her hair was greasy, falling in lank wisps about her pale face, her dress stained with spots of beer or wine. She glared at me when I suggested that she get the bath out while I was gone.

'If you think I'm havin' a bath for that snooty Miss Elton to walk in on me when she likes you're mistaken.'

'She's out,' I said. 'She won't be back for hours.'

'I can't be bothered to bring that bath in from the yard

and fill it,' Lainie grumbled. 'I don't know why we can't live somewhere with a proper bathroom.'

'Come into a fortune? If you can't be bothered to have a bath wait until I get back and I'll help you. I'll wash your hair and your dress for you anyway.'

Lainie glared at me. She was so sullen and bad-tempered these days that there wasn't much to choose between her and Mam. I supposed she wasn't feeling well because of the baby, but any attempt to ask was shouted down so I didn't try.

The street leading to the market was busy that morning, crowded with shoppers, horses and carts and a young lad on a bike with a delivery basket on the front. He whistled at me as he passed, whizzing precariously in and out of the traffic. Two young girls were playing with a wooden hoop and a couple of mothers stood gossiping with a group of noisy children causing havoc on the pathway beside them.

Maisie lived in a small terraced house just behind the market and her door was always open on a Saturday morning. Maisie didn't believe in locking her door, she had lived here all her life and was adamant that no one would dream of stealing from her.

That morning, I was surprised to find her door shut and when I tried the latch, I discovered it was locked. That just wasn't like her. I lifted the knocker, rapping it against the door a couple of times.

'Yer won't get an answer,' a voice said and I turned to see Maisie's neighbour standing just behind me. 'She were took bad in the week and they come and fetched 'er away.'

'Where did they take her?' I asked. 'Is she very ill?'

'Crippled up with pain she were,' the woman replied and frowned. 'She seemed in a bad way when I fetched the doctor to 'er – couldn't 'ardly stand. Poor old bugger, she ain't got no family.'

'Maisie has been like family to me,' I said, feeling upset that I hadn't known my friend was ill. 'Do you know where they've taken her?'

'To the infirmary I reckon,' the woman said with a shrug.

'Leastwise, that's where they usually takes 'em round here what are on their last legs. It were the workhouse once, but they call it a 'ospital now – ain't much difference as fer as I can see.'

I was feeling upset as I walked home three hours later. The matron at the infirmary had allowed me to see Maisie, though she had warned me not to expect too much.

'She may not know you, Miss O'Rourke,' she told me as she summoned an orderly to take me to the old people's ward. 'I'm afraid it was almost too late when she was brought in. It's a sad case, but one we meet so often. The elderly are afraid to call the doctor or they simply can't afford to pay the fees, and then when someone finds them . . .' She shook her head over it. 'But of course you are welcome to see her.'

'Thank you, I shall,' I said. 'But while I am here may I inquire about Rosie Brown? Has she shown any signs of recovery?'

Matron shook her head. 'I am afraid her condition is deteriorating fast, Miss O'Rourke. We do not expect her to live much longer.'

'That is very sad,' I said. 'Thank you for telling me. I'll go and see Maisie now if I may?'

I sat beside Maisie's bed for more than an hour, holding her hand and talking to her, but I had been shocked by the change in her. She had saliva running over her chin and her mouth was slack. It was obvious that she had no idea where she was or what was happening around her.

Perhaps that was a good thing, I thought as I walked home afterwards. It was very sad, but it would have been worse if she had known where she was. Maisie would have hated to end her days in the infirmary and so would Mam.

I knew now that I could never walk out and leave my mother. It didn't matter how much she pinched or yelled at me, she was my mother and I wouldn't condemn her to die in that awful place.

Maybe I would try to make peace with her. If I really tried, I might learn what had made her the way she was, and perhaps we could even be friends. It was surely worth trying?

I called out to Lainie as I walked into the house, but there was no sign of her. As I moved towards the kitchen, Maggie came out to meet me. One look at her face told me that something was wrong.

'What is it?' I asked. 'Is it Lainie? Is the baby coming early or something?'

'It's your mam,' Maggie said and her face was white. She looked as if she might have had a few tears. 'I don't know how to tell you, Bridget . . .'

'Mam?' I felt a sickness in my stomach. 'What's happened? Did she fall out of bed and hurt herself?'

'I think she had another stroke,' Maggie said. 'A massive one this time so the doctor says . . . She's dead, Bridget. I went up and found her lying there, her eyes staring. I sent Mick for the doctor, but he said there was nothing anyone could do.'

'Is Lainie with her?' I sat down to catch my breath as a wave of dizziness went over me. 'Mam dead . . . I don't understand. She seemed better . . .'

'I heard them shouting at each other about an hour after you left,' Maggie said. 'It sounded somethin' awful. Yelling they were and I heard a crashing sound as if your mam had tried to get out of bed.'

'So where is Lainie then?' I asked.

'She went off soon after the row. Your mam was still alive then, Bridget, 'cause I heard the door slam and then Martha yellin' at the top of her voice about Lainie being a lazy slut.'

My chest felt tight and I was breathing hard as if I had been running very fast. It all seemed like a bad dream. Surely I would wake up in a moment. Mam couldn't be dead . . . Not just like that.

'They were always yelling at each other, but Lainie was in a bad mood this morning.' I stared at Maggie but there was a mist in front of my eyes. This wasn't real. It couldn't be! 'What happened then?'

'I didn't take much notice then, but after an hour it seemed quiet and I thought I would pop in and make sure Martha was all right and that's when I found her. I'm sorry, Bridget. I feel I've let you down.'

'It wasn't your fault. I shouldn't have left her so long.' I felt swamped by my guilt. 'Maisie was taken into the infirmary this week. I went to visit her and . . . it was my fault. I shouldn't have left Mam.'

'Now don't you start that, Bridget O'Rourke,' Maggie said sharply. 'You're not to blame for what happened between Lainie and your mam and we don't even know if that's what caused Martha to have another turn. She's been going downhill for a long time now and if you're honest you'll admit it.'

Mam had often made my life a misery, but the shock of her death had left me feeling stunned.

'She complained of being stuck in bed, but I was sure she was feeling better in herself. I hadn't been letting her drink too much and she sometimes got angry with me over it, but things hadn't been so bad lately . . .'

'And why was that?' Maggie said. 'I'm after thinkin' your mam just couldn't be bothered to shout at you the way she used to. Lainie got her mad and they went at it hammer and tongs for a while. It probably got Martha worked up and that's what started it off.'

'If I'd been here it might not have happened.'

'And she might have lain for months like a cabbage,' Maggie said. 'I've seen it, Bridget. Believe me, it was better this way. You should know that if you've come from the infirmary.'

I remembered the old people I had seen lying in narrow cots side by side, some of them calling out and being ignored by the orderly as she hurried about the ward. The tales I'd heard of places like that and my own experience looking after Mam told me that Maggie was right, but that didn't ease the shock or take away the feelings of guilt. What hurt the most was the fact that she had died alone, perhaps calling for help.

'I shall have to let Jamie know,' I said as my thoughts struggled to cope. 'And Lainie, too. She might have quarrelled with Mam but I have to tell her what has happened.'

Maggie nodded. 'You could send one of them telegrams to Joe Robinson,' she said.

'I wouldn't know how to go about that,' I said. 'No, I'll go down the corner shop and ask if their lad will go over and see Joe. If I give him half a crown he'll go for me.'

'You'll want to spend a little time with your mam,' Maggie said as I stood up. 'I'll fetch Maud Browne, she'll do what's right by Martha, Bridget.'

'Yes, thank you, that would be kind. I don't think I could . . .'

'And it's not right you should,' Maggie said. 'Go up and say goodbye to her and then leave it to Maud and me.'

I nodded but my throat was too tight to say anything. I walked slowly upstairs dreading what I was going to find, but it wasn't so bad. Maggie had already cleaned up around Mam, and her eyes were closed, her face relaxed by death into something approaching peace. I went over to the bed and stood looking down at her.

'Why couldn't you wait until I got back?' I asked, tears stinging my eyes. 'It's just like you to go and do this to me.'

For the first time Mam couldn't answer me back and I discovered that hurt, it hurt a lot more than I had imagined. There had been times when I'd almost wished her dead, times when she'd driven me to tears, but now it just seemed such a waste.

I bent down and kissed her forehead, then I turned away. I couldn't do anything for her now and I ought to let Jamie know. He could call and tell Lainie on his way over. I wanted my family with me so that I didn't have this awful feeling of loneliness.

I left Mam's room and went into mine. The money Joe had given me was in the chest beside my bed and the pendant was with it. I hadn't worn it yet and I probably never would, but I was glad to have it to remind me of Fred. And the money would be useful now.

The drawer was slightly open. I frowned as I saw it, sure that I had closed it before I went down that morning. I pulled it open wider, a sinking sensation in my stomach as I saw what I had half expected. The money had gone and so had the pendant.

Searching frantically through the drawer, I found ten shillings that I'd put by for the rent in a little purse, but the rest had gone. I could hardly believe it. That ten pounds had meant so much to me; it was the money I was planning to use to go down and visit Tommy, and my nest egg for the winter when I would need to buy more fuel for the fires.

Miss Elton had gone out early as she was spending the day with friends in the country. She hadn't been back to the house and that only left one person who could have taken the money. I didn't even consider Maggie, because she would rather give me a shilling than take one, but Lainie was different. Lainie had been envious of my pendant and she had been in a very strange mood that morning.

How could my sister do that to me? I could understand and forgive the row with Mam, even though it had probably led to her seizure, because they had always quarrelled. Lainie couldn't have known that this time it would bring on a seizure. But the theft of the money and Fred's pendant was harder to bear.

'Oh, Lainie,' I whispered. 'How could you . . . ? How could you do that to me?'

'She's gone off somewhere,' Jamie told me when we sat in the kitchen having a cup of tea that evening. He had already been up for a moment to see Mam laid out in her coffin upstairs. 'I went to the pub where she'd been working and they told me she hadn't been there for several days.'

'Maybe that's why she looked as if she had been neglecting herself,' I said and frowned. 'She was in such a mood this morning when I went out. I wish I had asked her what was wrong, but I thought she might have got over it by the time I came back.'

'I should think twice about takin' her back next time if I were you.'

'I couldn't turn her out if she needed help. I'm sorry, Jamie.

I haven't got the money to bury Mam. I don't like to ask, but I'll pay you back when I can.'

'You will not. Who else but me should bury her? I'm the eldest, and it's little enough I did for her or you when she was alive, but I'll pay all the expenses and she'll have a proper send-off, Bridget me darlin'. You can buy whatever you need and invite all her friends and neighbours to the wake.'

'Oh, Jamie,' I said, my eyes wet with tears. 'I feel so shocked by what's happened that I can't think straight. I knew she was ill but I didn't expect her to die. It was so sudden . . .'

He put a brotherly arm about my shoulders and gave me a hug. 'I've five pounds in me pocket for you, Bridget, and there'll be more where that came from when you need it.'

'And where would you be getting that sort of money, Jamie?' I gave him an old-fashioned look.

'Joe has helped me a lot these past months,' Jamie said. 'I'm earnin' good money now, Bridget. Much more than I ever thought possible. Joe says if I keep on this way he'll let Mary and me marry sooner than the end of the year.'

'That's lovely, Jamie,' I said. 'But I don't like takin' the money from you.'

'It's yours,' he said. 'You've done enough for Mam and that Lainie. Trust her to run off just when you need her.'

I hadn't told Jamie that she had taken most of my money and the pendant Fred had given me. He would have been furious over it, and I thought Lainie might need help again one day.

Joe came to see me the day before Mam's funeral. He brought me two bottles of good whisky, three of sherry and a tin full of sausage rolls his mother had made for the next day.

'I'm sorry I couldn't get over before,' he said. 'I know Jamie gave you some money, Bridget, but I thought this might come in useful.' He laid six gold sovereigns on the kitchen table.

'You can't give me that, Joe,' I said. 'No, please take it back. I don't want your money. Jamie is going to pay for everything. He has already told me how good you've been to him.'

'I've helped him get a start,' Joe said. 'But Mary wants him and I couldn't do less for him for her sake. That money is yours by right, Bridget. I sold some bits and pieces out of Fred's house. I was going to give it to you when I came over anyway.'

'Are you sure it isn't your money?'

He grinned and made the sign of the cross over his heart. 'The honest truth as I live and breathe. It's your money. Fred would want you to have it.'

'I . . . somehow I've mislaid the other money you gave me,' I said, not looking at him. 'And Fred's pendant. I dare say I shall find it when I'm not looking.'

Joe was silent. I sensed that he didn't quite believe me, but he didn't question me and I was glad. I hadn't told Jamie about the theft and I didn't want to tell Joe either.

'Mary would have come to the funeral but she's got a bad chest,' Joe said. 'But I'll be there, Bridget.'

'It's a Catholic service – will you mind that?'

'It's all the same to me,' Joe said and shrugged. 'I'll be there for you – tomorrow and in the future.'

'Thank you.' I looked at him and then away quickly as I saw the expression in his eyes. I'd seen something similar in another man's eyes. 'I . . . I'm not sure what I'm going to do in the future. I shall have to go down and see Tommy. I want to tell him about Mam myself and find out if he can come home soon.'

'Would you like me to come with you?'

I hesitated for a moment and then shook my head. 'I think I want to go alone, Joe, but it was a kind thought.'

He nodded, seeming not to mind one way or the other. 'Well, don't forget that I'm there if you need anything – even if it's just to talk.'

'I shan't forget,' I promised. 'You've been a good friend, Joe. My brother – well, he's like a different person since he met you. You trusted him and you helped him, and that means a lot to me.'

'Don't feel that you have to be grateful,' Joe said. 'I don't want gratitude, lass, but I would like to think that we were friends?'

'Yes, of course we are.' I smiled at him. 'I like all your family, Joe – and maybe I'll be able to see more of them in future.'

I went down to Skegness the day following Mam's funeral. I was glad it was over, but I hadn't been able to force myself to clean her room yet. It made me feel strange to walk in and see her empty bed, but perhaps I'd feel better once I'd been to see Tommy.

'You were warned that you couldn't see your brother for a while,' the matron said and frowned at me. 'This is most irregular, Miss O'Rourke.'

'I'm sorry but my mother died. I have to tell Tommy. I couldn't put that in a letter – could I?'

She stared at me in silence for a moment. 'Well, you will have to wait here. I'll speak to the doctor in charge.'

'Yes, of course. I didn't mean to break the rules. I am very sorry, but he should be told about his mother – and by me. Something like this cannot come from a stranger.'

Matron gave me a look that seemed to convey both frustration and sympathy. 'Very well, I'll take the responsibility myself and bring Tommy to you, but only for ten minutes.'

'Thank you. You are very kind.'

My heart ached as Tommy was led in a few minutes later. He was wearing a nightshirt that looked too big for him and a linen mask over the bottom half of his face.

'Ten minutes,' Matron warned and went out again.

'Take that thing off your face, love,' I said and held my arms out to him. 'Come here and let me give you a cuddle.'

Tommy shook his head and hung back.

'I'm infectious,' he said. 'It's a killer disease, Bridget. If I give it to you, you might die.'

'Don't be daft. You used to sleep in my bed.'

'Matron said I'm not to come near you.'

'Bugger Matron!' I went over to him, kneeling on the

cold flagstones to put my arms around him. 'I love you, our Tommy.'

He broke away from me, retreating a few steps. 'Why are you here? You shouldn't have come. I wish you hadn't.'

His eyes were bright with unshed tears, but he was determined not to break. I suddenly understood how hard this was for him. He had been through one parting and now he was suffering all over again.

'I had to come, Tommy,' I said. 'I had to tell you. Mam had another seizure and she's dead. I wanted to tell you myself.'

'I don't care,' Tommy said and his mouth had set in a sullen line. He looked so young and so vulnerable that my heart twisted with pain. 'Most of us in here are goin' to die anyways.'

'Who told you that – not Matron?'

'No. She says if we do as we're told we'll get better, but she tells lies. I've seen them takin' the poor beggars out the back. Jim says they're the dead ones. He says he'll be dead before the winter.'

'How old is Jim?'

'Fifteen.' Tommy stared at me. 'He says all the treatment is a waste of time because we're going to die soon.'

'He shouldn't say such things to you. I'll ask Matron to move you away from him.'

'I don't want to move,' Tommy said. 'Go away, Bridget. I wish you hadn't come and I don't want you to come again.'

'But you'll be better soon and then you will be able to come home.'

'Time's up,' Matron said, coming back into the room. She looked at Tommy. 'Are you ready now?'

'Yeah.'

He turned his back on me. I watched as he was led away, my eyes gritty with tears. I was hurting too much to shed them. Tommy was wrong. He had to be! I would never have brought him here if I hadn't believed he would get better.'

'What are his chances?' I asked as Matron returned. 'Is he going to die?'

'We shall do our best for him,' she said and looked annoyed. 'This is precisely why we do not allow relatives to visit at first. Tommy is very upset and so are you.'

'Why do you let him see things – the dead being carried out the back?'

'I see Jim has been up to his tricks again.' Matron frowned. 'What your brother has seen from his window are bags of laundry. Don't worry, we treat those who do not recover with respect. I'll talk to Tommy and I'll put him in with someone older.' She paused, then: 'Our rules may seem strict, but we are not heartless monsters. Some of the treatment seems severe, but it helps in many cases – though not in all I am afraid. We are a long way from being able to cure the worst cases. However, Tommy was sent here before his illness took too firm a hold, and in these cases we often see what we call remission. This means that the illness disappears and the patient feels well again, though it would not be true to say that they are cured. I have great hopes for Tommy, Miss O'Rourke.'

'Thank you.' I blinked back my tears and managed a smile. 'Please take care of him. I love him very much.'

'We shall do all that is possible and perhaps God will do the rest.'

'Yes, perhaps He will,' I said. 'Though I sometimes wonder if He gets tired of listening to our prayers.'

'Now, Miss O'Rourke, that will not do,' she said in a rallying tone. 'Have you never heard the saying that it is always darkest before the dawn? Once the worst has happened, things usually get better.'

Twelve

The house seemed so empty and I had too much time on my hands now that Mam had gone. Miss Elton was out most of the time, and though we spoke most days, we had little in common. She suggested that I should go to an evening meeting of the Movement with her but I refused. Somehow I seemed to be drifting, unable to settle or think what to do now.

Mam was gone but I still had to clean the house and find the money for the rent man, which wasn't easy now that Lainie wasn't bringing anything home. I ought to look for work, but for the first few days I couldn't make myself think about it. I had hated Mam sometimes, but my life had revolved around her. I didn't know what I wanted to do now. If Tommy had been at home I would have had a purpose, a reason to make things nice and keep going, but for the moment I just felt drained and empty.

I had lost Tommy too, at least for the time being, and the memory of his bitter words and hurt eyes was something that would never leave me. There was also another ache in my heart that I refused to let myself think about. I still hadn't seen anything of Ernie since his wedding and I believed he was deliberately avoiding me. Perhaps it was best that he did. I was so lonely sometimes, so desperately lonely that I wasn't sure what I would have done if he'd turned up on my doorstep and asked to come in.

My mood of despondency lasted for perhaps ten days after I'd returned from visiting Tommy, and then I woke up one sunny morning in June and decided I was feeling better.

I needed to go shopping. While I was at the market I might

ask if there was any work going on the stalls. I had enjoyed working with Maisie and I missed my friend. I thought that it might be nice to have a market stall of my own one day.

'Sorry, luv,' I was told by the man who ran the market. 'There ain't any stalls for hire or sale as far as I know. If I 'ear of anythin' I'll let yer know.'

I hadn't really expected to be given a stall at my first attempt. They were always in demand and often passed down from father to son. A couple of the traders I knew offered me a Saturday job and I was feeling more cheerful as I walked home, my basket heavy with shopping.

I could please myself what I did now. Now that I had begun to adjust to the idea, I realized that there were several options.

It was as I entered Farthing Lane that I saw her: Grace Cole. She was weaving about from side to side as if she were drunk, her movements slow and unsteady. It took me a few minutes before I realized that she wasn't drunk; she was ill.

I began to run towards her as I saw her sway and clutch at herself as if she were in pain. Of course, it must be the baby! She looked as if she had gone into labour there in the street.

Grace looked terrible. Her hair was lank with grease and her dress was stained down the front, but it was the way her face was creased with agony that shocked me. She really was about to give birth!

'Give me your arm,' I said. 'I'll help you get home.'

Grace looked at me sullenly. 'Mind yer own business,' she muttered. 'I'm not drunk.'

'I know that. Let me help you or you will end up having the baby in the street.'

Grace gasped and doubled up as a pain ripped through her and, dropping my basket, I moved swiftly to put my arm about her waist. She was trembling and sweating, and she seemed almost to collapse against me.

'What's wrong?' Tilly Cullen came hurrying up to me at that moment. 'Blimey! Her water's breakin'. You'd better get 'er 'ome fast or she'll drop the brat in the street.'

'There's no time,' I said. 'I'll take her into my house. Help me with her, Tilly. We need to get her to a bed fast.'

By this time, Grace was beyond resistance. She was weeping and swearing at us like a trooper as we managed to support her across the street towards my house. She was half fainting and I wasn't sure we were going to get her there, but then a couple of men realized what was going on and left their coal wagon to lend a hand.

'Look's like she's Jimmy Riddled all over yer,' one of them said to me, his blackened face splitting in a grin. 'We'd better get 'er up them apples and pears quick.'

'You can put her in the first room at the top of the stairs,' I said. 'It is mine and the bed is aired.'

The men were carrying Grace between them now and I went ahead with Tilly behind me as they carried her up the stairs. I pulled the top covers off the bed. Grace was writhing in agony as they laid her down on the bottom sheet and they went off as quickly as they could once I had thanked them.

Tilly was eyeing Grace nervously. 'I'll fetch Jean to 'er, Bridget,' she said. 'You stop wiv 'er. I can't stand to 'ear 'er.'

She clattered down the stairs after the men and I smiled wryly. I could hear them all laughing in the street and it made me angry. Did they imagine that what this poor woman was going through was funny?

Tilly was making sure she didn't get asked to do anything, but at least she had stopped to ask what was the matter and that had probably saved Grace from giving birth in the gutter.

Another terrifying scream from the bed made me move instinctively towards her. I'd never been in the room when a woman was giving birth before and I wasn't sure what I ought to be doing to help her through this ordeal. I took Grace's hand as she began to buck and writhe in agony, screaming abuse at me. I ignored it, feeling sympathy for her.

'I think you're supposed to push down hard,' I said, trying to remember what I'd heard Maggie say at various times. 'Grip my hand, Grace, and push as hard as you can.'

'It hurts too bleedin' much!'

'It won't stop hurting until it's out,' I said. 'Go on, push. Really try this time . . .'

Grace was struggling with her underwear. I helped her pull the soaking wet drawers down over her knees. As I lifted the dress clear, I could see a fuzz of dark hair between her thighs as the baby's head started to poke through. We had only just got her here in time!

'I can see the head,' I said and saw that blood and more water had soaked into the bed around her. 'It's coming, Grace. Push again if you can – try harder!'

'I'm trying, bugger it! You want to bloody try and see how you like it!'

Grace screamed like someone demented and suddenly in a whoosh of blood and slime, the baby shot out on to the bed. I bent over it, excited by something I had never seen before. The child looked red and ugly but also strangely beautiful.

'I'll see to 'er now,' Jean's voice said behind me. 'I've brought me things with me. I've been prepared fer days; the silly cow had no right to go out in her state. Tilly is bringing a kettle of hot water.'

Jean worked quickly and calmly to cut the cord and wrap the child in a clean towel. It started to cry as soon as it was separated from its mother. Jean gave the warm bundle to me, then turned her attention to Grace.

'You stupid girl,' she said. 'Why didn't yer tell me this mornin' that yer 'ad started yer pains?'

'Yer never believe me when I say I don't feel well,' Grace muttered resentfully. 'What is it?' she asked me as I brought the baby closer for her to see.

'A girl,' I said, feeling my throat tighten as I looked at the child in my arms. Ernie's child or not, she was beautiful and I felt a tug at my heart as I wished that she was mine. 'Do you want to hold her, Grace?'

'Nah,' she muttered, lying back against the pillows. 'You wash 'er and put 'er down. I'm tired. I want to sleep.'

Jean had cleared up the mess, and was slipping the soiled clothes from beneath her daughter-in-law.

'I'm sorry, Bridget,' she said. 'These sheets are ruined. You'll never get the blood out of them. I'll give you some more to replace them.'

'It doesn't matter,' I said. 'I never use the best sheets for myself. These have been patched several times.'

'I'll still give you some more. I think she'll 'ave ter stay 'ere fer a couple of days. I'll come in and see to 'er and the baby.'

'I don't mind her being here,' I said. 'And I don't mind looking after Grace, but you had better show me what to do for the child.' I carried the baby over to the washstand and poured what was left of the hot water into a bowl, adding cold until it was just warm. Tilly and Jean watched as I washed the baby and patted her dry. 'She's beautiful . . .' I turned towards the bed. 'You're so lucky, Grace. What are you going to call her?'

'I don't care,' she muttered. 'Leave me alone. I want ter sleep.'

'I think I would call her Katherine,' I said. 'If she were mine. Yes, she's a Katherine.'

'They will call her Kathy,' Grace muttered, 'but it's as good a name as any other.' She closed her eyes, clearly uninterested and falling asleep.

Jean had turned away from the bed now that she had finished clearing up. 'She is lovely,' she said. 'I think I may as well take 'er 'ome wiv me, Bridget. You've got enough to do and you don't want a baby screaming all night and upsetting your lodger.' She glanced at my dress. 'That looks a bit of a mess.'

'It will wash.' I shrugged. 'There are worse things than a spoiled dress. I thought she might die.'

'Not 'er,' Jenny said. 'She'll be all right fer a while now. I've left Ernie's tea on the stove in me 'urry and it will burn if I don't get back. Will yer walk back with me, Bridget?'

'Yes, of course I will,' I said. 'Let me carry the baby, Jean.

157

Are you sure Grace won't mind you taking her with you? She might ask where she is when she wakes up.'

'She won't bother 'er 'ead over the poor little mite,' Jean said and pulled a face. Her mouth was drawn into a thin line, her expression one of disgust. It was obvious that she heartily disliked Grace. 'That one don't care about nothin' but 'erself. She's worse than I thought she would be, and that's sayin' somethin'. Sulky, lazy – and that child ain't my son's.'

'How can you be so sure?'

'It's nearly six weeks too soon.'

'Babies are born early sometimes.'

'Not that one. She's full term, believe me. I've 'elped a few babies into the world and I know the difference.'

'You won't tell Ernie? It would only hurt him to know the baby wasn't his.' And it would make his sacrifice turn to ashes in his mouth. I had felt the pain of knowing that it might be his child as Grace gave birth, and the longing to hold a child of my own.

'I think he knows in his 'eart, Bridget, but I shan't say. They row enough as it is.'

We had reached Ernie's house. I could hear the sizzle of pans boiling over and Jean rushed into the kitchen to move a pan of greens from the heat, the smell of burning pervading the house.

She came back and pulled a face at me. 'I've saved some of it, but 'e'll be eating burnt tatties tonight.'

'Well, I'd better go,' I said, handing the baby to her. 'You're welcome to come whenever you like, Jean. I expect you'll have to come often to feed Kathy? I'll leave the door unlocked if I go to bed and you can come and go as you please.'

'We'll see 'ow she goes on with the child,' Jean said. 'I'll try bottle-feeding 'er as well fer a while, just in case. When a mother rejects her child the milk often goes sour so they say.'

'She hasn't rejected Kathy. She was just exhausted.'

'Maybe.' Jean pulled a wry face and I could see that she didn't have much faith in Grace's desire or ability to mother

158

the child. 'Stay a few minutes while I take Kathy up. I've got some cakes in the oven. You could keep an eye on them for me if yer like. I shan't be a moment.'

'All right,' I said. 'I don't mind a few minutes.'

I noticed that she had been setting the table before Tilly fetched her and I finished it for her, then caught the smell of the cakes – about right in my judgement. I opened the range and took a thick cloth in my hands, turning back to the table with a tray of rock buns in my hands.

Ernie was standing in the doorway staring at me. Straight home from work, he was in his shirtsleeves, his jacket slung over one shoulder, and he smelled of the horses and leather. He looked stunned, like a man in a dream.

'Hello,' I said. 'I was just watching the cakes for your ma.'

'I thought I'd gone mad and was seein' things,' he said and grinned at me. 'Where's Ma? Is she all right?'

'She's settling Katherine down.'

'Who is Katherine?' He went over to the stone sink to wash his hands, his head turned to look at me.

'Your daughter,' I said. 'Grace nearly gave birth in the street opposite my house. We had to carry her inside. She's still there but Jean brought the baby home so that she wouldn't upset my lodger with her crying. She's going to bring her back when she wants feeding and Grace will come home in a couple of days.'

'Grace should 'ave stayed home if she'd started,' he said and looked annoyed. 'I'm sorry she was a trouble to you, Bridget.'

'It isn't a trouble to me,' I said. 'Besides, she was early. She probably didn't realize it was coming.'

'No, she wasn't early,' Ernie said harshly. 'The child isn't mine. She lied to me, Bridget, and I fell for it.'

'You don't know that for sure.'

'Yes, I do. She shouted it at me once when we argued, told me I was a mug and that she wished she'd never met me.'

'Perhaps she was just saying it to upset you?' He shook his

head and I saw the anger in his face. 'I'm so sorry, Ernie.' For some reason I found myself standing very close to him, gazing up into his eyes. He looked tortured, as if he were suffering the torments of the damned. 'I had hoped you might find some happiness when you were married.'

'Without you? I'll never be happy without you, Bridget.'

'Ernie . . .'

I couldn't move as he reached out for me. He drew me closer and then we were kissing . . . Not as he had kissed me once before, but hungrily, desperately. It seemed to go on forever and yet as I broke away from him, I wanted it to continue. I gazed into his face, seeing the longing reflected there.

'I was a fool,' he said. 'I should have given her money and told her to clear off like Ma said.'

The tears stung my eyes and my throat felt tight. It was too late. He had a wife and child to care for – even if the child wasn't his own. Katherine was still his responsibility, and she was innocent. She needed a family to take care of her. Now that Mam was dead, I was free, but Ernie wasn't.

'I must go,' I said. 'I have things to do.'

'Yes,' he said, but the expression in his eyes told me he wanted me to stay. 'Bridget.' He was interrupted by Jean coming down the stairs.

'You had better go up and see Kathy,' I told him, 'because she is yours, Ernie. You took her on when you married Grace and gave her your name. She is beautiful, a lovely little girl and you have to love her for her own sake.'

Grace was still asleep when I got back that afternoon, but Jean came round about six and brought the baby for a feed, and again late in the evening. Katherine seemed to cry a lot and Jean told me she would be giving her a bottle when she got home because Grace didn't seem capable of feeding her.

'It's a good thing I was prepared,' she said and sniffed. 'I might 'ave known 'ow she'd be.'

I didn't go up while Grace was nursing her baby as I wasn't sure I could bear to see them together. My heart ached as I remembered the look in Ernie's eyes and the way he had kissed me.

It should be me holding a child in my arms. I should have been Ernie's wife. The thought kept on echoing in my mind and the pain of loss was a nagging ache in my heart.

Grace only stayed in my room one night. In the morning when I went up to take her a cup of tea, she was already out of bed and wearing my best dress. She gave me a shamefaced look as I put the tea down on the chest beside the bed.

'Should you be out of bed yet?'

'I'm all right.'

'Well, you know best . . .' I said coldly. 'Is there anything else of mine you would like to borrow?'

'I can't wear the dress I 'ad on,' she said. 'Jean took it away with 'er. I'll wash this and bring it back to yer.'

'Keep it,' I said, thinking I would never wear it again. 'I'll be making myself a new one soon. Yes, keep it, Grace.'

It was too tight for her and I could see that she had already split the seams getting it on. That should have made me angry, but somehow I didn't care.

'I suppose yer in the money now you've got that Joe Robinson in tow,' she said and looked at me with dislike. 'Yer bloody lucky, Bridget. They say you'll marry 'im now yer ma's dead.'

'And who told you that?' I asked. 'Joe is just a friend and I have no intention of marrying anyone at the moment.'

'Then yer a bigger fool than I took yer for,' she said. 'If yer 'ankering after that bloody Ernie yer welcome to 'im. I wish I'd never seen the bugger.'

'Why?' I stared at her. 'Is he unkind to you?'

'He still bloody wants you,' she said. 'It were allus you 'e wanted. Used to talk about yer all the time.' She laughed nastily. 'I queered your patch, but I made a bloody mistake. I should 'ave got rid of the brat. That old cow is allus on at me and 'e's a pain in the arse. Soon as I'm on me feet again . . .' She broke off as though aware that she had said too much. 'I'm orf then. Don't expect me ter thank yer.'

I stood where I was for a moment, then I began to tear the clothes from the bed. I took an armful down and put them in the copper to boil, then went back upstairs and turned the room inside out, scrubbing it until I could scrub no more. I wanted every last trace of her gone, but I knew she would linger in my mind.

She was the woman Ernie had married instead of me and nothing could change that.

I felt better when I had scrubbed my room free of the smell and taste of Grace, but I couldn't forget the taunts she had thrown at me or the leer on her face. She had known it was me Ernie wanted but she had deliberately set out to trap him.

He had told me she'd had a terrible life and I had felt sorry for her because I knew what it was like to have an unhappy home life, although Da had never laid a hand on me. Getting what she wanted hadn't made Grace grateful and I could imagine that she made life as uncomfortable as possible for Ernie and his mother. It hurt me that the man I loved was trapped in a loveless marriage, but it was too late to change things.

It wasn't all Grace's fault. I had to admit that it was partly mine. If I had only given him some encouragement he would never have got drunk and ended up misbehaving with her, but regrets would not turn back the clock. Ernie was married and for me that meant for life.

Over the next few days I tried to put the memory of Ernie's desperate kiss from my mind. It was madness to dwell on it or to ache for it to happen again. He was forbidden to me and it was best to forget him if I could. I must also forget the feelings of longing I'd experienced when I held Grace's child in my arms.

Having been present as Grace gave birth made me think about Lainie. I was still angry with her for taking Fred's pendant, but I couldn't help wondering where she was and whether there would be someone to take care of her when her time came. If I had known how to contact her, I would probably have told her to come home, at least until the child was born, but I had no idea where she might have gone. She was often in my thoughts and I alternated between anger and regret that we should have parted with this hurt between us.

'I've heard rumours that they might be pulling the houses down in Bullocks Lane,' Maggie said to me a few days after that night, 'and some of them warehouses by the river.'

'What do you think they are going to do?' I asked. 'Build a new dock area?'

'You never know what they might take it into their heads to do once they start,' Maggie said looking anxious. 'When they constructed St Katherine's they tore down whole streets of slum housing to make way for it. I've lived in the lane all my life, Bridget. I don't know what we should do if they decided to pull our houses down too.'

'Surely they wouldn't?' I was shocked at the suggestion. 'What good would it do them?'

'It's if they want to clean up the area,' Maggie said. 'Our houses ain't too bad, but we're in a slum area and they might decide to start fresh. They might build new houses and shops if they're cleaning up the riverside. The rent would go up that's for sure. Mick's fightin' mad over it.'

'I hope they don't come this far. I'm not sure I could pay more rent.'

'We should probably have to move away and I don't fancy one of them tenements. It's hard to find anythin' else round here now.'

I agreed with her, feeling anxious. I wasn't sure what I would do if I had to leave the lane. As yet I hadn't settled on a job, although I'd had a couple of offers of part-time work. I thought I might write to Jamie and ask him what he thought I ought to do about keeping the house on, but before I could do it the matter was decided for me.

I opened the door to the rent man on Monday morning as usual, handing him my book and the money. He looked at me oddly as he handed it back.

'You've always been regular with the money, Miss O'Rourke,'

he said, 'except for that one lapse . . . and I don't like to tell you this, but it's me orders. You've got to go.'

'What are you talking about?' I stared at him in dismay. 'I'm not behind with my rent?'

'That's what I was saying, but I've been told to give you one month's notice.'

'But why? I don't understand.'

'Your mother was the tenant, Miss O'Rourke. And you are considered too young to take it over.' He looked embarrassed as if he hated doing his job at that moment. 'I spoke up for you but it didn't do any good.'

'But that's not fair! Surely you can't do that?'

'I don't make the laws, miss. I just do me job and there are times when I bleedin' wish I didn't. But I've got a family to feed. You'll get a letter from a lawyer I expect, but I've given you warning.'

'But what am I going to do?'

'A young woman like you don't want the trouble of keeping a house,' he said. 'Find yourself a room somwhere or get married. I dare say there's a young man somewhere who wouldn't mind taking you on.'

I stared after him as he walked away, feeling stunned and disbelieving. How could this happen? It was so unfair that the landlord could just decide to turn me out of my home because my mother was dead!

I ran round to Maggie's house and asked her if they could do that. She looked horrified, but her answer was in the affirmative.

'Them varmints can do what they like with us,' she said. 'We've hardly any rights and I've heard of whole families being put out on the street just because the landlord wanted the house for someone else. It's wrong, Bridget, but it's the way things are.'

'Then it's time someone sorted things out,' I said.

'My Mick says there's somethin' called the Labour Party,' Maggie told me and screwed up her mouth. 'It's politics and I don't reckon on that much. Mick says when they get into government things may change for the common folk, but until then we ain't got a hope in hell!'

Maggie pulled a face and I laughed, but I thought her belief in miracles was probably as forlorn as Miss Elton's desire to see women in the Houses of Parliament. As far as I could see, it was money and power that decided the way things would be and I couldn't see those that had it letting that change.

'I don't know what I'm going to do when Tommy gets better,' I said. 'The rent man told me I should look for lodgings, but that won't help me find a home for my brother.'

'I would take you in,' Maggie said. 'Tommy could share with our Billy and we'd find a corner for you somewhere, but I reckon we'll probably be in the same boat before long.'

'Oh, Maggie, no,' I said looking at her in shock. 'Surely not?'

'If I were you, Bridget, I should see this as a sign,' Maggie advised. 'Make a break – go and live somewhere else. Start a new life . . .'

'Yes, perhaps,' I said. 'Jamie did well by going away. I think I shall write to him and ask him what he thinks.'

'You do that,' she said and made a wry face. 'Why any of us want to stay in a rotten place like this beats me anyway.'

Joe Robinson came to see me three days later. I heard the knock at my door and expected it to be Jamie, but Joe told me he was busy.

'He had a big job on, Bridget,' Joe said. 'But I wanted to come anyway. We've talked things over, Jamie, Mary, Ma and me, and we want you to come and live with us.'

'Live with you . . . ?' I stared at him in surprise. 'But there's Tommy to think about. I need more than just a room . . . I mean I'm very grateful for the offer, Joe, but I have to think about when my brother gets well again.'

'Yes, we have thought about that and this is just temporary,' Joe said. 'This is what we want to do . . .'

He outlined his plans for the future. He was going to move into the rooms above the flat while they were being renovated for Mary and Jamie. I would use his room until the wedding and in the meantime Joe was going to look for a bigger house to buy for himself.

'I've been wanting something bigger and nicer for a while now,' he said. 'It was easy for Ma and Mary to walk to the market where we were, but I fancy a better area. I'll use the next few months to look for something, and by the time Tommy comes home I'll have plenty of room for him. You'll be able to have your brother to live with you, Bridget. I promise you that.'

'I don't know what to say, Joe. It sounds like the answer to my prayers, but why should you do so much for me?'

'Because I want to,' Joe said. 'I like you and Mary is set on having Jamie so I expect she will get her way. Besides, I do have an ulterior motive.'

'That's a big word for this time of the mornin',' I said and laughed at him as I saw the way his mouth twitched at the corners. 'Go on, tell me the catch.'

'Mary isn't always as well as she might be,' Joe said. 'She wanted that shop and I let her have it and she's done well. But she was off sick the other week and she often goes in when I know she should be in bed. I employed a girl I know to help out, but Mary said she got things in a muddle and nearly lost her a valuable customer. I wondered if you would like to work with Mary and learn how she does her arrangements?'

'That isn't a catch,' I said. 'It's the most wonderful thing that has ever happened to me. Oh, Joe . . .' Tears stung my eyes and my throat caught with emotion. 'I don't know how to thank you.'

'You'll be doing me a favour,' he said and grinned, clearly delighted that I was pleased. 'Mary told me you were the one she wanted, but I didn't think you would come until Jamie got your letter.'

'Yes,' I said. 'Yes, I shall come, Joe. I like your family, and it will be an ideal solution to my problem.'

'I shall tell Miss Elton when she comes in this evening,' I said to Joe. 'She will want a couple of weeks to find herself a new room and that will give me a week to get the house clean.'

'I shouldn't bother too much with that after the way they've treated you.'

'I wouldn't dream of leaving it dirty,' I said. 'What about Mam's things, Joe? She hadn't got much, but there are a few bits that might be worth keeping.'

'Would you consider letting Mary and Jamie have them for over the shop? The furniture anyway. Anything else you could keep at our house.'

'Yes, I hadn't thought of that,' I said. 'Jamie can have the stuff out of the parlour. I'll probably ask the rag and bone man to take the mattresses away, but the bedstead in Mam's room is solid brass. Jamie could have that too.'

'That's settled then,' Joe said and stood up. 'Jamie will bring his wagon over the last week and clear his stuff and whatever you want to bring, and I'll come and fetch you the last day.'

'I can come to your house on the omnibus, Joe.'

'I'll be here,' he said and gave me a grim look. 'Just in case the landlord's agent tries to give you any trouble.'

'Thanks,' I said. 'Yes, that would be helpful, Joe. I'll let you know as soon as I'm ready then.'

After Joe had left, I went upstairs to my mother's room. I had only been in to clean it once a week since she died, but now I knew that I would have to tackle a job I had been dreading.

Miss Elton was most put out that I was giving her notice. 'Well, you might have told me before, Miss O'Rourke. This is most inconvenient. Most inconvenient.'

'I am very sorry,' I said. 'I was only given notice on the house a few days ago, and I wasn't sure what I was going to do until today.'

'I do not like moving,' she said, glaring at me as if it were my fault. 'I am not sure I shall find anything else as convenient.'

'I've been thinking about it,' I told her. 'Maude Brown is a widow. She lives on her own since her husband died, in a house at the far end of the lane. It's a bit better than the others around here. I think she owns it; her husband had a little money. She might consider taking you on.'

Miss Elton nodded and thanked me for my advice. I knew she wasn't very pleased, but three days later she told me she would be leaving at the end of that week.

'Mrs Brown has told me I can move in straight away,' she said. 'So I shall pay you until Saturday, and then leave, if that is all right with you, Miss O'Rourke?'

'Yes, of course, if that's what you want.'

It would mean that I would only just have enough money left to manage the next few weeks, but I would go down the market and take a Saturday job and see if I could find something else to bring in a little money until I was ready to leave.

In many ways I would be sad to leave the lane and the people I had known all my life, but I would enjoy working in Mary's shop. Besides, what else could I do?

I returned to my task of clearing out Mam's room after Miss Elton went out that last evening.

I had left the big chest of drawers in Mam's room to the last because I knew that was where she had kept her personal things.

Most of it went straight in the ragbag, but in the bottom drawer I discovered several items wrapped in yellowed tissue. When I unwrapped them carefully, I found two pretty lace tablecloths that had never been used, and I thought I would keep those for myself. In another parcel was a lace blouse, which also looked almost new and very expensive. Not the sort of thing I would ever have expected Mam to own. It looked as if it might have come from a West End shop.

There was also a small wooden jewel box of the kind they sold cheap on the market and inside it amongst the jumble of broken beads and junk was a gold brooch with a turquoise and pearl centre. I had never seen Mam wear it.

I would keep the blouse and the tablecloths, but I thought I would give the brooch to Maggie.

'You can't give me this,' she said when I took it next door a few minutes later. 'It's lovely, Bridget, but it was your mam's. Don't you want to keep it?'

'I want you to have it,' I said. 'You've been good to us, Maggie. I think Mam might have wanted you to have it and I certainly do.'

Maggie embraced me with tears in her eyes. 'I'm going to miss you, Bridget. You won't forget us when you're livin' with them posh friends of yours?'

'As if I would! I shall visit when I can, Maggie,' I promised. 'And I'll send you a postcard sometimes – a naughty one that will shock the neighbours.'

'You're a wicked girl, Bridget O'Rourke,' she said and kissed me. 'But I love you.'

'I love you too, Maggie.'

I was smiling to myself as I left Maggie's house and went next door, but I jumped with fright when a man loomed out of the darkness just as I was opening the door.

'Bridget . . .' My heart stood still as I heard the note of desperation in Ernie's voice. 'I had to see you. I had to see you once more before you go away.'

'Ernie . . . ?' I looked at him doubtfully. I had a suspicion that he had been drinking. 'You shouldn't have come. You know you shouldn't.'

'Please . . . ?' he said. 'Just a few minutes . . . Just to say goodbye.'

I hesitated and was lost. It was wrong and we both knew it, but I felt almost as desperate as he did as I saw the misery in his face. For days at a time I would manage to subdue my longings and force the thought of Ernie to the back of my mind, but at least I had something to look forward to. I knew there was nothing for him but work and a sullen wife to come home to of an evening.

He reached for me as soon as we were in the kitchen and the door was closed, pulling me into a hungry embrace that almost drove the breath from my body. I knew I ought to resist, but I couldn't. I clung to him, letting him kiss me, wanting it to go on – wanting more.

'I love you, Bridget,' he murmured huskily as his mouth released mine for a moment. 'I want you so much . . . I need you . . .'

'Ernie, we mustn't . . .' I said breathlessly. 'You know we mustn't.'

But my protest sounded weak even to my own ears. I made no real resistance as he took me down to the rug before the kitchen range, his hands moving beneath my dress, searching out that part of me that throbbed for his touch. For a moment I remembered the night Harry Wright had tried to rape me, but this wasn't Harry; it was the man I loved and my body was on fire for him.

All that I had ever been taught warned me that I was a fool and that this was wrong. I should not let it happen. Ernie was married. We had no right to do this, but I was young and my body clamoured for his as his demanded mine. All thought of sin and consequence was drowned in a wave of desire.

'You're so lovely, so sweet,' Ernie murmured against my hair. 'You smell so good, Bridget . . . so good.'

'Ernie . . .' It was no longer a protest as I whispered his name, rather an entreaty. I wanted him to love me, to make me his own. I wanted this night to remember whatever happened in the future. 'I love you. I love you so much . . .'

'Bridget my darlin' . . .'

Ernie's kisses were tender and sweet as he explored my body, his caresses bring me to a quivering readiness and when he finally entered me I was ready and wet for him. Perhaps there was pain; I had always been told that it often hurt the first time, but if it did I was swept up by the magic and excitement of my feelings and I did not want him to stop.

His loving was not hasty or selfish and I discovered something in my lover's arms that night that I had never known or expected to know. I had thought that the act of love was always selfish, that it always took rather than gave, but now I knew that it could be beautiful.

Afterwards, I lay my head against his chest and wept.

Ernie stroked my hair, which had broken free from its usual

bonds, and lay about my shoulders in a dark mass. 'I'm sorry, so sorry,' he said. 'I was selfish.'

'No,' I said and sat up to look at him. 'Don't think that. I'm weeping because you made me happy.'

'Oh, Bridget,' he murmured brokenly as he got to his feet and reached out to help me up. He looked down into my eyes. 'What are we going to do? How can I bear to go back to her after you?'

I touched his cheek, my fingertips trailing across his lips, stopping him from saying more.

'You know that what we did was wrong,' I said. 'I am not blaming you, Ernie. I wanted it as much as you did, but it can't happen again.'

'I could leave her. We could go away.'

'Don't!' I cried. 'You know it can't happen. You have to look after your ma and Grace and little Kathy needs you. You have her, Ernie. If you have nothing else, you have her.'

'She is beautiful,' he said. 'You made me see that, Bridget. I do love her as if she were my own. I try to pretend that she's yours and mine.'

'Yes, I felt the same,' I said and smiled. 'I held her after she was born, Ernie, and I wanted her to be ours.'

'Then she will be,' he promised. 'I shall look after her. I shall love her as if she is ours.'

'Then you will find happiness,' I said. 'And you must try to be kind to Grace, but I know you will.'

Ernie nodded, his eyes intent as he looked at me. 'Are you goin' ter marry Joe Robinson?'

'What made you ask me that?'

'It's what people say,' Ernie said and for a moment there was anger in his eyes. 'He's got money, Bridget. He'll look after you.'

'No, I'm not going to marry him,' I said. 'Joe hasn't asked me and I wouldn't if he did. How can you ask after what just happened between us? Do you think I would have done that with you if I was going to marry Joe?'

He looked at me for a moment, and then accepted it. 'I

shouldn't have asked, Bridget. I know you're not like Grace. I'm sorry. It's just that I can't bear to think of you with someone else.'

'I'm not going to marry Joe,' I said. 'At the moment I don't know if I shall ever want to marry anyone, but it might happen. I want children, Ernie, and I want a home of my own. Is that so terrible?'

'No, of course not,' he said. 'I had no right ter say that – no right ter come here the way I did tonight. I'll go now and I shan't trouble yer again.'

'You have to go,' I said. 'But we won't part in anger, Ernie. We won't part with bad words between us. I love you and I want you to be happy. Won't you wish the same for me?'

He stared at me for a moment and then he shook his head. 'I can't, Bridget. I'm not as good or forgiving as you. I'm angry and bitter. I hate Grace and I hate myself for marrying her and if you marry Joe Robinson or anyone else I shall hate them. I don't want yer to be happy without me. I want yer to be as miserable as I am.'

Thirteen

'Well, there you are, Bridget. You know where the bath-room is if you need it,' Alice Robinson showed me the room that was mine for the time being. 'Joe cleared his things out this weekend and the bits and pieces you sent over are all here. I didn't unpack them because I thought you would want to do that. I hope you will be comfortable here?'

'Oh, I'm sure I shall, thank you,' I said. Her house was sheer luxury to what I'd been used to, with a proper flush toilet and a real bath with hot water! There was linoleum on the floor downstairs and a thick cord carpet along the stairs and landing. 'You are very kind, Mrs Robinson. It was good of you to let me come.'

'Now then, none of that,' she replied in her no nonsense way. 'My name is Alice and I want you to use it. You're a part of the family now. Mary and me are looking forward to having you here.'

'I want to be a help to you. How is Mary feeling today?'

'She's gone to her shop,' Alice replied and frowned. 'I begged her to stay home a few more days but I might as well have saved my breath. She's a stubborn girl, Bridget.'

'I expect she was worried about the shop. She wants it to be a success.'

'I think that's exactly what she's worried about. She's had several large orders for flowers for a hotel and no one but Mary can see to that. She's so clever at arranging them – neither Joe nor I could help her with anything fancy.'

'Do you think Mary would teach me?' I asked. 'Then I could stand in for her when she isn't well and she wouldn't need to worry so much.'

'I know she will be glad of your help. She's talked of nothing else for days. Joe will show you how to find the shop after we've had a bite to eat.'

'I'll unpack a few bits,' I said. 'But I'll come as soon as you're ready and I'll help you when I get back later.'

'You concentrate on settling in first,' Alice replied. 'The kettle is on the go – ten minutes, all right?'

I glanced round the room after she had gone, taking it in properly now that I was alone. It was bigger than my room at home and the stained wooden floorboards were almost fully covered with two big woven rugs. The candlewick bedcover was a duck egg blue and the wallpaper was the same colour with a ribbon pattern running through it; the curtains were a darker blue.

I began to put away my things: Mam's blouse and the table-cloths, my clothes and a few keepsakes. Alice was soon calling from downstairs. It was time to put the past behind me.

'It's lovely of you to come straight away,' Mary said as I walked into the shop an hour later. 'I've been so busy this morning. People popping in to say how much they like the window display and buy little things. I've sold several bunches of flowers, but I've got to finish these arrangements before five. That's when the deliveryman is coming to pick them up.'

'What can I do?' Mary was working at a little bench at the back of the shop. She had lots of bits of chicken wire and all kinds of containers – little pots, tall, elegant vases and straw baskets – from which she was contriving the most magical arrangements I had ever seen. 'You're so clever, Mary. I would never have thought you could do things like that with flowers. All I've ever done is stick a few sprigs in an empty jam pot.'

'You're not the only one to say that,' Mary replied, a faint flush in her cheeks. 'I suppose some of them are very different to what people are used to – especially round here. I first got the idea when Ma took me up the West End. It was a birthday treat and we were going to a music hall show, but when I saw the flower shop all I wanted to do was stand and look at the wonderful flowers. I spent all my money on them and didn't bother to go to the show at all. Joe thought I was mad, but I started trying to make the sort of thing I'd seen and found I could do it.'

'I think they are wonderful, but who buys them?'

'They have arrangements like these in the reception areas of posh hotels,' Mary said. 'I've been round some of the hotels just to look and I was amazed. I think they are better than all the diamonds and jewels in the big jewellery shops. When I came home, I kept plaguing Joe to buy me flowers and I tried selling a few on the market, but it was too cold for me and I couldn't stand all day. So when he told me about the shop . . .'

'It was a good idea,' I said. 'Where do you get the flowers? These are better than the ones Maisie used to sell.'

'Joe gets some of them from his regular suppliers, but we're buying a lot in from specialist suppliers now. Especially the roses.'

'I would never have dreamed there was so much to selling flowers. Joe is very clever at what he does and so are you. What can I do to help you, Mary?'

'You can tidy the bench,' she said, 'and make sure all the tubs of flowers have water. If someone comes in you can serve them. All the flowers have price tickets on them so you can't go wrong.'

I started to pick up the bits and pieces Mary had discarded, tidying them into the bins behind her counter. Then I found a jug and filled it with water from a tap in the little back room. I was filling the vases in the window when a man stopped to look in. I smiled at him and he hesitated and then came into the shop.

'Hello,' he said. 'So we meet again, Miss O'Rourke. How nice to see you in a shop like this – much better than the market, I think.'

'Good afternoon, sir,' I said. 'And how are you?'

'Very well thank you,' Philip Maitland replied. 'I hadn't noticed this was a flower shop until this morning.'

'Miss Robinson only opened it a few months' back,' I said. 'May I be of assistance, sir?'

'Yes, you may,' he said. 'I want a dozen of your red roses. I hope they smell nice.'

I took one of the roses from the vase in the window and inhaled the perfume. It was delicious and I held it out for him to smell.

'Ah yes, delightful. Could you wrap them for me?'

I glanced at Mary and she indicated some tissue on the front counter. I laid the twelve stems on the paper, making sure that they looked attractive, and then carefully rolled the paper, fastening it with a little twist at the bottom.

'Yes, very nice,' Mr Maitland said. 'Now, what do I owe you?'

'I think . . .' I looked at the price again to be sure. 'Yes, that's six shillings.' I took the three half crowns he offered and put them in the tin under the counter, giving him one shilling and sixpence change. 'Please call again, sir.'

'Yes, I certainly shall,' he said. 'It was a pleasure to do business with you, Miss O'Rourke.'

'Thank you,' I said and blushed as he tipped his hat once more.

I turned to Mary as he went out, the bell clanging loudly. 'Was that all right? I've only ever served someone on the market before. I wasn't sure what to do.'

'You were very good,' Mary said. 'Anyone would think you'd been doing it for ages and that was the best sale I've had in the shop. Most people buy a sixpenny bunch of violets. It's only the ordered flowers that keep me going – that's why I worry so much if I am ill.'

'Yes, I can understand that,' I said. 'But you'll have me to help you now.'

'If you sell more roses I shan't need to worry so much.'

'Well, the roses are a lot of money. I nearly died when I saw how much they were for each bloom. How can anyone afford that for flowers? When it was Lainie's birthday I used to buy her a bunch of pinks from the market for sixpence and I thought I was spending a fortune then.'

'I know it seems a lot,' Mary agreed looking anxious. 'But

you have to allow for expenses and you get some wastage and those roses are specially grown to have long stems. They're not just off someone's allotment like some of the flowers you buy in the market.'

'Oh, I didn't mean to criticize. It just seems a lot to me. I could feed the family for a week on what he paid me.'

'But he is a gentleman,' Mary pointed out. 'Did you notice the suit he was wearing? That must have been made to measure by a West End tailor. You could probably feed a family for a year on what that cost.'

'Yes, I suppose so. Does that seem fair to you, Mary?'

'No, of course it doesn't,' she said. 'I don't envy what other people have, but I sometimes think a lot of people have a hard time of it.'

'Yes, so do I, but I don't suppose there's anything we can do.'

'We could go to the political meeting in the exchange next month,' she said, surprising me. 'It's partly to do with the suffragettes, but also new rights for workers' groups. I'd like to go but Joe isn't keen on that sort of thing. He says it's a lot of hot air about nothing.'

'I expect he's right, but there's no reason why we shouldn't go – as long as you feel up to it.'

'I'm better now,' she said and promptly had a fit of coughing. 'Take no notice of me, Bridget. I'm always like this for weeks after I've had a cold. It was my own fault. I got wet walking to the market in the rain and instead of hurrying home to change, I came back here and did some work. There's nothing really wrong with me.' She looked at me sympathetically. 'Not like your Tommy. I was so sorry he had to go away.'

'It hurts to think of him there, Mary. I write to him and send him little things, but I know he's miserable and I feel guilty.'

'They say it's bad housing and deprivation that causes illness in so many children. I think if something could be done to help save just a few of the children that die each year, these meetings would be worthwhile, don't you?'

'Yes, I do.' Mary seemed to care about the things I thought

mattered and I could tell that we were going to get on really well. 'I'm going to enjoy being with you, Mary. We could do a lot of things together – at least until you and Jamie get married.'

'I sometimes wonder when that will be. Jamie works all hours. I hardly see him, Bridget, but Joe just keeps saying we need a bit by us before we marry. I suppose he's right, but now and then I get a panicky feeling inside and I think something will happen before we can be together.'

'Oh, Mary,' I said and laughed. 'Nothing is going to happen. Jamie loves you. It's a good thing he's working hard for you. He used to be terrible, always drinking and fighting, but he's a different man now.'

'I know I'm daft to worry,' she said. 'And if I don't get on I shan't have these flowers finished on time. Come and watch how I do them, Bridget. They're not hard really, just a bit fiddly. When we've got more time I'll let you have a go.'

I watched as Mary shaped the wire, cleverly making wonderful creations out of flowers and greenery. Several times during the afternoon I had to leave her to serve customers. Some of them just came in to ask the price of something and stayed for a chat, but most bought a small bunch of violets. Mary told me they came in off a ship from the Channel Islands that very morning. A young man bought a single rose for his girlfriend and another man bought a huge bunch of pinks for ninepence.

'It's the best day in the shop so far,' Mary told me when I helped her add up the takings later. 'You've brought me luck, Bridget. It's because you're so pretty and that smile of yours makes them buy even if they only came to look.'

'Oh, I'm sure it's not me,' I said and blushed. 'It's just that people are getting to know you're here.'

'What can I do to help?' I asked after the supper dishes were washed and put away in the large pine dresser that evening. 'Is there any ironing, Alice? I could do that for you, or I'll scrub the kitchen floor if you like? I want to do my share in the house now that I'm living here.'

'You've done quite enough for one day,' she said. 'We're all going to have a cup of tea in the parlour now. We usually do in the evenings. Joe tells us what he's been up to on the market and then we read a book or find some sewing to do.' She smiled at me as I looked doubtful. 'Mary loves to read novels – something by Jane Austen or perhaps one of Mr Charles Dickens' books. I go to the library every week and bring a selection for us both. I brought something for you this afternoon, but you must tell me what you like to read, Bridget.'

I was embarrassed to tell her that I hadn't read a book since I left school, so I just said that I was sure I would like anything Mary liked and left it at that. It was a very different way of life for me, but I thought I would enjoy it once I had settled in.

'Would you mind if Mary and me went out one evening next month? There's a meeting we should like to attend.'

'One of those political things?' Alice questioned. 'Mary mentioned it. Joe wasn't keen on going with her, but the two of you together don't need him. As long as you come straight back afterwards and don't hang about the streets or talk to strange men.'

'Oh, we wouldn't do that,' I said. 'It's not safe for a woman to be out too late at night – at least I never feel safe on my own.'

After we'd drunk our tea, I went upstairs to unpack my things. I sat on the edge of the bed, looking about me and thinking. For a moment my thoughts went back to the night Ernie had come to the house and we had lain together on the rug before the kitchen range.

It had been wrong. We had committed a sin, but I wasn't sorry. Maybe I would go to hell for my sins, but I hadn't confessed it to Father O'Brien.

I had wondered if there might be a child. Some women fell straight away, but it hadn't happened to me. I knew it was a good thing, because I couldn't have stayed on here in Alice Robinson's house if I had been carrying a bastard child and yet I knew I would always carry an ache inside me, a longing to have Ernie's baby in my arms.

Over the next few weeks I gradually found a routine for myself.

I was up early in the morning and had the kitchen and front doorstep scrubbed before the others came down. And on washdays I lit the fire under the copper in the scullery for Alice to boil the sheets.

However, I had discovered that it was pleasant to relax sometimes in the evenings, and I was steadily reading my way through Elizabeth Gaskell's novels, which Alice had introduced me to when I arrived. I was also making myself some new clothes with Alice and Mary's help, and sometimes the three of us measured and cut out patterns on the floor of the parlour. Joe always groaned when we had a dressmaking session and took himself off to the pub for an hour or so.

I went to the shop with Mary every day, doing all the jobs Mary might have found hard. The windows were cleaned inside and out every morning, the floor brushed and mopped, and when Mary wasn't busy with special orders, I went upstairs and tidied the rooms for Joe.

He was still doing the jobs that needed attention and the place smelled of paint and wallpaper paste. It was gradually coming on, and though it seemed odd to see Mam's bits and pieces in an unfamiliar setting, I was glad Joe was making use of them until Jamie and Mary moved in.

'When shall you let them have the wedding?' I asked Joe once when he came back as I was cleaning the sitting room.

'Not for a while yet,' he said. 'I want to make sure he can provide for her, Bridget. He's doing well, but this is the first time he's held a steady job for longer than a few months. Perhaps at the end of the year.'

Mary pulled a face when she heard this. 'I'll have to start working on him,' she said. 'It's all right for Joe to talk, but I don't know how many years I'll have, Bridget. I don't want to waste what I've got.'

'Don't say things like that!' I was alarmed. 'I thought you were feeling better?'

'I am,' she assured me. 'But I'm not as strong as I ought to be and I don't want to waste even a bit of the time I have.'

It made me anxious when Mary said things like that. We had

become friends and the thought that she might die young upset me. But she didn't often talk that way. Most of the time we were happy and laughing together. I missed Maggie and my friends, of course, but there was so much to learn and see.

Suddenly life seemed to have become brighter for both Mary and me. Neither of us had been used to the freedom we now enjoyed. We had little to restrict us now and we often went out together to a music hall show or just walking in the park on a sunny Sunday afternoon. Sometimes Jamie or Joe came with us, but if they were busy then Mary and I simply went alone.

Mary was always teasing me these days because she said that her shop was getting a lot of young men as customers.

'It's because Bridget charms them,' she told Joe and Alice in the parlour one evening. 'Some of them stand outside the window staring at her like lovesick calves.'

'Oh, Mary, don't,' I cried and pulled a face. 'They're just plucking up the courage to buy flowers for their young ladies.'

'And what about your admirer then?' she challenged. 'He's a gentleman, Ma, and comes into the shop at least three times a week. He always buys a dozen of the most expensive roses and he waits for Bridget to serve him. I think he fancies her.'

'You do talk nonsense!' I blushed. 'He obviously has some-one special or he wouldn't buy all those flowers.'

'I think they are just an excuse for him to come and see you. He's too shy to ask you out so he just keeps buying flowers.'

'I hope he doesn't ask me out. I should have to say no and it would be so embarrassing.'

'When does he come in?' Joe asked and frowned. 'I'll keep an eye out for him – make sure he's not up to any funny business. You want to be careful of that sort, Bridget.'

'You're just jealous because Bridget has an admirer,' Mary mocked. 'What could he possibly be up to in a flower shop?'

Joe scowled at her. 'Gentlemen don't belong in our part of town. What's he doin' here, that's what I'd like to know.'

Mary went into a fit of giggles and looked at me, her teasing having prompted exactly the reaction she wanted.

*   *   *

181

The hall was packed for the political meeting that night and Joe had done his best to persuade us not to attend.

'You'll get a rough element there,' he'd warned. 'In any case I don't know why you want to go. It's all a lot of daft talk. They'll stand up and make fine speeches and then nothing will happen.'

After the first hour I was inclined to agree. The first speaker had been a plain-faced woman who had reminded me of Miss Elton. She had gone on and on about rights for women until I felt like standing up and asking her where it was all leading.

Eventually, the woman had sat down to unenthusiastic applause. The next speaker was someone called James Keir Hardie, who, the audience was told, was the founding member of the Scottish Labour Party. Following him was a young Englishman who had spent his life working on the docks but was now about to enter politics. He talked about poverty in the East End and the need for a minimum wage for unskilled labourers.

'Until we get powerful unions, the bosses will defeat us every time,' he said. 'At the moment the union can be sued for money lost by the bosses during a strike and that spells ruin. Take away our power to strike and you silence us. We have to repeal unfair laws and the only way we're goin' to do that is to elect men like ourselves into government.'

'Oh, yeah – 'ow yer goin' ter do that then?'

'We've got to have a powerful political party for the working man to vote for at the next general election.'

There was some applause from the audience but also jeering and heckling from the back of the hall. It was obvious that there was a rowdy element just as Joe had forecast.

'They've probably been paid to cause trouble,' Mary whispered. 'If they start a fight the police will be called in and then the papers can discredit the speakers.'

Some fighting and scuffling had already started at the back. Several large, burly-looking men had moved towards those who were causing the disturbance and after a struggle the troublemakers were thrown out.

I listened to the remainder of the speeches, but although some of them were interesting, none of the speakers seemed to have any new ideas. They all condemned the poverty and the unfair wages paid to workers in many jobs, particularly the unskilled labourers in the factories and sweatshops, but no one appeared to know what ought to be done about it.

'Joe was right,' I whispered to Mary. 'Let's leave before everyone starts to move, shall we?'

Mary agreed and we left our seats, beginning to walk down the aisle. Others had the same idea and ten or twelve people left at the same time. As we went outside, I noticed a group of men hanging around the street. They looked the rough sort and I sensed trouble brewing.

'I think they're the ones they threw out.'

Even as I spoke, the jeering started and the rough element began to jostle those who were leaving the hall. Mary and I were caught in the middle of it and found ourselves being pushed from the back as some of the men inside rushed to meet the challenge.

'Look out!' I yelled as I saw one man start to hit the people around him with a wooden club. I was frightened for Mary and pushed her out of the way, catching a glancing blow on my shoulder. I turned on my assailant in a fury. 'You just watch who you're hitting! Someone could get badly hurt here.'

'Get out of the way if yer don't want ter get 'urt!'

'I was trying to.' I was looking for Mary and couldn't see her. Somehow we had got separated and I was anxious for her. 'Mary . . .'

I felt a hand on my shoulder and turned in alarm, my heart thudding with fear. Joe was right! We shouldn't have attended the meeting. If Mary was hurt . . .

'Come with me, Miss O'Rourke. My man already has charge of Miss Robinson. We'll get you out of here. This is going to turn very nasty.'

'Mr Maitland . . . Were you at the meeting?' I asked as he forced a way through the crowd for us towards a very smart, horse-drawn carriage that had pulled up at the side of the road.

'We were just passing when we saw the trouble,' he replied. 'It was fortunate that I chanced to see you. Barrett, open the door for the young ladies.'

'Yes, sir.' He cast a disapproving look at us as though he thought we were not of his gentleman's class. 'I was waiting for you, sir.'

'It is very kind of you to offer us a lift,' Mary said. 'But we shall be all right now – shan't we, Bridget?'

I looked at Mary. 'Are you all right? I was a bit worried.'

'Yes, of course.'

Turning back to our rescuer, I said, 'As long as Mary is all right we can get home by ourselves, sir. We only live round the corner.'

A little smile tugged at his mouth. 'Just as you wish, Miss O'Rourke.' He glanced over his shoulder. 'If you are sure, I ought to go. I am expected somewhere and I am already late.' Police whistles could be heard now and the crowd was beginning to break up.

'Miss Clarissa will be wondering where you are, sir,' his man said.

'Yes, you do right to remind me,' he said and tipped his hat to Mary and then to me. 'This evening is rather important. You see, it is my fiancée's engagement ball . . . and mine, of course. But these things matter to ladies so much more, do they not?'

'Congratulations,' I said. 'So that's who the roses were for. We did wonder.'

'Yes, they were for Clarissa.' He smiled and glanced at his pocket watch, which was gold and not silver like the one he wore when he came to the shop. 'Excuse me, I must go.'

'Have a good time, sir.'

He nodded and got into his carriage. We stood for a moment, watching as it drove away.

'Well, that's a shame,' Mary said. 'I thought he was sweet on you.'

'Can you see me married to someone like that? His fiancée will be a lady and wear elegant clothes and go to posh places.

Did you see the way he was dressed? He's rich, Mary, and a gentleman. I could never marry someone like that – it just wouldn't be right.'

'I'll bet you're as pretty as she is,' Mary said as we linked arms and began to walk home. The disturbance was almost over, the rowdy element having fled into the night before the police could arrive to arrest them.

'But I'm not her. I wasn't brought up to speak properly, though I try to remember. I'm not an accomplished young lady. I can't dance or play the piano – or do any of the things that ladies do. Besides, I wouldn't want to marry Mr Maitland. I think he's nice, but he's not my sort.'

'What is your sort, Bridget? Have you met someone you specially like?'

'There was someone I liked,' I said. 'I wasn't ready to think about courting and then he married someone else.'

'Oh, poor you,' she said and hugged my arm. 'But he couldn't have been worth having, Bridget, or he wouldn't have looked at anyone else. Joe wouldn't. If he wanted a girl he'd wait forever if he had to.'

'Joe is different. He's been a good friend to Jamie and me.'

'I don't suppose we'll see Mr Maitland again now he's got his young lady to say yes. He won't need to buy her roses, will he?'

'Mean thing if he doesn't,' I said. 'I think he should buy her more.'

'Specially if he gets them from us,' Mary said and laughed.

We crossed the road to the pool of light thrown out from the pie shop, sniffing at the enticing smells coming from inside.

'I shouldn't say anything to Joe about being jostled and then offered a lift,' Mary said as we carried off our purchases. 'I'm not sure I want to attend any more political meetings, but we don't want him saying we can't go out at night on our own.'

'Oh no,' I agreed. 'I wouldn't tell Joe. We might go to the theatre next week, Mary. Joe and your ma might like to come, too.'

'We'll ask them, but if they say no we'll go on our own.'

Linda Sole

'I'm thinking of going to night school,' I told her. 'I want to learn bookkeeping. I used to do accounts for Mr Dawson, but Joe's books are a mystery, Mary. I asked him if he wanted some help when I saw the books upstairs at the shop. He said it would be a big help to him, but they don't seem to add up.'

Mary giggled. 'That's because he doesn't want anyone to know what he's up to,' she said. 'My brother runs deeper than you think, Bridget. He's got his fingers in a lot of pies. He thinks Ma and me don't know, but we guess a lot more than he realizes.'

'Yes, I expect he has a lot of business deals one way and another. Joe is very clever, Mary.'

'Yes . . .' She pulled a face at me. 'He is and he isn't, Bridget. He's good at making money and we've never been without anything, but I don't like some of the people Joe deals with.'

'Why? What's wrong with them?'

'They frighten me,' she said. 'There's a man called Hal Burgess – he's a small-time crook and I often see him hanging round the market. Joe says he uses him when he wants an errand, but I don't trust that man. I've heard he works for someone else . . . someone people are afraid of. They say this man is very rich and controls half the crooks in the East End. He never gets involved in anything dirty, of course, but he controls the men who run the protection gangs and if anyone is planning a big job they have to get his permission if it's on his territory.'

'Mary . . .' A cold shiver ran down my spine. 'Joe wouldn't get involved with someone like that? I'm sure he wouldn't.'

'No, but he might upset the apple cart, Bridget. Joe has been branching out a lot recently, buying a bit of property and taking on more market stalls. The man who owns half of the property around here might not like to see Joe moving in on his patch . . . and Hal Burgess is a bully and per-haps worse.'

'What do you mean worse?'

Mary glanced over her shoulder nervously. 'Sometimes people get killed if they don't do what the Big Man wants.

186

That's what they call him, the one behind everything. No one knows his name. He's just the Big Man.'

'That is a bit worrying,' I agreed, and thought about Fred Pearce. The police had never discovered who had murdered him – just as they hadn't solved the mystery of the attack on the watchman at the docks, or what had happened to Rosie. But as far as they were concerned, Rosie was just a girl of the streets who had been beaten up by one of her customers. And perhaps she had, but I couldn't help wondering sometimes if it had been for a different reason. 'Can't the police do anything to stop him?'

'Half of them are probably on his payroll,' she said. 'And the other half are either too scared or too stupid to do anything. They arrest the petty criminals and the girls who walk the streets, but they let the big ones get away with it.'

'Maybe they're just biding their time,' I said. 'Until the Big Man makes a mistake.'

'You don't understand the way things work,' Mary said. 'There's a criminal underworld, Bridget, and they all look after each other. If you're in with them they take care of you but –' she shrugged her shoulders – 'that's why I worry about Joe. He says he can take care of himself, but he might not if he gets in someone's way.'

Mary was busy with her orders for the hotel when the doorbell rang out a few mornings later, so I went to serve the man who came in. It was a week after we'd been to the political meeting and a glorious summer day.

'Yes, sir. Can I help you?'

'How much are them violets?' he grunted and squinted at me.

'Sixpence a bunch,' I told him, feeling uncomfortable as I felt his eyes on me. I didn't like him one little bit. 'Would you like to buy one?'

'Bleedin' robbery!' the man said and wiped his running nose on the sleeve of his coat. 'No wonder Joe Robinson is coinin' it.'

'This shop belongs to Miss Robinson,' I said, feeling more

and more uneasy. Shooting a glance at Mary, I saw that she was staring at us and her face was as white as a sheet.

'Same thing ain't it?' He glared at me. 'You watch yer lip an' all. Maybe I'll be back . . .'

As soon as he had gone, Mary got up and came over to me.

'That was him,' she said in a hushed voice. 'Do you remember me telling you about Hal Burgess the other night? Well, now you know why I worry about Joe.'

'He asked about the violets, said they were too dear and that Joe must be making a lot of money from them.'

'I hope he isn't going to demand protection money,' she said. 'I can't afford to pay him. We're managing but not making lots of money yet.'

'Surely he wouldn't? I thought it was big clubs and restaurants that had to pay . . . Places where they have a lot of money through the door.'

'Do you think I should tell Joe?'

'I think perhaps . . .' I broke off as the door opened, breathing a sigh of relief as I saw who had come in. It was nearly a week since he had bought flowers from us and I went to serve him. 'Good morning, sir. How are you today?'

'Very well, Miss O'Rourke.' He looked at me thoughtfully. 'You are rather pale – is something the matter?'

'No . . . just that a man was in here a moment ago. He was a little abusive.'

'That rough fellow I saw leaving just now?' His brows rose. 'Shall I send for the police, Miss O'Rourke? Did you happen to know him?'

'Miss Robinson knows who he is,' I said. 'Not a very nice person, but I don't think we should trouble the police, Mr Maitland. He didn't do any harm, just made vague threats.'

'Well, my advice is to call the police if he comes near you again,' he said. 'Now, I must buy two dozen of your best roses today. I have been busy this past week and Clarissa will feel neglected unless I make amends.'

'We thought we hadn't seen you for a while.'

He smiled at me and nodded. 'You may perhaps have

wondered why I come this way so often? I have been involved in setting up a charitable home for orphans. It has taken a great deal of my time, but we opened it this week.'

'I think someone mentioned that,' I said. 'Though I didn't know you were involved. I think that was a lovely thing to do. We need more people like you to take an interest, Mr Maitland. You should have been at that political meeting the other night. All they did was talk.'

He looked amused. 'I am glad you approve, Miss O'Rourke. It is a particular thing with me. I do not care for the way children are treated in the workhouses. We take children into care and we give them good food, adequate clothing and a home. We do not work them half to death to pay for their lodging.'

'You should be in parliament, sir.'

'I am constantly telling those who will listen how to improve the lot of the poor,' he said. 'For a start we need to clear the slums. Until we get decent homes and proper education for all we shall never live in a civilized world.'

I wrapped his roses and he handed me the money.

'I don't suppose we shall be seeing much of you in future, sir?'

'Oh, I still have business around here, Miss O'Rourke. There are many things that interest me, but I wanted to ask you something. I have been told that you supply flower arrangements for hotels and businesses?'

'Yes. Mary does them. She made that lovely arrangement of lilies and roses in the window.'

'I noticed it,' he said. 'I own a hotel in the Mayfair area. I have had a regular order for flowers for the reception and some of the better suites. I wonder if you would like to send me some samples of Miss Robinson's work?' He took out his card and handed it to me. 'This is the address to which the flowers should be directed. I have not been pleased with our supplier of late. Floral arrangements make all the difference to a room, but not if they are half dead before they arrive. The flowers I buy from you last several days.'

'They are always fresh. I am sure Mary will be pleased to

send you something, sir. We have someone who delivers them in a closed van so that the wind doesn't blow them about on the way.'

'Well, I shall look forward to seeing something soon. Goodbye, ladies.'

'What do you think of that?' I asked as I went back to where Mary was finishing an order for a large wedding. 'You'll soon be so busy you'll be needing more help.'

'Not while I've got you. It wasn't true what you said to him. You made that display for the window.'

'Well, you showed me how,' I said. 'I couldn't have done it before I came here, Mary. And he didn't say he particularly liked it, did he?'

'He must have done or he wouldn't have asked us to send him some samples,' she pointed out. She gave me a sly look. 'I still think he likes you, Bridget, even if he is going to marry Clarissa.'

'Don't be daft,' I replied and laughed. 'It will be good if you get his order though. You're doing much better than I ever imagined you could.'

'Joe thinks the same.' Mary looked anxious again. 'I just hope Hal Burgess isn't going to make trouble for us.'

Joe listened in silence as I told him what Hal Burgess had said to me when he came in the shop and then he frowned.

'I'm glad you told me,' he said. 'Don't worry, Bridget. He won't trouble you again. I'll see to that.'

'You won't do anything silly, Joe?'

'Of course not. He's a bully and some people are frightened of him, but like all bullies he backs down if you stand up to him. Besides, I have friends and he knows it. I'll make sure he doesn't come near you again.'

'Thanks, Joe,' I said. 'But don't get into any trouble yourself. Mary thinks that man might be dangerous.'

'Hal is a mere pussycat compared to some of the men I deal with every day on the market,' Joe said. 'Hal knows he would be in hot water if he upset me.'

'You sound fierce,' I said and he grinned. 'I told Mr Maitland about the way Hal Burgess made threats and he thought I should go to the police.'

'He's the gentleman Mary thinks is sweet on you . . . ?'

'Of course he isn't, Joe. He is just pleasant and he has given Mary a chance to make some arrangements for his hotel in Mayfair. I've told her she'll be needing someone else to work for her if she keeps on this way.'

'She is doing well,' Joe agreed. 'I was thinking of getting a delivery van myself. Either Jamie or I could do the deliveries for Mary. I asked Jamie whether we should get one of those new-fangled things with engines, but he said he would rather stick to horses. I think automobiles are the thing of the future, though. You see more of them about now.'

'That's a good idea,' I said. 'You'll be getting another flower shop before you're finished, Joe.'

'I would need someone with Mary's skills to make it a success,' he said. 'But I've got ideas about more shops and I've been looking for that house for us all. I think I may have found one. It's in a nicer area with a bit of land all round it and sheds at the back where I could keep stuff. It backs on to the river, but not the dock area. I'll take you and Mary to see it when I'm more sure I'm going to get it.'

'That sounds nice,' I said. 'But won't it be more difficult for me to get to work at the shop?'

'I could always take you in the van,' Joe said. 'Or maybe there's a tram you could use. We shall have the Tuppeny Tube all over London before long. Then everyone will be able to get where they want in no time.'

The London Central Railway had just opened the Tuppeny Tube, which ran from Shepherd's Bush to the Bank. I hadn't been on it yet, but I knew Jamie and Mary had used it one Sunday when he took her out for tea at a posh restaurant up west.

'Have you heard anything from Tommy?' Joe asked suddenly. 'We could go down and visit him one Sunday if you liked?'

'I should love to go,' I said. 'But I'm not sure, Joe. Last time I went Matron was annoyed, and Tommy got upset. I don't want to upset him again.'

'Why don't you write to Matron and ask if you could take him out for a few hours?' Joe said. 'We could walk by the sea and have something nice to eat somewhere.'

'That would be lovely. I'll write to her and see what she says.'

'Good.' He smiled at me. 'And don't you worry about that Hal Burgess, Bridget. I'll see he doesn't bother you again.'

Despite Joe's promise, I couldn't help worrying in case our unpleasant visitor returned, but after a couple of weeks and he hadn't reappeared, I stopped worrying.

It was August now and we were having a hot dry spell, which wasn't good for the flowers. We had to keep them cool and well watered, and they soon wilted if they weren't bought within a day or two. It meant that some of them got wasted, but Mary was pleased with the way the shop was going.

Mr Maitland had given her a regular order, just as I had thought he would, and either Jamie or Joe delivered three large displays to his hotel twice a week. His account was always settled promptly and Mary thought he was her best customer.

Jamie had been lodging at one of the pubs, but now he had moved in with Joe to help get the rooms ready. Joe had decided that they could have the wedding in September, and Mary was excited.

'It's going to be lovely living here,' she said. 'I can pop upstairs and do whatever I want while you're in the shop, Bridget. And if Jamie is busy, I can always get on with my arrangements in the evening.'

'I'm so pleased for you, Mary. Joe says he's nearly sure he's bought the house. He's going to take us to see it soon.'

'Joe seems more content lately,' Mary said and looked at me. 'I think he's about ready to settle down, Bridget. Ma and me have been on at him for years to find himself a wife, but he wasn't interested . . . You've changed all that.'

'What are you talking about?' I blushed as I saw the teasing look in her eyes.

'You must know Joe is sweet on you?'

'No, of course he isn't,' I said. 'We're just friends.'

'You take it from me, it won't be long before my brother asks you to marry him. I think he has just been waiting to get the house settled.'

'Oh, Mary . . . You don't mean that?'

'Of course I do,' she said. 'I've always known that was what he wanted . . . Right from the moment he asked you to come and live with us. Think about it, Bridget. It would make everything cosy, all tied up in the family. Joe likes things to be neat – and he cares about you.'

I turned away as someone came into the shop. I hadn't thought Joe was on the verge of asking me to marry him. He was always generous to me, and willing to have a laugh, but marriage was something else. It was a lifetime's commitment, and I wasn't sure how I felt about that.

I liked Joe a lot, of course I did. He had been so generous to Jamie and to me, but I still loved Ernie. Despite all my efforts to forget him, he was there at the back of my mind, and the memory of our loving was fresh in my mind.

Fourteen

I was laughing at something Mary was saying as we went into the shop one morning and bent down to pick up a letter on the mat, hardly looking at it as I handed it to her. We didn't often get letters and I waited expectantly thinking it might be someone wanting her to do more flower arrangements. The colour drained from her face as she read it and I could see that she was very upset.

'What's wrong, Mary?'

She handed me the opened letter, her hand shaking. It was written in a large, childish scrawl and its message would make anyone feel anxious.

'"Tell that bugger Joe Robinson to stop playing with fire or his fingers will get burned."' I read aloud. 'It doesn't say who it is from or what Joe is supposed to have done.'

'It's horrible,' Mary said with a shudder. 'Throw it away.'

'I don't think we should do that,' I said. 'I'm going down to the market. Joe will be at one of his stalls. He ought to see this straight away, Mary.'

'He'll go mad,' she said. 'But take it if you want to. I can manage here for a while.'

'We can't just leave this, Mary. If someone is threatening Joe he has to know about it.'

'Yes, I expect you're right. I'm just afraid it will stir up more trouble. I know my brother, Bridget. He won't just let this go.'

I left Mary to open up the shop alone and ran almost all the way to the market, startling one or two people I knew as I hurtled past them. When I saw Joe he was talking to one of the men who worked on his stalls, but he finished his business and came up to me quickly. I was still trying to recover my breath and it was a moment or two before I could speak.

'What's the matter, Bridget? Has Mary been taken ill?' He was looking at me in concern, knowing that I wouldn't have run like that unless it was urgent. 'Take your time . . . Get your breath back.'

I thrust the letter at him. 'This was at the shop this morning. Mary wanted to forget it, but I thought you should see it at once.'

Joe read the letter swiftly and swore. 'Is Mary very upset?' he asked. 'I'll kill the bugger who wrote this if they've made her ill.'

'No, she isn't ill, but it was a shock and naturally she's upset. Who would do that, Joe? Why is someone warning you?'

'I don't mind being threatened myself,' he said, looking angry. 'But I don't like them using you and Mary.'

'But why should anyone want to threaten you, Joe?'

He glanced over his shoulder. The market was coming to life, people pushing all round as they searched the stalls for a bargain, so there was little chance of talking privately. It was difficult enough to hear what Joe was saying over the general noise of costers shouting and the normal buzz of a crowd.

'We'll have a cup of coffee in the café over there and I'll tell you,' Joe said and took hold of my arm.

I thought I ought to get back to the shop, but Joe seemed as if he wanted to talk and I certainly wanted to know what was going on. I'd never come up against anything like this. In the lane people would say what they thought, but no one would send threatening letters.

Joe was silent as we crossed the busy road, dodging a dray wagon with a team of four black horses in shiny harness.

He directed me to a table in the corner while he fetched two thick white china cups of coffee. They were chipped and stained and the liquid inside looked like tar. He took a sip of his and pulled a face, pushing it to one side.

'It's not very nice, Bridget, but I thought we could talk in comfort here.'

'What's going on, Joe?'

'I'm in a bit of bother,' he replied. 'I've bought a couple of cheap properties recently, Bridget. And I was after another house – the one I told you about? It was almost sold for next to nothing until I stepped in and offered quite a bit more. My offer was accepted, but this morning I was told I couldn't have the house. I went round to see the lawyer and his clerk told me they'd had a small fire in their office. No one was hurt and they put it out before it did too much damage, but apparently it was a warning of what might happen if I got the house. They've had to accept the first offer.'

'But that's terrible,' I said. 'How can they do that? Surely it's not legal?'

'It's the way things work sometimes,' Joe said and grimaced. 'Especially around here. A lot of the property in this area belongs to the same person. Most of it was bought years ago for very little. The man who owns it controls everything. Shopkeepers, restaurants, pubs – they all pay for protection and everyone knows that one man is behind it, even though no one knows him.'

'Someone must know who he is.'

'If they do they are too damned scared to say. No, they prefer to pay up and live quietly.'

'Do you pay protection money, Joe?'

'No, I don't,' Joe looked grim. 'I have friends, and we protect ourselves. Until recently I haven't been approached but . . .'

He paused and I guessed what was coming. 'They've demanded money from you, haven't they? That's why that man, Hal Burgess, came to the shop.'

'He's just the organ-grinder's monkey,' Joe said. 'I can handle him and his kind. It's the man behind him that I would like to meet! But no one gets near him.'

'Oh, Joe. You shouldn't even try. It could be dangerous.'

'I'm willing to take risks for myself, but not for you and

Mary.' He looked at me strangely. 'I've been meaning to tell you, Bridget. I've been asked to sell Fred's house.'

'Fred's house? I didn't know you owned it.'

'I bought his house and the shop for less than half what they were worth,' Joe said. 'It was the lawyer's idea. He said it would save the bother of a legal wrangle over the will. I was going to tell you.'

'I don't understand. I thought you said Fred's will wasn't right?'

'It wasn't done professionally and the lawyer told me it would be difficult to prove. He said that the shop was worth hardly anything as it stood because I'd got such a watertight lease. And he wangled it so that I paid a hundred pounds for the two properties. The money simply went to the Crown and everyone was happy.'

'Oh . . .' I wasn't sure what to make of this. 'So it was easier and better for you that way?'

'It might have cost more than the property was worth to fight the case,' Joe said. 'These things can take years. I thought it was the best way out and I was going to give you the profit I made on Fred's house. I was planning on having it done up a bit to make it sell better, perhaps put a flush toilet in and maybe a bathroom.' He paused for a moment, then, 'I reckon it should be worth a hundred or a bit more when it's finished – but the offer is only for seventy-five. I turned it down, but now I'm not sure what to do. I've been told the offer came from a man who owns a lot of property in the lane.'

'And you're wondering . . .' I stared at him. 'Maggie said that there was a tale about our houses being pulled down . . .'

Joe nodded. 'I don't know for sure, but I think that may be the reason Fred was murdered. He was so stubborn, Bridget. He wouldn't have sold his house whatever they said to him. I offered to buy the shop in the first place, but he didn't want the money. He said he had no use for it. He was a long time making up his mind to let me repair it and take out a lease, and he only did that because we became friends. I liked him and I used to take him a bottle of whisky. He told me about his wife and son dying of diphtheria and I think he trusted me.'

'He must have done or he wouldn't have given you his box. He must have been afraid something would happen, Joe, and he thought you could take care of things.' I stared at him. 'But why would someone murder him because he wouldn't sell his house? What was so important about one house?'

'If one person – or a syndicate set up by powerful men – owns all the houses in an area they control what happens. They can either put all the rents up high, or if there's a slum clearance on the cards, they stand to make a lot of money by selling the land the old houses stand on. It can be big business, Bridget. Think about what happened when they cleared all the slums to make way for the docks.'

'But that's so unfair! Why should people be turned out of their homes so that someone can make money and why should you have to sell the house for less than it is worth?'

'It's just one of the rackets that go on all the time,' Joe said. 'Money and power can be corrupt in the wrong hands, Bridget. I may have no choice but to sell, but I shall try to push the price up. I don't see why you should lose out just because someone thinks he has a right to do what he wants.'

'The money would be useful,' I said. 'But it doesn't matter, Joe. You and Mary are more important. Don't do anything foolish for my sake. Really, I don't care about the money.'

'I knew you would say that.' He smiled at me. 'You must know that I care for you, Bridget? You are very important to me. Whatever I do, I shan't put you or my family at risk.'

'You and Mary mean a lot to me – Alice too, of course.'

Joe hesitated. I sensed that he wanted to say more, but he held back whatever it was and looked rueful.

'Whatever I get from the sale of the house will be yours. I've got my shop at a bargain price and Fred wanted you to have all of it.'

'You've already done too much for me, Joe. You bought the house, the money is yours.'

'When you need it, you have only to ask,' he said. 'I've done very little so far, Bridget. One day I hope I shall be able to do much more.'

I was thoughtful as I began to walk back to the shop. What would I say if Joe asked me to marry him and what would happen when Jamie and Mary got married?

Joe would want to come home. His hopes of buying a better house were dashed for the moment. Would he try again or would he find another way of finding space for Tommy?

If I married Joe, we would share a room and that meant there would be room for my brother. It would solve the problem, at least until we had children of our own.

But, was I prepared to marry Joe just for the sake of a home?

'Well, well – wot 'ave we 'ere?'

The hateful voice broke into my thoughts. I whirled round, feeling chilled as I found myself staring at Harry Wright. It was a long time since I'd thought of him, but panic swept over me as I recalled his attack on me the night Lainie left home.

He grinned at me in that cocky way of his, obviously sensing my fear. 'Don't run away, Bridget. I've been waiting fer this fer a long time.'

'What do you mean?'

'I've seen yer before,' he said, leering at me. 'But she's always wiv yer, that bleedin' Joe Robinson's sister. Just you wait . . . one of these nights I'll catch yer alone, and then we'll take up where we left off.'

The horrible look of triumph in his eyes left me in no doubt of what he meant, and I felt chills trickle down my spine.

'If you touch me again, I'll tell Jamie.'

'I ain't afraid of 'im – gone soft 'e 'as,' Harry said. 'Nor that bleedin' Joe Robinson. 'Sides, if yer were goin' ter tell you'd 'ave done it by now.'

'Stay away,' I said, holding up my hand as he reached out to grab me. I backed away from him, my heart racing. It wasn't likely that he would try anything much in broad daylight in a busy street, but my stomach was churning with fright. 'Stay away from me or you'll be sorry!'

I yelled the words at him, then turned and ran blindly down the street, wanting to get as far away from him as possible, but in my panic I bumped into someone and almost fell. I smothered a gasp as a man caught my arm to steady me.

'What is wrong, Miss O'Rourke?'

I was breathing hard, my chest tight as I gave a little cry and then looked up. As I saw who it was my fear eased and I took a deep breath, telling myself to calm down.

'Someone frightened me.'

'That man?' Mr Maitland looked towards Harry Wright, who was still standing there grinning at me. He had known I was scared and he was enjoying his triumph. 'What did he do to you?'

'He . . . he threatened to come after me when I'm alone.' I wasn't sure why it all spilled out, except that I was upset, both by Joe's revelations earlier and Harry's sudden reappearance in my life. 'He . . . he attacked me once before. He tried to . . . but someone came and he ran off.' I blushed and stopped abruptly.

Philip Maitland's eyes narrowed. 'He tried to abuse you, is that what you are saying, Miss O'Rourke?'

'Yes . . .' I was hot all over now and embarrassed. What on earth had made me tell him? 'I've never told anyone else. I was afraid people might think I had encouraged him. And I didn't.'

'I am certain you didn't – a nice girl like you, Miss O'Rourke. Does this man have a name?'

'Yes, but you mustn't go to the police. My brother would go after him if he knew.'

'Just leave this to me. His name was . . . ?'

'Harry Wright . . . but please don't go to the police, sir. They won't do anything and it will just cause trouble. I shouldn't have said anything. I was upset, that's all.'

'Mr Wright will receive a polite warning from my solicitors. I believe we can make him think before he upsets you again, my dear.'

I blushed furiously at the tone of his voice. 'You – you've made me feel better simply by being here. I wish you would just forget what I told you. I was startled, frightened, but I shall be all right now.'

'Then of course I shall,' he said. 'We shall not mention the matter again. And now perhaps you would like to sell me some of your beautiful roses?'

'I should love to,' I said, thinking how nice he was and what a pity it was that there weren't more men around like him. 'Have you been pleased with the arrangements for your hotel, sir?'

'Very pleased,' he said and there was a flicker of amusement in his eyes. 'In fact I am going to ask Miss Robinson if she will do all the flowers for my wedding. We shall have the reception at the hotel and I shall want something extra special. She may have to come to the hotel that day. Do you think she would agree?'

'I should think so,' I said. 'But you must ask her yourself, sir.'

'Of course,' he said. He looked at me with gentle concern. 'Are you feeling better now?'

'Yes, much better. You've been so very kind. May I ask, when are you getting married?'

He nodded and we went into the shop together, talking about his wedding and the special flowers he required.

We were busy in the shop all that day and I managed to forget about the incident with Harry Wright until I was undressing that evening, and then it suddenly hit me and I felt the sickness whirl in my stomach. I sat on the edge of the bed shivering and clutching my arms about myself. The first time he'd attacked me it had been a shock and I hadn't really been frightened until the last moment, but I'd had time to think about what had happened since then and it had made me realize what a lucky escape I'd had that night. If it happened again I might not be so lucky.

I felt as if a heavy weight was pressing down on me and I wondered if perhaps I ought to tell someone about my fears –

Joe or Jamie. The trouble was that they wouldn't simply let it go. One or the other of them would go after Harry, and that would lead to trouble.

I didn't want Jamie to get into trouble with the police now that everything was going so well for him and Mary. And perhaps if I were careful nothing would happen. I would simply have to make sure I didn't go anywhere late at night on my own.

My mind travelled on to what Joe had told me that morning and the threat in that letter we had found in the shop. It seemed wrong to me that anyone could have that much power, and I saw the Big Man as a huge fat spider sitting in the middle of his web, his tentacles stretching into our lives, controlling us and so many others.

Maggie and my other friends were living in fear of losing their homes, just because he might make some money from pulling down the houses. And perhaps he had killed Fred . . . but no, he wouldn't have done it himself. One of his thugs would have done that.

I was suddenly angry, my fear vanishing as I thought of what I would like to do to the man who had threatened Joe and probably killed an old man simply because he wouldn't sell his house.

Of course, I couldn't be sure that this was what had happened, but it seemed to fit. And then I thought about Lainie and what had happened to her and my anger was so fierce that it tasted like gall on my tongue. And there was Rosie, too. She had been beaten to death.

'This is fun,' Tommy said as he ate the ice-cream Joe had bought for him. The wind was whipping across the beach and though it was still summer it was cold, but that didn't matter. I was almost bursting with happiness, and I could hardly believe we were all here together. Matron's letter saying that we could take my brother out for a day had come like a blessing from heaven, making me feel better than I had for a couple of weeks. 'What we goin' to do next, Joe?'

'We'll find a café and have a pot of tea and fish and chips,' Joe said and grinned at him. 'What do you think of that, young Tommy? It's a bit cool out here for me. You're tougher than me, young 'un.'

Tommy laughed in delight. He had taken a shine to Joe, the two of them hitting it off instantly, and all the constraint and bitterness of my last visit might never have been.

'Matron says fresh air is good for us,' he said. 'She opens all the windows wide. Jimmy and me thought she was tryin' to do us in.'

'What happened to your friend?' I asked.

'He went to stay with a family last month. They say he ain't infectious no more. He'll be able to go home by Christmas.'

'So he didn't die then?'

'Nah – he were having me on for a bit of a laugh,' Tommy said and looked at me sheepishly. 'I'm sorry, Bridget. I shouldn't have said them things to you when you told me about Mam.'

'You were upset.'

'Not over Mam. I thought you had left me here to die – that I was too much trouble to you . . .'

'How could you ever think such a thing?' I asked, my eyes stinging with tears. 'You know I love the very bones of you.'

'Jamie sent me a letter and told me all you'd done for Mam and that you were upset I was stuck here. I know he was right, Bridget.'

'Of course I care about you,' I said and put my arm about his shoulders as he looked up at me. 'I love you, Tommy, and it hurt me that I had to leave you here. As soon as they say you can come home I want you to be with me.'

'Jamie says I can go with him and Mary if I like,' Tommy said. 'But I'd rather be with you and Joe – if that's all right?' He looked at Joe anxiously. 'I wouldn't be a lot of bother.'

'You're always welcome in my house,' Joe told him. 'Now let's get in out of this wind. It's bleedin' cold on the East Coast even in summer.'

'You're a softie,' Tommy said and grinned at him, sticking out his chest and breathing deeply. 'You want Matron round you for a few days.'

'Well, young imp, we'll have to see if I'm soft or not when it comes to your education. I shall expect you to do well in school and find a good job when you leave.'

'I'd like to be a doctor,' Tommy said. 'But I don't suppose I'm clever enough.'

'I think you might be,' I said. I had noticed such a difference in him. He was bright, eager and he spoke so much better than he had a few months ago. His stay at the sanatorium had done him good in more ways than one. 'We'll see what you want to do when the time comes.'

'It ain't so bad here when you get used to it,' Tommy said. 'They give us lessons and show us how to make things – weaving baskets and sticking wooden racks together. And I'm not infectious now. I'll be coming home in the spring.'

'I can't wait for you to come home, darlin'.'

'I'm hungry and frozen to the bone,' Joe said. 'Let's go and have them fish and chips!'

'He seems cheerful,' Joe remarked as we sat on board the train carrying us back towards London. 'I never knew he said unkind things to you, Bridget.'

'I didn't tell you – or anyone. There was no point. I knew he was upset and I hated leaving him there.'

'But that was the best thing for him. You can see it has done him good being there, Bridget.'

'Yes, I saw that today.' I smiled at him. 'Thank you for today, Joe. He really enjoyed himself.'

'We'll come again as soon as we can.'

'Yes,' I agreed. 'I spoke to Matron. She says he will probably stay with a family for a month or so just to get used to being with people again, and then go back for more tests. If the disease has really gone, they may let him come home sooner than he thinks.'

'Well, we shall find room for him. We'll have to see how

things work out. Mary and Jamie are going to get married next month and I'll be moving back to the house. I'll have Mary's room. Yours is bigger and we could always put a little bed in there for Tommy until I find us something bigger.'

'You haven't heard any more about Fred's house I suppose?'

'I told them I wouldn't go any lower than a hundred pounds.' Joe frowned. 'So far I haven't had a reply.'

'If you meant it – about the hundred pounds –' I took a deep breath – 'I might be able to buy a house of my own somewhere.'

'Ma would be upset if you left us,' Joe said. 'She says you're a real help to her in the house, Bridget.' He hesitated, then reached out to take my hand in his. 'You could think about marrying me, Bridget?'

'Oh, Joe . . .' I didn't take my hand from his, but he sensed my hesitation and let it go. 'I don't know.'

'I shouldn't have asked,' he said. 'I know you wanted time to think about things for a while and I understand you're not in love with me. I'm offering you affection and a home, Bridget. I love you. I think you know that, but I wouldn't ask more than affection from you.'

'If I married you it would be a proper marriage,' I told him. 'I want children one day, Joe, and with me marriage is for life.'

'But you still want to think about it?'

'For a while, yes. I'm sorry. I know it isn't the answer you want.'

'I'm a patient man,' he said. 'I shan't rush you, Bridget. I want you to be happy and if there is someone else . . .'

'There was,' I replied, looking into his eyes. 'There was someone I ought to have married, Joe, but it didn't happen. It can't happen now because he has a wife and child.'

'I see.' Joe nodded and looked sad. 'I'm sorry, Bridget.'

'No, don't be. It's over. I've accepted that, but I still need a little more time before I'm ready to marry anyone.'

'Then I shan't ask you again just yet, but I'll be waiting if you change your mind.'

I went over to see Maggie that Sunday afternoon. She was pleased to see me and we hugged as she pulled me into her kitchen and looked me over.

'My, you do look posh,' she said. 'Where did you get that blouse? It must be pure silk and that's a lovely skirt, Bridget. Real good stuff.'

'The blouse was Mam's,' I told her. 'I don't think she ever wore it, just kept it wrapped in tissue in the drawer. I've been able to make myself a few things, Maggie, and Alice Robinson made this skirt for me. She's very good with her sewing machine. Alice made Mary and me similar ones for in the shop.'

'You wear that smart skirt for work?' Maggie was amazed. 'What else have you been doin' with yourself then?'

'I've been to night school a few times recently. I've been taking lessons in bookkeeping and I've had a go at typing, but I don't like that as much as I thought I would. Alice gets me books from the library and I read a bit in the evenings and Joe takes us all to the theatre now and then on a Saturday night. It's mostly the music halls, but we went to a big theatre once and saw Lillie Langtry in a play . . .'

'The Jersey Lily?' Maggie said and stared at me. 'My oh my, it will be tuppence to know you soon!'

'You know me better than that,' I said. 'I'll never forget you, Maggie.'

'I was just havin' a laugh, me darlin',' she said. 'I miss you so much, Bridget. They've left your house empty, you know. It ain't the only one either. Old Mr James died last month and they ain't let his house again – just boarded up the windows. Mind you, that was in state, but it just shows.'

She sounded so odd that I looked at her. 'You think it's true about them pulling these houses down then?'

'I reckon so,' she said. 'Mick says they'll wait until they can turn us all out and then they will level this lane and a couple more all the way down to the river.'

'What about the brewery?'

'I heard as Dawson had been offered to sell it,' Maggie said.

'Ernie Cole told me he was in a fearful temper over it, said the price was too cheap and he was damned if he would sell for that. And Maude Brown had a letter from a solicitor offering to buy her house, but she says she's not goin' to sell whatever they offer her. Mick says if the government want the scheme to go ahead, they will probably put an order on it and she'll have to sell whether she likes it or not.'

'That's not fair!'

'There ain't much fair in this world, Bridget. Mick says it's what happens and he's heard quite a bit about the scheme at work. Some bigwig is pressin' for it, he reckons. It were turned down once, but now it looks as though it might go ahead.'

'I think it is probably true then and they will pull the houses down when they can. What will you do then, Maggie?'

She shrugged. 'Mick is all for going back to the old country. Says he'll find a job on a farm.' She pulled a face. 'I'm not sure I shall like that, but we'll see when it comes to it.' She hesitated and then looked at me. 'Have you heard about Ernie and Grace?'

'What about them? I don't hear anything unless you tell me, Maggie.'

'She's gone off and left him,' Maggie said. 'Took stuff that belonged to Jean Cole and left little Kathy with them. Jean is savage over it, though she loves the baby. She says Kathy will be better off without her mother, but Ernie was looking a bit down in the mouth.'

'Well, it's very rough on him and his mother, especially if . . .'

Maggie nodded. 'That's what most of us think. Ernie got took in good and proper, but Mick says he knew what he was doin' when he went with the girl and it's his own fault.'

'Yes, I suppose it is,' I said, 'but it seems hard on Jean, doesn't it? She's got stuck with the job of looking after the baby.'

'Yes, that's what she says. It would be different if Grace

207

had died, because Ernie might have married again, but he's stuck – no wife and no prospect of one either.'

'He's not a Catholic, Maggie. He might be able to get a divorce.'

'If he could find her and if he could afford to pay a lawyer,' Maggie said. 'I can't see him doin' either. No, he'll probably wait a few years to make sure she isn't coming back, then find someone to move in with him. There's a good few would jump at the chance – married or not. 'Sides, if they move away who will know he's not a widower?'

'Ernie will,' I said and frowned. 'I suppose it wouldn't matter to some . . .'

'But it would to you?' She sighed. 'That's what I thought. You'd best settle down with that nice Joe Robinson and forget him, lass. I know you thought something of Ernie once, but if he hadn't been a fool he could have waited and married you after your mam died.'

Mary was full of ideas for Mr Maitland's wedding flowers and we spent a part of every day planning the various arrangements we were going to make.

I usually helped with them these days because we were busier than ever and Mary seemed to get tired. The weather had become cooler all at once and I noticed she seemed to have the sniffles a few days before the big event.

'I must not be ill,' she said, a desperate look in her eyes. 'I can't let him down for his wedding, Bridget. He's brought such a lot of trade to this shop.'

'We were lucky he happened by that day,' I agreed. 'Don't worry, Mary. If the worst happens I'll go to the hotel alone. Jamie can help me carry all the stuff in, and I'll make any last minute alterations to the arrangements when they're in the various rooms.'

'Yes, I know you wouldn't let me down,' she said, 'but I'm looking forward to seeing his hotel myself.'

'Well, don't worry,' I said. 'You will probably be fine.'

I spoke too soon. The next morning Mary woke with a

raging fever and we had to have the doctor to her. He said that she had a nasty cold, but that she would be all right if she stayed in bed.

'I have to go to work,' she said to Alice when she thanked the doctor and said Mary would do as he advised. 'We've got so much work to do – and Bridget can't manage the shop alone.

'I can manage for the next couple of days,' I told her. 'If you're feeling better by the next day you can come down and give me a hand with the more intricate arrangements, but I don't think it would be a good idea for you to come to the hotel. Just leave that to me this time, Mary.'

She was reluctant to agree, but there wasn't much choice. Even if she had tried to get out of bed, she wouldn't have been able to manage it.

I felt a little odd walking to work on my own. We were usually there by half past eight, but I left a little earlier so that I could have things ready when the customers came in. It was going to take time to make all the frames for the arrangements and I might even have to stay late in the evening, but I wouldn't think about that. I needn't be scared as Harry Wright hadn't bothered me since that day I'd seen him in the market. I wondered if Mr Maitland had asked his lawyer to send Harry a letter warning him to leave me alone, but I thought he probably hadn't as I'd asked him not to.

A few customers came in for bunches of flowers that morning, but I was able to concentrate on the work for Mr Maitland's wedding most of the morning.

I didn't go out for lunch, but sat and munched at the sandwiches Alice had packed for me and thought about what I was going to do that afternoon. I was annoyed when the doorbell went, realizing that I'd forgotten to lock up for my lunch break, but as I looked at the woman who entered, I gave a gasp of surprise.

'Lainie . . .' I said and sprang up to go and meet her. 'How did you know I was here – and where have you been?'

'One question at a time,' she said and gave me an odd look.

'I hardly dared to come and see you. Are you mad at me for what I did?'

'I was! I could've hit you that day, Lainie. I had to ask Jamie for the money for Mam's funeral.'

'Do you blame me for that?' she asked. 'Maggie thinks I caused it. She didn't want to tell me where you were, but I persuaded her in the end.'

'No, I don't blame you,' I said. 'Mam was ill. It could have happened at any time. The doctor told me so, but the quarrel may have brought it on sooner.'

She looked ashamed of herself. 'I was feeling so wretched that morning, Bridget. I'd been livin' rough all week after they threw me out . . .'

'Why didn't you come straight home?'

'I don't know,' she admitted. 'I just felt so miserable, and then you started on about the way I looked . . .'

'I just wanted to help you. It isn't like you to let yourself go, Lainie.' She was looking slim and pretty again, her hair freshly washed and her dress clean. 'You had the baby then?'

'Yes . . .' She took a deep breath. 'I had it adopted, Bridget. I could never have loved it – and that was another reason I cleared off, apart from the fact that Mam told me to . . .'

'You knew I would tell you to keep it?'

Lainie nodded. 'You wouldn't understand, Bridget, but I should have felt unclean every time I looked at it.'

'Was your child a girl or a boy?'

'A boy, but it's no use you thinkin' you'd take it on. The adoption people wouldn't let you have him, and he's gone to a good home.'

'I'm sorry, Lainie.'

'I'm not. I can start fresh now, and I'm goin' to keep straight this time, Bridget. I've found myself a job up west in a dress shop and I love it. It's like being in another world. The owner doesn't know I've had a child and she likes me – says she'll make me a senior salesgirl if I keep on as I am.'

'I'm glad for you, Lainie,' I said and then hesitated. 'Have you heard from Hans?'

'No . . .' Her face had gone white. 'I don't want to see him – I just couldn't, Bridget. I have to forget and find a new life.'

'I thought you might feel differently now.'

'No. I just came to give you this . . .' She took something out of her jacket pocket and handed it to me. I saw that it was Fred's pendant and I slipped it into my pocket, glad to have it back. 'I shouldn't have taken that. I'm sorry. I thought I might need to sell it. But your money's gone. I needed it.'

'I would have given you the money.'

'Well, I can't pay you back, but I wanted to give the pendant back.' She looked round. 'This is a nice shop. What are all those wire things at the back?'

'I'm making the frames for the flower arrangements for a wedding up west,' I said. 'It's at a big hotel and Mr Maitland is one of . . .' I stopped as I saw the colour drain from her face. 'Is something wrong, Lainie? You're not ill?'

'Maitland . . .' she whispered and her eyes were dark with remembered horror. 'Is that . . . Philip Maitland? The one who used to visit Bridie Macpherson?'

'Yes. I met him once coming out of there and . . . Who is he, Lainie? Why are you looking like that?'

'He . . . he's the one,' she said in a hoarse voice that I could hardly hear. 'Be careful, Bridget. He seems so nice . . . but don't trust him, not for a minute. You don't know how evil he is.'

I stared at her, feeling a mixture of disbelief and horror. She couldn't be talking about the man I knew. It wasn't possible!

'Are you sure, Lainie? He's a gentleman . . .'

'You think I don't know that?' she asked and her eyes were bright with anger now. 'Why do you think I fell for his lies? He seems so kind and generous but cross him and you will see what he is really like.'

'Lainie . . .' I could hardly believe her. 'He wants us to finish off the flowers at his hotel. I'm goin' there . . .'

'Don't trust him,' she said. 'I'm tellin' you, Bridget. That man has his fingers in so many pies. Do you know why he was after tryin' to charm round Bridie? He wanted to buy her hotel, but he didn't offer her a fair price and she said he got nasty with her when she refused, but I didn't believe her. I thought she was just jealous because he preferred me to her. I knew she fancied him, but he didn't look at her. He likes them young, Bridget.'

'He wanted to buy her hotel?' The cold was spreading right through me. Surely this couldn't be true? 'Did he happen to mention any other property he owned in the area?'

She shrugged carelessly. 'I don't know what he owns and I don't care. I just know he's dangerous.'

'Oh, Lainie,' I said. 'I am so sorry for what he did to you. I know you didn't want to tell me who he was, but I'm glad you did. I shall be very careful when we go to the hotel.'

'You're never still going to go?' she asked and looked upset. 'I only told you because I thought he might be after you, too. Be careful of him, Bridget. Don't let him hurt you the way he did me.'

'Don't worry,' I said. 'I might have been in danger if you hadn't happened to come today, but I shall know now. And yes, I am going. Mary can't do the flowers because she's ill, and this means a lot to her.'

But I hadn't told Lainie the truth. I had other reasons why I intended to keep my appointment with Mr Maitland . . .

I brooded about what Lainie had told me after she'd gone and the suspicion lingered like a crawling maggot in my brain throughout that evening. How could Mr Maitland be the man who had tempted and then forced my sister into prostitution? How could he have had her beaten and raped, and then sold her to other men? It seemed like a nightmare; a violent, improbable dream that I would wake from at any moment, yet in a strange, sinister way it made sense of so many things. It made me wonder why he had gone out of his way to help Mary and me.

A man who was capable of such evil just didn't do things like that out of kindness. What did he want from us? There had to be a reason behind his frequent visits to the shop – or was I letting my imagination run away with me?

Something else was haunting me. Someone had murdered Fred and ransacked his home. Joe had told me that Fred had refused an offer for his house . . . and then there was what had happened to Rosie. Had she been beaten so savagely so that she couldn't tell me the name of the man who had taken Lainie away?

Surely it wasn't possible that these incidents were all connected? It made me feel sick to imagine what kind of a person could do these things. It was all so horrible.

Yet if Philip Maitland was the Big Man . . . No, that was ridiculous! It couldn't be true. No one had ever known who the Big Man was. It was unlikely that I could just stumble across the truth. But it made sense. A man who could force Lainie into prostitution after enticing her away from Bridie's hotel could easily be involved in all kinds of criminal activities.

Now that I thought about it, the clues were there and had been there under my nose all the time. I hadn't suspected anything, but why should I? I should have questioned more! Why would a gentleman like Mr Maitland visit the Sailor's Rest unless he had business in the area, and what kind of business might that be? It could have been at the docks of course, and Lainie could have the wrong man, but that was too much of a coincidence. It wasn't possible that two men of the same name had visited the hotel at the same time.

Everything was slotting so neatly into the puzzle that it was unreal. I wasn't sure what to do about it. Joe ought to be told of my suspicions, but at the moment that was all they were. Once I spoke them out loud they would be real – and what then?

If Jamie discovered what had happened to Lainie he would go after the man who had so nearly destroyed her, and that would ruin any chance he had of happiness with Mary.

Joe would handle things differently. He thought about things for a while before he acted. Joe was the one I should tell, but what could he do? If Mr Maitland really was the Big Man he was well protected. And if Joe went up against him he might be in trouble himself.

What was I thinking? Was I expecting Joe to take some kind

213

of revenge? My own thoughts shocked me. Was I planning murder now? Yes, there was a part of me that wanted that – an eye for an eye . . .

I remembered the vengeful thoughts that had kept me awake the night Lainie first told me of her ordeal.

I had wanted the man who hurt Lainie dead when she had told me, and I still wanted it, but if he was a criminal and a murderer, the law should be able to punish him. The thought rushed into my mind that hanging was too good for him! Bloody thoughts of torture and inflicting pain were filling my head. Yes, yes, I wanted him dead! And I wanted him to suffer . . .

Yet it would be better if the law dealt with him, because that way it would expose the whole corrupt empire he ruled over. There was no proof, of course. No proof that any of my suspicions were true. The police could say Lainie was lying and that the rest was just in my mind. Unless I could find something at his hotel . . .

Fifteen

'Are you tired, Bridget?' Joe looked at me with concern as he carried the bits and pieces I would need out to his van. He'd bought one of the new-fangled things with an engine he'd told me about and I was a bit nervous of riding in it because it popped and banged when it started, but he said it was faster and better than horses. 'You look pale and there are shadows under your eyes. I know you've had a lot to do, and Mary hasn't been able to help you much . . .'

'It isn't the work,' I told him. 'I've loved doing it, Joe. I've had a couple of sleepless nights. I've got something on my mind, that's all.'

'Anything you want to tell me?'

'Not for the moment.' I had lain awake all night, my thoughts going round and round as I tried to decide what I ought to do, without success. 'Don't worry, Joe. I'll tell you when I'm ready. I promise.'

I did desperately want to tell him; this secret fear was like an ache in my guts, nagging at me all the time, but I had to see what I could discover first. I had to be sure I wasn't imagining it all.

My stomach was churning as we set out that morning. It was very early and most of our flowers were fresh off the milk train, ordered for the wedding from specialist growers outside London. Some of the arrangements – the usual ones for the lobby and guests' rooms – had been made up the previous day and kept in the cool overnight; the other expensive wedding flowers would be arranged once we got to the hotel.

It was a two o'clock wedding which gave me plenty of

215

time to make sure everything was perfect for the reception at three.

When we arrived at the hotel, I asked for Mr Maitland and was told by a rather snooty receptionist that he would not be in until much later that morning.

'You can use a room at the back of the kitchen. We can't have people running all over the hotel on such an important day.'

'Some of the arrangements are too large and delicate to be moved,' I said. 'Particularly those for the private lounge and Mr Maitland's own apartments. That is why he particularly requested I should come and do them here – to make sure they are perfect.'

'Well, really,' she said and looked annoyed. 'I can't be expected to supervise you the whole time. I have far too much work.'

'I assure you I am very respectable,' I told her. 'All you have to do is to let me into the various rooms and leave me to get on.'

'I shall come with you,' she said. 'You will do the dining room and the lounge first, and then I'll take you up to Mr Maitland's suite.

'Whatever suits you,' I said carelessly.

I desperately wanted to be left alone in the private suite. It was probably the only chance I would ever have of finding proof of my suspicions – if there was anything to find. It wouldn't be easy. If he had shielded his identity successfully for so long then he wasn't the careless type.

To insist that I must work alone would have made the receptionist more suspicious. I could only hope that she would grow tired of watching me.

It took me nearly three hours to finish the arrangements for the dining parlour and downstairs reception rooms where the guests were to be entertained, and when the snooty desk clerk came back she looked impressed.

'Well, I must say these are beautiful,' she said. 'Those banks of white lilies are spectacular, and they smell wonderful.

I've had the porter take everything you requested up to Mr Maitland's private suite. I shall take you up and stay with you.'

She was so pompous and sure of herself. I wondered what she would do if I told her she could be working for a murderer.

'Have you worked here long?' I asked as we went upstairs together. 'This is a nice place, isn't it?'

'We only have the best people here,' she said. 'I don't suppose you've ever been in a hotel like this.'

'No, I haven't,' I agreed. 'I think you are lucky to be employed here, but I expect it takes a lot of hard work to please someone like Mr Maitland. Is he difficult to please?'

'He is most particular about who he employs,' she said. 'Only the best will do for Mr Maitland.' She looked at me consideringly for a moment. 'I suppose you are good at what you do. Your flowers are better than we used to have from our last supplier.'

'Thank you. We try to please, but arranging a few flowers can't compare with what you do here. It must be a huge responsibility looking after the guests and making sure things run smoothly.'

'Well yes, it is,' she said and I could see she was mellowing slightly. 'Here we are then. How long will it take you to finish up here?'

'These arrangements are the most important of all,' I said. 'I should think an hour or two. I don't mind how long I spend on them as long as they are right. They have to be perfect. Mr Maitland was most particular about that. You know he and his wife are spending the night here in the suite before they go to Paris.'

'Yes . . . but surely . . .'

She looked horrified at having to spend up to two hours supervising me. I started work immediately, not wanting her to think I was trying to waste time, but I deliberated over every flower, although I knew exactly where each one ought to go.

As I worked, I was taking stock of my surroundings, thinking about where I might search if I did get the chance. It was a lovely room with high ceilings and a charming decor in shades of green, cream and gold. The furniture was all antique as far as I could tell, and I thought valuable. I had never seen such pretty cabinets; they were made of a pale wood that looked almost satiny and the front panels had pictures of birds or musical instruments inlaid in different woods. The tables and chairs were all elegant and very fine, and it looked as if it had been furnished to please a lady.

'Aren't the cabinets pretty,' I said to my watchful companion. 'I've never seen anything quite like them.'

'That's because they come from France. Mr Maitland had this room refurbished to the highest standards quite recently.' She glanced at the little silver watch pinned to her dress uneasily. 'How long before you finish in here?'

'Oh, another half an hour at least. I've still got flowers for the bedrooms.' There were two bedrooms, both of which were to have flowers, which I thought a little odd. Surely they only needed one on their wedding night?

'I ought to go down now. There's so much to do . . .'

'I could lock up and bring the key to you.'

'No – I'll come back in about fifteen minutes. Please try to be finished.'

'I mustn't hurry or I might spoil the flowers. These were very expensive. Mr Maitland wouldn't be pleased if they were damaged.'

She gave a sniff of disgust but didn't say anything more as she went out. As soon as I was sure she had gone, I went over to the desk I had picked as being the only place in this room where I might find something private.

None of the drawers were locked and most were empty. Obviously, it had been provided for Mrs Maitland's use when she stayed here. I knew that they had a large house in the country and that the suite was only for when she came up to town.

I rushed back to place a few flowers into my last arrangements, working at a feverish pace, then I carried one into the first bedroom, which was beautiful and had lots of lace everywhere. Clearly this was for Mrs Maitland and I didn't waste time on it. My nerves were jangling as I carried the last arrangement through into the second bedroom, which was more masculine and furnished in deep colours of crimson and gold.

I placed my flowers and took stock quickly. A large dressing chest in dark mahogany, two bedside chests, and a desk were the most likely places to hide something . . . but what?

I had no clear idea of what I was looking for as I made a quick, careful search of the bedside chests and found nothing that made me think it might be a clue.

What did I need? Papers . . . A secret accounting book perhaps? Even a letter with Fred Pearce's name on it. It might not be enough proof to get him arrested, but it would be enough for me.

I decided to try the desk next. The top drawer was locked. This was more like it! A tingle of excitement went down my spine as I hunted for a key, first in the drawers on the right-hand side. I found stationery, pens, ink, a sheet of postage stamps and various things that did not interest me, but no key or account books.

Turning to the drawers on the other side, I slid open the top one and my blood froze as I saw the pistol lying there. It was small and shiny and deadly; I stared at it in fascination for some seconds. Why would anyone keep that in their bedroom unless they thought they might have a use for it one day?

It was a moment or two before I noticed that the pistol was lying on top of a letter from a firm of solicitors, and as I moved the pistol with the tip of one finger I saw that it concerned a house in Farthing Lane.

It was true! It was all true. I hadn't conjured up a fairy tale in my mind. The sickening proof that my suspicions were at least partially true rushed over me with such force that my head reeled. It was if I were turned to stone, my feet fastened to the floor.

If this much was as I'd thought it might be, then the rest

would probably follow. The Big Man had sent his bully-boys in to frighten Fred into selling his property, and the result had been murder. He was probably behind the beating that had caused Rosie to become little more than a cabbage as well. What else was he capable of? How many other people had he had killed for his own ends?

The sickness washed over me in waves as I struggled to take in all that my mind was telling me was true. Surely I had to be wrong! It was too horrible to accept . . . Too frightening.

It was my sense of shock and horror that made me slow to react when I heard something from the next room. Even as I started to push the drawer shut it was too late. Philip Maitland was standing in the doorway staring at me. I swallowed hard as I saw his eyes narrow in suspicion.

'I – I was looking for a pin,' I said. 'For your buttonhole . . .'

My excuse sounded stupid even to my own ears, and my heart was beginning to race wildly, thudding against my chest so hard that it sounded like drums in my ears. He came slowly towards me, his gaze moving towards the desk, where the drawer was still slightly open. I felt sick with fear as he looked at me, eyes narrowed in a way that made my legs feel as if they would give way.

'And of course you found this,' he said, pulling the drawer wide to reveal the pistol. A shiver went through me as his eyes seemed to go cold. I had never seen him like this and I remembered what Lainie had told me. 'Or was it the letter you were looking for, Bridget?' His voice had a sinister edge to it as he used my first name. 'I have wondered how long it would take you to make the connection.'

'What do you mean?' I looked at him, trying to appear ignorant of his meaning.

'Come, my dear, please do not insult my intelligence – or your own.' His smile was terrifying. 'I have admired your good sense. It amazed me that two sisters could be so different. She told you, of course, and now, finally, you have begun to wonder about me. I am only surprised that it took you so long. I enjoyed testing you, and it was necessary to keep in touch so that I would know when you began to understand.'

'Told me what?' My mouth was dry and I was wondering if a dash to the door would get me out of this. 'I'm not sure . . . ?'

'But of course you are, that's why you have been searching my rooms. I admire your spirit, Bridget. Knowing what I did to Lainie, you must know what I could do to you if I chose?'

'I . . . I wasn't sure,' I said as I met his mocking gaze proudly now. 'I didn't know it was you until recently, though I knew some beast had done unspeakable things to her.'

'Such passion, Bridget? I have thought for a long time that I chose the wrong sister. Was what I did so very terrible? She was a whore, and all I did was put her to work – that is what she is good at, whoring. Now if it had been you . . .'

I reacted instinctively, my hand shooting out to slap his face, but he caught my wrist, his fingers biting deep into my flesh as he jerked my arm up and spun me round so that my arm was behind my back. The pain almost made me cry out, but I bit it back, determined not to show fear.

'It would never have been me,' I said, panting as he increased the pressure. He was hurting me and I knew that he could probably break my arm if he wished. He would surely seek to punish me? He couldn't let me go knowing what I knew now. 'I wouldn't have been stupid enough to listen to your false promises.'

'Oh, but they wouldn't have been false for you,' he said and then I felt his warm breath on my neck and his mouth against my skin. 'You smell wonderful . . . better than any perfume Clarissa uses. But then my wife-to-be is useful in other ways. She does not need to feed my base passions, but you do it just by defying me. I have thought for some time that I would enjoy knowing you better.' He kissed the back of my neck. 'You do understand what I mean by knowing?' He laughed as I made a sound of disgust and renewed my efforts to get free. 'Quite useless, my dear. How do you make yourself smell so good, Bridget? Or is it simply you? Is it your flesh . . . Such firm smooth flesh I'll swear—'

'Take you filthy hands off me!' I cried as his free hand encircled my breast, squeezing it. His only reaction was to squeeze harder so that it hurt. 'Let me go, damn you! You're an evil monster and I would like to see you hang.'

'Oh, but there's no chance of that,' he said, jerking my arm a little harder. 'You see, I was never there, Bridget. A dozen people will testify that the night Pearce was murdered I was at a dinner party with several rather important people. When Rosie was beaten senseless for poking her nose into my business, I was at a dance attended by royalty. I have power and influence, you see.'

'But you sent those bullies to ransack Fred's house and you had Rosie beaten . . .'

'That is something you can never prove. Just because I like you, I shall set your mind at rest and tell you that I am all the things you imagine, and perhaps some that even your fertile mind cannot.' He laughed huskily, gloating in his triumph, so sure that I could never touch him. 'Have you heard from Mr Wright lately? But of course you haven't. He won't come near you again in a hurry. You should thank me, Bridget. I sent my bullies – those same men you so heartily dislike – to teach him a little lesson . . . Wasn't that nice of me? I could be so good to you . . . Or not, as I please.' He licked at the back of my neck, making me shudder with revulsion.

'I could believe you capable of anything! You'll hang for what you've done.'

To my amazement he laughed, and let go of my arm. 'You really would have been the better choice,' he said. 'Do you know, I think we might have got on well . . . I should have enjoyed taming you, my little firebrand.'

'I would never have let you touch me.' I rubbed at my arm where his fingers had bruised me.

'I can be very persuasive,' he said. 'But no matter, there are enough willing girls for me to take my pick from without forcing you.'

'You forced Lainie!'

'Not to sleep with me; she was willing enough. So willing that I soon tired of her and thought I would set her up in a career most suited to her talents. I made a mistake. I should have disposed of her.'

I felt sick as I saw the expression in his eyes, or perhaps it was lack of expression. He sounded as if Lainie were a gnat he could simply brush aside when he had no use for her.

'I wish you were dead! You deserve to be hung!'

'Possibly you are right,' he said, 'but I don't think it will happen, do you?' He was laughing at me, sneering as he taunted me with my impotence. He was so sure of his power, so sure that I could not harm him. I believed he enjoyed telling me his secret just to see my reaction. 'So what are you going to do, Bridget? Tell your friend Joe Robinson? I don't think that would be very wise, do you? He might get into serious trouble . . . And that brother of yours . . . such a terrible temper! Now, he might find himself serving a long prison sentence for assault. These things can be arranged – or not as I please.'

'You devil!' I was beyond reason as I suddenly darted towards the desk and snatched up the pistol from the drawer he had left wide open. 'I can kill you.'

'Would you dare? I wonder . . . ?' He was still laughing in that hateful way, still mocking me. 'How amusing. If it were not my wedding day, I might be tempted to teach you a lesson . . . A very pleasurable lesson – at least for me.'

He started towards me and I raised my arm, pointing the pistol at his chest. 'Don't come near me or I'll shoot.' I reached for the letter and put that into my pocket. 'I'm going now and I'm going to the police.'

'That letter is a perfectly legitimate piece of business,' he said and seemed more amused than alarmed by my threats. 'Take it by all means – and the gun – but be careful, Bridget. I make a bad enemy.'

'You won't get away with this,' I said.

'Why don't you just shoot and have done with it? It would be so easy . . . If you have the courage?'

He was moving towards me again, but I backed away. My hands were shaking and my mouth was dry. My finger hovered over the trigger and I was close to pressing it. I am not sure what might have happened had I not heard the snooty receptionist calling to me from the sitting room, and I knew it was too late. I put the pistol into my pocket and went out to meet her.

'Oh, there you are,' she said. 'I was wondering where you'd got to . . .' She broke off as Philip Maitland followed me out of the bedroom. 'I'm sorry. I didn't know you were here, sir.'

'I have been admiring the excellent flower arrangements Miss O'Rourke has done for us,' he said, the smiling gentleman once more. 'Do you think Clarissa will be pleased with them, Miss Smythe?'

'Oh yes, I am sure she will, sir. Miss O'Rourke spent such a long time doing them.'

'Yes, I am certain she did.' He shot me another mocking glance. 'Will you arrange for the account to be paid immediately, Miss Smythe? I shall not have time to see to it myself.'

'Of course, sir.'

He nodded and smiled again. 'Thank you for coming, Miss O'Rourke. Please don't imagine I shall forget you. You can be sure to expect a visit from me on my return.'

His words seemed so acceptable, so much what he would be expected to say in the circumstances, but I was shaking as I left his suite and followed the receptionist downstairs. I knew he had been making a threat.

I had told Joe I would make my own way home on the Tuppeny Tube and the tram, and it was past four when I reached the shop. Joe had arranged for a girl to look after things while I was away, and I wanted to make sure that everything was all right.

We checked the money together and then I went round

all the tubs with the water jug just to make sure the unsold flowers were not suffering. At six o'clock I left and walked home, glancing over my shoulder every now and then to make sure I wasn't being followed.

Mr Maitland would make me pay for my impudence in challenging him. I knew that it was only a matter of time, but I still wasn't sure what to do. His threats against Joe had made me reluctant to share my secret with him. At the moment it was only me that was likely to suffer because of what had happened, but if I told Joe . . .

He was sitting in the kitchen with Alice and Mary when I got in. Alice was roasting a big joint of pork and had just taken it from the oven to baste it. Mary still looked pale and shaky but she seemed better and she looked anxiously at me as I went in.

'How did it go?' she asked. 'I ought to have come with you.'

'No!' I said sharply and then checked myself as both she and Joe looked at me. 'You weren't well enough, Mary. You know I'm right, besides, there was no need. I managed very well and Mr Maitland is very pleased. He told one of his employees to settle the account straight away.' I smiled, forcing myself to behave naturally. 'You would've laughed, Mary. She was such a snooty thing. She insisted on staying with me most of the time – I believe she thought I was going to steal the silver.'

Mary laughed, but Joe was looking at me oddly.

'I wish I'd been there,' Mary said wistfully. 'Was it lovely in the private suite – did the flowers look right?'

'They were wonderful,' I replied. 'Even the snooty Miss Smythe said so, and the suite was so posh. You should have seen the fancy cabinets. She said they came from France and that he had the room done specially for his wife. I've never seen anything so fine.'

I told Mary about the pretty bedroom and the fact that they had two. 'Don't you think that's strange?'

'It's the way the wealthy live,' Joe said. 'Separate rooms.

A lot of them marry someone suitable from a good family and take a mistress for their fun.'

'Joe!' Alice looked at him in surprise. 'You just wash your mouth out. I won't have such talk in my kitchen.'

'Sorry, Ma,' he said and grinned at her. 'I'm off out. Bridget, can I have a word before I go? I want your opinion about something. It's in the parlour.'

I saw by their faces that it was one of Joe's surprises. He was always bringing things home that he thought we might like, and when I followed him in I saw that he had a large music box with metal rolls and a handle that you wound up to make the tunes play.

'I bought this for Tommy. Do you think he will like it?'

'I am sure he will,' I said. 'It was good of you, Joe. I hope it wasn't too expensive?'

'It came cheap with some other stuff,' he said, and he gave me a straight look. 'What's wrong, Bridget? I know something is troubling you. Won't you please tell me? There is something on your mind, isn't there?'

He had to know the truth because after the confrontation with Philip Maitland there was bound to be trouble – and not just for me.

'I will but not here,' I said. 'I can't risk your ma and Mary hearing.'

'It's that bad?' I nodded and he frowned. 'Would you like to come out for a drink with me, Bridget? I've been meaning to ask, and we could talk on the way.'

I hesitated, then nodded. 'Yes, why not? I think I could do with a drink, Joe.'

Joe sat and stared at me for a full five minutes when I came to the end of my tale. We were on a bench outside the pub where we'd brought our drinks to be sure of finding a quiet corner, and the wind was a bit chilly. I shivered and pulled my coat collar up around my neck.

'You're cold,' he said. 'Are you sure you don't want something stronger than a shandy?'

'No, that's fine for me. I ought not to have told you, Joe –

there's nothing you can do. I should have left well alone, tried to forget it. I've made a mess of things and he's laughing at me. He's too clever.'

'He thinks he is. But he made a mistake, Bridget. In fact, he made two. He should never have let Lainie live – or you for that matter.'

'I'm not sure he would have, but for this.' I took the pistol out of my pocket and showed it to him. 'I threatened to kill him, Joe. I think I might have tried if that receptionist hadn't come back. I wish I had!'

'Give it to me, Bridget.' I handed it over and he slipped it into his pocket. 'And the letter – not that it's proof of anything. He was right about that. The police would laugh at us if we went to them with this evidence. He needs the gun for protection – well, a lot of rich people have them – and the letter is just a business deal. He was simply making an offer for a piece of property.'

'We can't do anything, can we? I told him I would like to see him hang but he just laughed.' I felt frustrated and angry. 'He's so powerful – he can do anything he likes.'

'His sort always think they can get away with everything,' Joe said. 'But maybe we can make him think again.'

Fear clutched at my stomach. 'You won't do anything silly, Joe?'

'I shan't do anything for the moment,' he said. 'And I certainly shan't tell Jamie. He would use his fists or something sharper, but that won't help against a man like Maitland.'

'I know, that's why I didn't tell him about Lainie. I want him to marry Mary and be happy.'

'Yes, and I think we should go ahead with the wedding soon,' Joe said looking thoughtful. 'I was going to make them wait a bit longer, but Mary is right – she should have her happiness now.'

'I'm so glad . . .' I leaned towards him and kissed his cheek. 'You're a good man, Joe, and I'm very fond of you.'

'I thought I'd upset you by asking you to marry me?'

'Of course not. I'm pleased you did, Joe. I think it might happen one day.'

He reached out and put a finger to my lips. 'You don't have to say any more, Bridget. I told you I could wait until you're ready – and I will.'

'Thanks.' I sighed. 'So, what will you do about this, Joe?'

'I'm not sure. I promise you he won't get away with this. There's more than one way of dealing with a snake.'

'Yes, that describes him well,' I agreed. 'He has such cold eyes . . . I never imagined he could be like that. He frightens me, Joe. I'm frightened of what he might do – to all of us.'

'That's how he gets away with it,' Joe said. 'No one would imagine he was the controlling power behind a corrupt criminal empire, and he controls those who do have contact with him by fear.'

'He knows he has power,' I said. 'He was taunting me . . . daring me to go to the police.'

'He knew he was safe, but maybe we can find a way to make him suffer. I'm not saying it will make up for what he did to Lainie, Fred or Rosie, but sometimes you have to settle for less than what you want in this world, Bridget.'

'Yes, I know.' I sighed. 'I wish I'd pulled that trigger while I had the chance.'

'And then they would have hung you for murder.' Joe shook his head. 'Just leave it to me. I'll see what I can do. This letter isn't proof of his guilt, but now I know who he is, I can probably discover a few things. He's been lucky for a long time, but he has enemies. Maybe his luck is about to run out.'

Mary was beginning to feel better again and she was excited about her wedding, and Alice was full of the plans and arrangements.

'We'll have a big tea,' she told me. 'A real good do with ham, tongue, boiled potatoes and trifles as well as cake. We'll be holding it in the hall behind the church – give her a proper send-off.'

'It will be lovely. I'm looking forward to it.'

'Would you like me to make you a new dress, Bridget? If you buy the material I'll get it done before I start on Mary's.'

'Are you sure? It will mean extra work for you.'

'You can help me cut and sew it. I might teach you to use the sewing machine when Mary is married. It's handy for a lass to know how to sew, especially if you have children.'

The look she gave me told me that she was expecting some more good news soon, and I wondered what she had guessed. Joe had taken me out for a drink a couple of times recently, and his mother couldn't know the true reason for our excursions.

But perhaps she wasn't so far wrong. Joe had asked me to marry him, and I was considering it. I knew that my love for Ernie had not gone away; it might always be there at the back of my mind, but that didn't mean I wanted to spend my life in regret. The time would come when I was ready to move on, and when I did it would probably be as Joe's wife.

Joe seemed fond of Tommy as well, and had begun to talk about going down to see him before the wedding. Tommy had sent me a naughty postcard with a lady showing her bloomers on the sea front as the wind blew her dress up. He'd written a cheeky message, saying that he and Joe had bought it specially for me when they went to the shop together. I laughed at the card, and it made me happy to know that my brother was feeling more like himself. Joe was amused over the card and said it had been Tommy's own choice.

'It would be nice if they would let us bring him home for a little visit,' he said. 'I'm sure he would like to go to Jamie's wedding, wouldn't he?'

'He would love it, Joe, but do you think they would let him come?'

'Well, why don't we go down this weekend and see?'

'Can we really, Joe?' I asked, looking at him in delight.

'I don't see why not. You write to Matron and tell her you're coming and ask if you can bring him here for a week or two. See what she says.'

'Yes, I will then,' I said. 'I'll post it on my way to work

this morning. I was going to the market anyway. I want to buy some material for a new dress.'

Joe nodded and smiled at me. I knew he thought everything was all right, but it was only three weeks since Mr Maitland's wedding and he probably hadn't had time to think up a suitable punishment for me yet.

I posted my letter off and then went to the market. I spent some time wandering around the market stalls, enjoying myself. I had always liked market folk. I felt comfortable with them, and the bustle and fast patter of the stallholders was exciting.

It was as I was walking back to the shop that I had a feeling I was being followed. I knew Joe had someone guarding me a lot of the time, but this was different. I had a horrible prickly sensation at the nape of my neck and when I turned round I saw Hal Burgess and my heart started to beat faster. This was what I'd been expecting. Was it just a reminder that Philip Maitland hadn't forgotten me – or was my punishment about to happen?

Hal leered at me and something in his look told me that he knew I was frightened. He was a bully and like all bullies he liked to intimidate his victims.

'Been shoppin' then?' he said as he caught up with me. 'That's right – enjoy yerself while yer can.'

'What do you mean?'

'You 'eard,' he said. 'Yer time's runnin' out. A friend told me to tell yer.'

My heart took a sickening lurch. It was a warning.

'What friend? I don't know what you're talking about.'

'Well, you'll get a surprise then, won't yer?'

'Tell me what you mean?' I demanded, but he just grinned and walked off.

I knew this was Mr Maitland's way of telling me that he hadn't forgotten me. He was intending to punish me for daring to challenge him, but he was biding his time.

'I'm going to have some flowers in the hall for my wedding,'

Mary told me that Saturday afternoon as we closed the shop. 'I shall do something similar to what you did at Mr Maitland's hotel, but using cheap blooms, of course. I couldn't afford those lilies.'

'Well, at least he paid for them.'

Mary looked at me. 'Was there a reason why he wouldn't?'

'No, of course not,' I said. 'But it was a large account and it's good to get it settled, isn't it?'

'Oh yes,' she said and looked happy. 'Everything is going so well, Bridget. We are beginning to make a profit at the shop. Not a huge amount, but much better than I expected, and it's only two weeks to my wedding.'

Her dress had been cut out and Alice was busily working on it. We were going to have a fitting session very soon and Mary's happiness was almost tangible. She glowed with warmth and a sense of expectation. The excitement in the house was mounting daily with Alice almost as thrilled as her daughter.

'Yes.' I hugged her arm. 'I'm so glad you're getting married at last, Mary, and I know Jamie is happy. You are the best thing that ever happened to him. Once upon a time I thought he would probably end up in prison or disappear like our father did, but now I can be sure it won't happen.'

'He'll be in trouble with me if he doesn't behave,' Mary said and gurgled with laughter. 'So, when are you and Joe going to name the day then? Don't tell me he hasn't asked, Bridget?'

'He did mention something,' I agreed. 'But we're waiting for a while, Mary.'

She nodded and hugged my arm back. 'Well, you know your own mind best, but I think it would be nice, Bridget. We would be a real family then. Not that we aren't now, of course.'

'We'll see,' I said.

I thought about it that night as I lay in bed. I would be silly to keep on refusing Joe. If I couldn't have Ernie, the next best thing was to settle for a man I liked and respected.

Sixteen

M atron wasn't willing for us to take Tommy back with us that weekend.

'I could agree to him coming for two days over the wedding,' she said, 'but longer than that would be unsettling. And I think it best if you don't tell him until you come to fetch him. He might get overexcited and make himself ill – and things don't always turn out as you plan.'

'What do you think she imagines might happen?' I asked Joe as we were sitting in the train going home. 'We wouldn't let him down.'

'Some people do,' Joe said. 'Besides, it didn't matter to Tommy. He enjoyed going out for the day, and it will be a nice surprise for him next weekend. You can come down on the Friday yourself, Bridget, and fetch him. We'll put a bed up for him in your room. It's not an ideal arrangement but it will do for the time being.'

However, when we told Mary what we were going to do, she said that she was going to sleep over the shop that night.

'No, that you won't,' Alice said. 'Whatever will people think – you and Jamie under the same roof on the night before your wedding. I never heard of such a thing!'

'Oh, Ma . . .' Mary went into a peal of delighted laughter. 'You didn't think Jamie was going to stay there with me? No, we've already arranged it so that he goes off somewhere.'

'But why would you want to sleep there on your own?' Joe said. 'It will make things awkward for you in the morning.'

'No, it won't,' Mary said. 'I want to work on my flowers

on Friday evening. Bridget is going to fetch Tommy, which means I'll need to mind the shop – and I shall work better when there's no one about. I'll be here by breakfast and you won't know any different.'

'I could come over and help you when I get back,' I offered but she shook her head and looked annoyed.

'Why won't any of you realize that I'm not a child and I'm not an invalid? The rooms over the shop are going to be my home. I want to do things – make it how I want. Surely you can understand that I would like to have a little time alone there? You can move into my room on Friday, Joe, and I can take some of my things over in the morning. The rest of my stuff will wait until we come back.'

Jamie was taking her to an undisclosed destination for a few days' holiday and she had been trying to guess where they were going for weeks but he wouldn't tell her.

I knew that Joe wasn't pleased at the idea, and nor was Alice, but Mary was set on having her own way.

'I'm getting married,' she said. 'You can't wrap me in cotton wool forever, Joe.'

'Well, if it's what you want.' Joe gave in reluctantly.

'It's exactly what I want,' she said. 'You'll see. You won't even know I'm gone.'

Tommy was thrilled to bits when I collected him from the sanatorium.

'This means I'm really getting better, doesn't it, Bridget?'

'Yes, of course it does,' I said and hugged him. 'You've got to come back on Sunday, Tommy, but it won't be long before they will let us have you home. Just a few weeks with one of the families down here to get you used to being away from the hospital, and then you will be living with me and Joe, and Alice.'

'Are you going to marry Joe? He's sweet on you, Bridget, and I like him. He's a lot better than that Ernie Cole who used to hang around after you.'

'Is he? What was wrong with Ernie?'

233

He shrugged. 'I don't know. Maybe nothin'. I just like Joe better.'

I wondered about that, but decided that Tommy hadn't really known Ernie so he couldn't make comparisons. Joe had been good to him, giving him things and taking him out for a day. It was natural that he should prefer Joe.

Alice made a big fuss of Tommy when I took him home. She had baked a lovely seed cake and some jam tarts for him, and he attacked them hungrily. After supper, I took him up to the bathroom and gave him a good wash before tucking him up in bed.

'It will save a bit of time in the morning,' I told him when he complained that I scrubbed his ears too hard. 'We're going to have such a lot to do tomorrow.'

'I've never been to a weddin',' Tommy said as I kissed him goodnight. 'I bet Jamie is excited.'

'Yes, I am sure he is,' I said. 'He loves Mary very much and I think they will be very happy together.'

'That's good,' Tommy said and closed his eyes sleepily. 'Goodnight, our Bridget.'

I struggled to open my eyes as I heard the knocking at the front door. It was still dark! Surely it was the middle of the night? I couldn't have been to bed more than a couple of hours.

I got out of bed and pulled my coat on over my nightdress, going out on the landing to the top of the stairs. Joe had gone down and was lighting the lamp in the hall. I saw him open the door and I could hear someone shouting at him.

'Your bleedin' shop's on fire, mate,' a man said. 'I live across the road and I see it from me window. Someone has alerted the fire brigade, but I don't reckon as there will be much left of it by the time you get there.'

'On fire . . .' My heart caught as I heard the stunned note in Joe's voice. 'Oh, my God! Mary – where's Mary?' He turned to look at me and I started down the stairs at a run. 'Tell me what happened to my sister!'

'I dunno, mate. We didn't know she was there. We thought

you were but someone said as you'd moved back 'ere. We all thought it was empty.'

'Joe . . .' I said. 'Mary is still in there. You have to go round. You have to do something!'

Alice had come to the top of the stairs. She had heard the commotion and I could see the fear in her eyes.

'I told her not to sleep there alone,' she said. 'I knew something would happen.'

'Look after Ma,' Joe said to me. 'I'm going round there, Bridget.'

'Let me come with you.'

'No, you stay here. I don't want to worry about you and Ma.'

I noticed that he had pulled on his trousers and a coat before answering the door. He wasn't going to stay to argue and I was still dithering as he shot out of the door. I started up the stairs to Alice, but she came down to join me.

'You go after him, Bridget,' she said. 'He'll go mad if anything . . .' Her voice broke on a sob. 'I don't want to lose them both.'

'I'm going like this,' I said. 'I can't wait to dress properly. If Tommy wakes, tell him everything will be all right.'

'Of course – I just hope it will.'

I followed Joe and the man who had roused the alarm through the empty streets, my heart beating like a drum. Oh, please let Mary be all right! I was praying as I ran. Please let her be all right.

My chest hurt and I could hardly bear to think about what might be happening at the shop. Perhaps it was just a little fire. Mary might have got out through the back yard. She must have . . . she must have . . .

My heart stopped as I got nearer and caught the acrid smell of burning, and then I saw it. Flames were shooting through the roof and the whole place was an inferno. The fire engine had arrived and men were trying to douse the flames, but it was clear that nothing could be done to save the shop or the rooms over the top.

'Mary . . .' Joe shrieked in his agony. 'My sister is in there . . . She's in there . . .' He started to run across the road towards the shop and his intention was clear.

'Stop him!' I cried. 'He'll go in after her.'

One of the men from the fire brigade moved to catch Joe in his arms, holding him as he fought like a wild thing to get free, but now others had come out from the houses and some of the neighbours joined in to restrain Joe.

'No one is alive in there now,' one of the firemen said. 'It must have been a while before the fire caught. The smoke would've killed anyone asleep upstairs long before the fire reached them.'

'I've got to get in . . .' Joe said, and he was sobbing. 'I've got to get her . . . She's my sister. She's getting married tomorrow.'

I saw the shocked, pitying faces of the people around him. They didn't know what to say or do, but the fight had gone out of Joe now and, as the roof suddenly caved in, he gave a moan of despair.

'Mary . . .' he said. 'Mary . . . I'm sorry.'

Tears were running down his cheeks as I went to him and took him in my arms. He was sagging with grief, helpless as the sobs broke from him, and he kept repeating her name over and over again. I'd never seen him like this, never known him to be so vulnerable, and my heart reached out to him.

'Mary . . . I'm sorry. I'm sorry, Mary . . .'

'There's nothing you can do here, Joe,' I said, pulling him away. 'Let's go home . . .'

He looked at me for a moment, then shook his head. 'You go back,' he said and his face had set in a hard line. His eyes were bleak, seeming to stare through me. 'I'll come later, Bridget. Jamie doesn't know . . . I have to see Jamie.'

'Not now,' I urged. 'Leave it until the morning.'

'No – he has to know,' he said and pulled away from me. 'Go home, Bridget. This is for me and Jamie to sort out.'

'Don't, Joe . . . please,' I begged.

He turned away without another word and the fear mounted

inside me as I knew what he was going to do. Joe knew this wasn't an accidental fire. It was meant to punish us for daring to challenge an evil man, as everyone had thought Joe was sleeping there.

Alice was sitting in the kitchen alone when I got back. She was staring into the fire and I could see by the way she was hunched up in misery that she already knew the worst.

'She's gone, hasn't she, my lovely Mary?'

'Yes. They said the smoke would have killed her long before the fire reached her. She wouldn't have suffered, Alice. She must have simply gone to sleep.'

'Never to wake up again.' Alice's eyes were bleak as she looked at me. 'I used to pray that it would happen that way sometimes, when she was suffering terribly as a little girl. I couldn't stand to see her suffer and I used to hope she wouldn't wake in the morning so that I didn't have to watch her in agony. It was wicked of me to pray for that, Bridget, and now God has punished me.'

'Of course He hasn't,' I said. 'You hated to see Mary suffer when she was little, but she grew up and she was happy. She was so happy, Alice.'

'She wanted to be married months ago,' Alice said. 'Joe made her wait. Why did he do that, Bridget? She might have had those months of happiness. Why did he deny her that?'

'Joe didn't know what would happen. It's not his fault.'

'My son has always done things I didn't approve of,' Alice said and her face was cold, harder than I had ever seen it. 'I put up with his scheming and his dealing, even though I knew some of his deals wouldn't bear close investigation, but if he's done something to cause my little girl's death . . .' A shudder went through her and she looked at me pleadingly. 'You promise me she didn't suffer, Bridget?'

'I'm sure the smoke killed her. She wouldn't have known anything.'

Alice nodded. 'I'll believe you,' she said. 'You're a good girl. Joe will be lucky if he gets you.' She suddenly buried her face in her hands and began to sob.

I put my arm around her shoulders. She stood up and I held her close until the fit of grief had eased and then she pushed me away, wiping her face on her apron.

'Crying won't bring her back,' she said. 'I'm going to put the kettle on. Your brother is sound asleep. Why don't you go up and take a look at him?'

'I think I'll just sit here and wait until Joe comes back. A cup of tea would be nice, Alice.'

She looked at me and then smiled oddly. 'I'm not going to hang myself over the banister, Bridget. I have to see that my little girl is buried proper.'

I wondered if they would even find a body, but I didn't dare to tell her that. Seeing the fire had made it even more real to me and I didn't want to inflict my nightmares on Alice. She had enough of her own.

We sat in silence to drink our tea, and then she went upstairs. I waited alone in the kitchen for Joe, but he didn't come and in the end I went up too. After all there was nothing I could do.

I couldn't imagine what Jamie was feeling now. My heart ached for his pain. Joe had loved his sister dearly, but she was Jamie's whole world. He would go mad. I knew, without being told, that both Joe and my brother would be looking for the man behind this terrible tragedy, and when they found him they would kill him.

Joe might have been willing to settle for less when it was just a matter of property. He might even have accepted the fire at the shop if Mary hadn't been sleeping there, but now he would have only one thing on his mind.

It was hard trying to explain to Tommy that there would be no wedding. He stared at me with huge, scared eyes and I could see that he was trying desperately to hold back his tears.

'What happened to Mary?'

'She . . . she died,' I said. 'The smoke must have sent her to sleep and she didn't wake up.'

'Jamie will go mad,' Tommy said. 'He won't know what to do, Bridget. He'll be hurtin' so bad inside.'

'Yes, I know. We all feel that way. We all loved Mary.'

My own pain was almost unbearable. I hardly knew how to look at Alice, who was walking about with a stony face, her eyes as cold as death. She had hardly spoken a word that morning, and I wouldn't have known what to say to her if she had. I knew she was blaming Joe, and that wasn't fair. If anyone was to blame it was me. I was the one who had threatened Philip Maitland and this was his reply.

Tommy asked me what was going to happen now, and I said that we would go out somewhere for the day.

'It might be best if Alice didn't have to worry about us,' I said. 'I tell you what, we'll go up west and have a ride on the tube. Then we'll go somewhere and—'

'I would rather see Jamie,' Tommy said. 'I'm not a child, Bridget. I know what's happened and I want to stay here.'

I had been trying to save him some of the upset that was turning this house on its head, but he didn't want that. My brother had grown up far too soon. He might only be eight years old, but he had seen suffering and death in the sanatorium and he understood more than I had given him credit for.

'All right,' I said. 'We'll see.'

The door opened at that moment and Joe came in to the kitchen followed by Jamie. Tommy got up and ran to his brother, flinging his arms about him and sobbing into his body.

'I'm sorry, our Jamie,' he wept. 'Sorry for your lovely Mary.'

Jamie hugged him tightly, his eyes meeting mine over Tommy's head. I saw the stark misery in him and I put a hand to my face, unable to bear it

'We've been to the shop,' he said. 'It's a burned-out shell. There's nothing left . . . nothing.'

Alice gave a moan of despair. 'My Mary . . . my little girl . . .'

'We'll have a funeral just the same,' Joe said hoarsely. 'We'll bury her ashes.'

'Damn you, Joe Robinson!' She rounded on him fiercely. 'This will be some of your doing.'

'No,' I cried. 'That's not fair. It wasn't Joe's fault.'

'Don't, Bridget,' Joe warned. 'Ma doesn't mean it. She's upset. I shouldn't have let Mary go. I shouldn't have let her stay there alone.'

'You couldn't have stopped her,' I said. 'Whatever happened, Joe, it wasn't your fault.'

He looked at me and nodded. 'We think we know what happened. People have seen things – they've told me things they wouldn't have told the police. I came back to get dressed properly and then we're off. Don't worry, Ma. I'll get to the bottom of this.'

She didn't answer him as he went upstairs, but her manner changed as she turned to Jamie. 'Don't take on too much, lad,' she said as he sat down at the kitchen table, burying his face in his hands. 'Tears won't hurt you, but they won't bring her back. You made her happy these last months and I'll always be grateful for that. She wasn't a pretty lass, but she said you made her feel beautiful.'

'She was beautiful to me.' Jamie raised his head, his face wet. 'I loved her . . . I'll always love her.'

'Jamie,' I said. 'I'm so sorry. I love Mary, too.'

'She knew that,' he said. 'She was always talkin' about you and what you were doin' at the shop. Full of ideas for the future she was.'

'The shop's gone then?' Alice said and pulled a face. 'Joe will have it insured but I don't know whether he'll set it up the way it was.'

'The shop doesn't matter,' I said. 'It doesn't matter to Joe. You know he would have done anything for Mary.'

She nodded but her eyes were unforgiving. She was blaming Joe, and I wasn't sure why.

'Jamie . . .' I said, turning to him. 'Joe told you the rest?'

He nodded, and his face was grim. 'You should've told me long ago, Bridget.'

'What's this then?' Alice asked but Jamie shook his head. He got up and grabbed Tommy, lifting him on to his shoulders.

'Tell Joe I've gone for a walk. I'll be back in half an hour.'

'What's going on?' Alice asked after he had gone. 'I knew Joe was up to something. What has he been up to now?'

'It isn't Joe,' I said again and then sighed. After what had happened, she had a right to know. I sat down at the kitchen table and told her everything: what had happened to Lainie, Fred's murder and the incident at the hotel. 'So you see, Joe had only a small part in all this. It would be unfair to blame him.'

'What has he been doing to make that man fire the shop? It was meant to be Joe asleep up there . . . and it should've been.'

'Yes, Ma, it should've been me,' Joe's voice said from the doorway. 'And the worst thing I've done is take my time. If I'd been less careful this might never have happened. The only way any of us can sleep safe in our beds again is for that bastard to die.'

I waited for Alice to reprimand him for swearing but she just stared at him, then she nodded and got up to go over to the stove. 'I don't know what we're going to do with all the food I've made,' she said. 'I can cancel the meat, but the cakes are made. Would you take some for the young lads in the hospital, Bridget?'

'Yes, of course, Alice.' I looked at Joe. 'Jamie has taken Tommy for a walk. I don't think he could bear to sit in the house.'

'I'll go and find them,' Joe said. 'We've got some talking to do.'

'Don't do anything silly,' I pleaded. 'Think first . . .'

'I want him dead,' Joe said. 'I should've done it weeks ago, as soon as you told me. Then Mary might still be alive.'

It was no use my telling him that his enemy had been in Paris until the last couple of days. He was hurting like hell over Mary's death, and I knew that neither he nor Jamie would listen to anything I had to say.

I was frightened for them both. If they were hung for murder it wouldn't bring Mary back or stop Alice from looking as if the light had gone out of her life.

Nothing could ease the grief we all felt, but it might get better in time. All I could do was to pray, and to be there when I was needed.

I took Tommy back to the sanatorium on the Sunday. Matron had heard about the fire and was very kind to both Tommy and me.

'I shall look after him, Miss O'Rourke,' she said. 'And you know you are always welcome to come down here when you wish.'

I didn't go straight back to London that afternoon. I had a little money in my pocket and I stayed for one night at a small hotel. I felt the loss of Mary press down on me like a great weight, and I couldn't face the thought of going straight back to that house of mourning. But the next day I knew I had to go.

Alice looked at me as I walked in. She had been blackleading the range and she looked exhausted. 'Joe was worried, but I told him you needed a little time to yourself.'

'It was selfish of me,' I said. 'Is there anything I can do to help you, Alice? Can I see to the washing or give the house a turnout?'

'I did that yesterday,' she said. 'I'm better working. I can't sit still a minute. If I sit down it all comes over me and I have to do something – anything rather than think.'

'I know how you feel,' I said. 'If you don't need me, I think I shall go and see Maggie for a few hours.'

'Would she let you stay?' She nodded as she saw the answer in my face. 'The memorial service isn't until Friday. Take a few days with your friends, Bridget. It will do you good.'

'What about you and Joe?'

'He's never in the house, and I'm better on my own. It's not that I want to get rid of you. I'll be all right when you come back – I just need some time to myself.'

'Yes, I can understand that,' I said. 'In that case, I shall ask Maggie if I can stay with her for a few days.'

Maggie took one look at my face and opened her arms. I

wept against her comforting chest and she held me until I calmed down.

'I couldn't believe it when I saw the paper,' she said. 'Jean Cole brought it up to me. It was a terrible thing, Bridget. A terrible thing. I don't suppose you know how the fire started?'

'I'm not sure, but it might have been deliberate. The shop belonged to Fred once.'

Maggie stared at me. 'Are you sayin' what I think?'

'Yes, but I can't tell you any more. It was connected, we're almost sure of it, but that's all I can tell you.'

She nodded. 'And what does your Jamie say to that?'

'I don't have to tell you, do I?'

'No.' She looked anxious. 'There will be more trouble before you're much older, lass.'

'Yes, I know. I don't know what to do, Maggie. Joe and Jamie – they've got that look in their eyes. I can't stop them. They won't listen to me. Nothing will stop them.'

'Good luck to them is what I say,' she declared, surprising me. 'I hope the bugger what done it gets what he deserves.'

'I'm very much afraid he will,' I said. 'But the man who set the shop alight isn't the only one to blame . . . There's someone else they might not be able to touch.'

'Isn't that always the way of it?' She shook her head. 'And what will you do now, me darlin', when this is all over?'

'I don't know, Maggie, but can I stay here until Thursday? I'll go back for the funeral and then I'll see what Alice says. She wanted to be alone, and I understand that.'

'Yes, of course you can stay,' Maggie said. 'We've been told by the rent man that we've got a couple of months before they throw us out, but I ain't goin' to worry about that. We'll go when they force us and not before. Mick says he and some of his mates are ready to fight and barricade the lanes, so we'll have to see.'

'Oh, Maggie. It's all trouble, isn't it?'

'No use cryin' until the milk's spilt,' she said. 'You just take your time, Bridget. You know you're always welcome here while I've a roof over my head. But if you're lookin' for work, I heard that Bridie Macpherson needs a bright girl to look after her hotel. Seems her mother's got to go into hospital for a while and she don't trust those she's got working for her.'

'I suppose I could live in there.' I thought about it. 'It would be somewhere to go for a while. I'm not sure about anything else at the moment, Maggie. Joe had asked me to marry him, but everything has changed now.'

'Well, you could walk over and see what Bridie says.' Maggie looked thoughtful. 'I dare say she would be glad of the help. Might take you on permanently if it worked out well.'

'I think it's an excellent idea,' Alice said when I told her that evening that I was thinking of taking a job elsewhere. 'I hardly ever see Joe and he hasn't a word to say for himself. You might as well be with people you can talk to, Bridget.'

'I told Mrs Macpherson that I would only go for a few weeks, just until her mother is on her feet again – and only if you don't need me.'

'To be honest, Bridget, I'm better on my own. I'm in such a mood that I might say something I didn't mean to you. I don't want to fall out with you, lass. I don't blame you for any of this.'

'I'm just as much to blame as Joe – perhaps more so.'

'No, it all started when he got big ideas about owning houses and shops,' she said. 'If he'd been content with his stalls on the market, this would never have happened.'

'It wouldn't have stopped Lainie being hurt . . .'

'I'm sorry. I was forgetting what happened to your sister. I'm so full of my own misery, I can't think of anyone else.'

'I would be the same if I were you,' I said. 'It hurts just to be in this house and not see her. I'm sorry, I shouldn't have said that.'

'It's what I think all the time,' Alice said. 'At least you're honest enough to say what you think. Joe won't speak to me.'

'I'm so sorry, Alice. He blames himself even though he must know in his heart it wasn't his fault.'

She looked at me but didn't say anything and I knew that she still blamed Joe. Mary had been her favourite child and the loss of her seemed to have made Alice bitter.

'If there was anything I could do for Alice or you I would stay, Joe,' I said to him when he came in that evening. He had eaten his supper after saying hello to me and he was about to go out again when I stopped him and told him about Bridie's offer. 'Do you want me to go or stay?'

'You go,' he said. 'There's things going on, Bridget. You'll be safer away from here for the moment. When it's all over . . . Well, we'll see what you want to do then.'

'Oh, Joe,' I said softly. 'I loved Mary, too. I want to help you. Is there nothing I can do? You know I would do anything if I could turn back the clock – stop what happened.'

'You're not the only one. I should never have let her stay there. I never dreamed they would harm her.' He broke off and looked at me sadly. 'I had it all planned, Bridget. The shop, a big house, and you and me married. Mary was getting what she wanted and things were sweet. Now it all tastes like ashes in my mouth. I wish I'd never seen the bloody shop.'

'There's nothing wrong with having ambition or wanting things to be better,' I said and reached out to touch his cheek. 'You're a good man, Joe – the best. Don't be too hard on yourself. It really wasn't your fault. I think they meant to kill you. Everyone thought you were there, no one knew Mary had decided to spend the night alone.'

'It should have been me!'

'Don't say that, Joe. It shouldn't have been anyone. It's the people who did this that are to blame – not you.'

'I love you,' he said. 'I think I loved you from the moment I first saw you. I wanted to kill that bugger for hurting you and I would if you'd told me who it was.'

'I didn't want anyone to know. I was too ashamed.'

'You've nothing to be ashamed of. If things were different . . . but I can't offer you anything now, Bridget. I might not even be around for much longer. This isn't going to end here. I'll get the man who fired the shop and that other devil, if it's the last thing I do.'

'Joe?' I stared after him as he went out, my heart aching. Joe had come to mean a lot to me these past months. I hadn't really known how much until I saw him trying to enter that burning shop after Mary. As he'd sobbed in my arms I had felt something stir inside . . . Pity or love, I hadn't been sure, but I knew it was something more than mere friendship. 'Oh, Joe.' The hurt was fierce inside me as I sensed his pain, but there was nothing I could do or say to help him. 'Oh, Joe.'

The tears were burning behind my eyes. I wanted to call him back and beg him not to do something that might lead to a violent death for him, too. But I hadn't the right. Mary was his sister and what he did now was for her.

I managed to see Jamie the next morning. He looked dreadful, his chin thick with stubble and his eyes bleary. I knew that look of old and I guessed that he had been drinking. He had slipped back to his old ways, and it distressed me to see him like that.

'Don't do this to yourself, Jamie,' I begged. 'Mary wouldn't want you to tear yourself apart like this.'

'Mary is dead,' he said bitterly and his eyes had no life in them. 'I want to die too, Bridget. Sure, I've nothin' to live for now she's gone.'

How could I tell him that he was young and strong and had his whole life ahead of him? Mary had been his world. Without her he was an empty shell.

'I'll be at Bridie's if you want me,' I said. He looked at me as if I didn't exist. It hurt me to see Jamie the way he was now and I wished I could turn the clock back.

If I had my chance again I would pull that trigger!

Seventeen

J oe took me to Bridie's in his van. I had brought only one bag with me, leaving most of my things in my bedroom at Joe's house.

'It's only for a while. I'll talk to you before I decide anything.'

'Yes,' he said. 'Just for a few weeks.'

'Goodbye, Joe.'

'Goodbye, Bridget.'

I stood watching as he drove away. It was a cool autumn day and the wind was blowing debris along the street. It was such an abrupt parting but we were both hurting too much to say more.

Sighing, I went into the hotel. Perhaps time would heal our grief.

Bridie was pleased I had come. 'You are free to use my apartments at any time during my absence. You will be in charge here, Bridget, so don't let me down.'

'I shall do my best for you. Thank you for giving me the job.'

'Well, to tell the truth you were the answer to a prayer. I shall feel much better with you here to look after things while I take care of my mother.'

'You must show me how you want things done, Bridie.'

She left me in charge the next morning. Seeming a bit nervous as she left and warning me to lock my door at night.

'We don't take the rough element here,' she said. 'But a pretty girl like you needs to take care.'

'Don't worry, I'll be fine.'

It seemed a bit strange after she had gone, but after that I began to feel that I had done this all my life. I enjoyed checking the guests in and out, seeing new faces and getting to know them all by name. Most were pleasant and they all treated me with respect. I suspected they knew Bridie wouldn't stand for any nonsense and I hoped my manner made it plain I wouldn't either.

I missed being with Joe, Alice and Mary. The hurt inside me was so raw that I wondered if I would ever recover from it. If I hadn't been able to keep busy I don't know how I would have got through that first two weeks at Bridie's.

I had heard nothing from Joe, though I thought about him a lot. Perhaps he was too busy or perhaps he just wanted to stay clear while he settled his business with Mary's killers.

It was two days before Bridie was due to return that it happened. I was about to lock up when a man entered the hotel.

'I am very sorry. I don't take in new guests after nine . . .' I began and then saw who it was. My heart missed a beat. 'Ernie . . . What are you doing here?'

'I wanted to see you. Can we talk for a while?'

I hesitated, then: 'As long as you only want to talk.'

'Just to talk, that's all I ask.'

'Come into Bridie's parlour then.'

He followed me inside, then stood staring at me. There was such a hungry yearning in his eyes that I felt my stomach clench.

'Are you back for good?' he asked.

'I don't know. I haven't decided.'

'I haven't heard from Grace. I don't think she will come back. I don't want her to.'

'She is still your wife . . . Kathy's mother.

'Kathy is mine. Grace abandoned her.' He stared at me hungrily. 'If they pull the houses down Ma and me are goin' to the country. I can find a decent job there and a good house. Come with me, Bridget.'

'I'm sorry, Ernie. It wouldn't work. I can't live with you in sin.'

'You've changed,' he accused. 'You aren't the same since you went away.'

'Perhaps I am different.' As I spoke I knew it was true. The old Bridget had gone and a new woman was emerging. A woman who suddenly knew exactly what she wanted out of life. 'I grew up.'

'You want him, but I can make you want me again!' He grabbed at me, pulling me roughly against him. His fingers bit into the flesh of my upper arms, bruising me. I pushed against his shoulders. 'You're mine, Bridget. I won't let you go to him.'

'I am not yours.' I struggled to free myself. 'I am not anyone's property. When we lay together I loved you, but that's over!'

'You bitch!' he muttered as I pushed him away. 'You're a whore like your sister.'

Before I could react he hit me across the face. It hurt and I recoiled, but I wasn't afraid. I was angry.

'Get out of here and don't ever come back,' I yelled. 'I don't want to talk to you ever again. Whatever we had is over.'

He stared at me for a long moment, then turned and walked from the room.

After he had gone, I went into Bridie's bedroom and washed my face. I was drying it when I heard something behind me and sensed that someone was in the room.

'I thought I told you not to come back!'

'That must have been the angry young man I passed just now, but I'll go if you want?'

'Joe?' I dropped the towel and stared at him.

He frowned as he saw the red mark on my face. 'Did he do that to you?'

'Yes, but it doesn't matter,' I said. 'I cared for Ernie once, Joe, but it's over and I just told him.'

'I'll go after him.'

'Please don't. Just forget it.' I went towards him. 'I was thinking about you earlier, Joe. I wanted to see you, to tell you something . . .'

'Hear me out first,' Joe said and I could see that it was serious. 'Hal Burgess is dead. I didn't kill him and neither did Jamie. The word on the street is that he overstepped his orders when he set that fire and the Big Man was angry. He ordered the execution.'

'Oh, Joe . . .' I felt cold all over and started to tremble. 'What does that mean?'

'I think it means Maitland got scared,' he said grimly. 'I've heard that the slum clearance has been turned down by the government and there's no longer any pressure on me to sell Fred's house.'

'You think he's trying to bribe you to step back?' My eyes went over his face, searching. 'Is that what you want, Joe?'

'I've been thinking.' He looked at me and his eyes were full of longing. 'I miss you, Bridget, and so does Ma. She told me to ask you to come back, but . . .'

'Yes, Joe?'

'Not to that house. I can't stay there, Bridget. I thought I might do Fred's place up, make it nice, and some of the other houses in the lane will be coming up for sale cheap. I might get another one for Ma.'

I smiled and took a few steps closer to him.

'What are you trying to say, Joe? If you're asking me if I'll marry you and live with you in Fred's house, the answer is that it's what I want more than anything else in the world.'

He gave me his crooked smile and my heart flipped. When did he become so dear to me? I hadn't noticed it creeping up, but then as Maggie was so fond of telling me – I was an idjit.

'I love you, Joe,' I said. 'It took me a while to realize it. I thought I was in love with Ernie, but he wasn't the man I imagined.'

'I love you, Bridget O'Rourke,' Joe said. 'I've loved you from the first moment you opened your eyes and told me not to touch you.'

I offered my face for his kiss and it was sweet and tender, but full of a hungry yearning.

'And are you content to let things go, Joe? Can you live with what happened – knowing that Maitland is free to carry on as before?'

'It won't be quite as before,' Joe said. 'Maybe some of his fine friends have got a wheeze of his criminal activities, but I know that others have started to move in on his patch. His empire will never be quite what it was before the fire, so maybe he's been made to suffer a little, though it isn't what I want. Yet, if he didn't order that fire . . .'

'Will Jamie forget it, Joe?'

'Jamie has gone,' he said. 'He gave me letters for you and Tommy. He's gone to America, Bridget. He says he'll write one day.'

'He loved her so much, Joe.'

But we had all loved Mary and it was going to take a while before any of us could begin to forget.

We waited six weeks for our wedding because we wanted Tommy to be with us. He was excited because he was coming home – and to the lanes.

'I'll be able to play with Billy Ryan again.'

'With all your friends,' I said. 'But it won't be like it was, Tommy. Joe has made it real posh for us.'

'It's great,' Tommy said. 'But I'm still going to college and I'm going to be a doctor.'

'If that's what you want Joe will help you – and we shall both be proud of you.'

'The doctors made me well again,' he said. 'I'd have been dead soon if it wasn't for them – I want to do that for others.'

'Then I am sure you will.' I hugged him. 'But you helped yourself, Tommy. You're an O'Rourke and a fighter and that counts for a lot.'

'Are you happy?' Joe asked as I snuggled against him on our wedding night. 'Was it all right?'

I reached over to kiss him in the dark. 'It was better than all right,' I said. 'It was lovely, and you know it.

I'm glad Tommy is stopping with Alice tonight. I wasn't exactly quiet.'

Joe laughed and nibbled my ear. 'Next time you call out like that I shall have to kiss you to stop you.'

'Just keep kissing me the way you do,' I said fervently. 'I dare say Tommy knows what it's all about – if he doesn't that Billy Ryan will soon tell him.'

'They are a pair of imps,' Joe said. 'I just hope Tommy doesn't lose his desire to be a doctor one day.'

'I don't think he will. Tommy knows he might have died. He is in what Matron calls remission which means that his illness appears to have gone but there is a chance that it may come back one day. They don't know enough about the disease yet to cure it, only to treat the patient's health. Matron told me they didn't know why tuberculosis goes into remission sometimes, but she says it can mean he might live well into his middle age or even longer. It could return suddenly, of course. Tommy doesn't know that, but he has known what it is like to experience death. I think that leaves a mark. In his case, it may help him to become something he would never have thought of if he hadn't been ill.'

'They say things happen for a reason,' Joe said. 'It might be right in his case but it isn't always so.'

He was thinking of Mary. His grief and pain would be a long time healing, and mine would always linger in the back of my mind, but I wasn't going to let it spoil our lives.

I wasn't an O'Rourke for nothing. I would fight for Joe as I had fought for Tommy and my mother.

Jamie had gone beyond me, but I believed he would fight in his own way, and perhaps be stronger for it. I hoped that someday Lainie would come to see me and become a part of my family again, but for now I had Joe and Tommy and my friends.

It was all I needed.